Love on Location

by

September Roberts

Love on Location

Contact Information: info@thewildrosepress.com

Cover Art by *Kristian Norris*

The Wild Rose Press, Inc.
PO Box 708
Adams Basin, NY 14410-0708

Visit us at www.thewilderroses.com

Publishing History
First Scarlet Rose Edition, 2018
Print ISBN 978-1-5092-1988-9
Digital ISBN 978-1-5092-1988-9

Published in the United States of America

**They couldn't be more different,
but when a ranger and a movie star meet,
they can't help but fall in love.**

He shrugged and stepped out of his boots, dropping them against the house. Next came the vest, which he draped over the stone wall that lined the walkway. "Carol, the prop mistress, will kill me if these get ruined," he said as he handed her his gun and holster.

"Okay," she said, her voice a little wobbly. When he peeled his skin-tight pants off and arranged them on the wall with his vest, her heart raced. He stood in front of her in boxer briefs that didn't leave much to the imagination. The words written across the front read: *#1 JOHNSON.*

"What? They're from a fan."

"Your fans send you underwear?"

"Among other things." He grinned again. "Can I come in now? I'm getting cold."

"Sure. Yeah. Come on in." She stepped inside, hung her hat on the doorknob, and scanned the living room quickly to make sure it wasn't too messy. "Can I get you something to drink, coffee, tea, or—"

"A beer would be great."

"I thought you said you were cold."

"A little."

Who was she kidding? A beer sounded amazing.

Dedication

I dedicate this book to park rangers everywhere.
I hope you never stop pointing at things.

Author Acknowledgments

This book wouldn't have been possible without the support of my amazing husband, Rich. Crystal, thank you for the hours you spent talking to me about your job. You're my favorite ranger. Laurie, I appreciate your love and editing. Both are invaluable. Monica, you are one of my favorite people and a spectacular editor. I also need to thank Megan, Brenda, and my local writing chapter for being my beta readers, and Johnny for encouraging me to query. Mimi from the Utah Film Commission helped more than she knew. Finally, I'd like to thank Sherri at The Wild Rose Press, Inc. for her patience and guidance.

Chapter One

Sweat beaded on Alex's forehead. What had she gotten herself into?

"Are you listening? I asked about set construction," Mr. Howard snapped.

The phone cord stretched taut across the office as Alex walked to the window overlooking the red rock canyon where the corner of a wooden deck jutted out into the sun. "They have most of the framing done."

"Are they on schedule?"

She shrugged. "I guess." As a park ranger, she didn't know the first thing about movie set construction. Up until a few days ago, Maggie had been taking care of everything for the upcoming project.

"You need to find out. If they're running behind, you must get in touch with the movie crew."

"I'm on it," she said, even though she didn't feel like she had anything under control. Mr. Howard had been lecturing her about her new job duties for the past twenty minutes, but it felt like an hour. The spotlight never suited her. Shy by nature, she didn't want to be in charge. She had actively avoided promotions, which is how she had ended up at Twisted Juniper State Park in the first place.

The park needed an assistant manager, second in command. Park manager was Maggie's job. Emphasis on *was*.

"The governor's office wants this to be a slam dunk," he said.

Alex frowned. "Right, a slam dunk," she repeated, since she had obviously missed the first half of his statement.

"Those letters carry a lot of weight, and during the next legislative session they will be used to decide how much money will be allocated to Twisted Juniper, specifically for raises."

She sighed again.

Mr. Howard's voice took on a sharp edge. "Maggie has assured me you are capable of handling being park manager. Your employees are counting on you. I'm counting on you."

"I understand, sir," she quavered.

"Don't screw this up," he ground out before disconnecting.

"Right." She cradled the phone and took a deep breath before walking out of her office. Next door, Maggie sat at her desk. Alex cleared her throat.

Maggie smiled over her computer monitor and then frowned. "What's up?"

"Mr. Howard just called to remind me how much is riding on the filming next week." Alex took a deep breath. "I totally spaced out and then he was talking about letters and the governor's office."

"It's ridiculous. We can't ask for them," Maggie said, rolling her eyes.

"Can't ask for what?"

"The letters of recognition from the film crew. They make us look good and then the governor gives the park money."

"So how do we get them?" Alex's mouth dried out.

Maggie's smile returned. "You charm the movie cast and crew and then they write letters telling everyone how great it was to film here and how awesome you are. It shouldn't be too difficult. You're nice and hard working. It'll happen. I promise."

Alex cleared her throat. "He told me there's a lot riding on it and the park employees are counting on me. He's counting on me. What if I screw up? What if no one gets raises because of me, or worse yet, what if they start laying people off? I'm not sure if I can—"

Maggie laughed. "Take a deep breath."

She complied while Maggie stood and rubbed her back before she laced her fingers together to support her rounded belly. "You're the hardest working ranger I know."

"Are you sure you can't keep him in there a little longer? I'm not cut out for this," Alex whined.

Maggie stared straight at her and shook her head. "He's due next week. I'm *so* done being pregnant. Besides, you're going to be fine. You know this job inside and out. You just have to trust yourself."

"Yeah, you're right." She tried to sound cheery but failed miserably. "I need to go check on the construction crew and make sure they're on schedule."

"Thank you for taking care of this. You've helped put my mind at ease," Maggie called out as Alex walked away.

The first thing Alex did was check in with the construction crew. Mr. Howard would be pleased to hear they were almost done, not that she planned to call him back any time soon. She spent the rest of the day maintaining the trails, helping visitors, and preparing for her full moon hike. She always looked forward to her interpretive programs, even if it meant working a longer day than usual. Nothing helped clear her mind more than being surrounded by pristine wilderness.

The night temperatures had been dropping for weeks, which meant changing into pants for evening activities. She walked through the parking lot from the Visitor Center and crossed the main road into the tiny neighborhood where all the rangers lived. When the park had opened fifty years earlier, a subdivision of houses had been built for the rangers—five houses for the full-time positions, and two triplexes for the handful of seasonals. The second house, reserved for the assistant park manager, was hers. She had worked at Twisted Juniper State Park for a year and a half and enjoyed it almost as much as her previous position in Oregon. Koko, a little mutt dog, had been a happy addition to the quiet house and gave her something to look forward to each night.

Koko whined from the front room window where she perched on the back of a squishy couch.

"Get down," Alex said through the glass as she unlocked the front door and bent over to hug her dog. Koko wagged so vigorously her entire body bent in half with each wiggle. "You saw me at lunch, silly. Come on, go potty before our walk."

Koko wove in and out of her feet with each step toward the sliding door. The pup bolted outside, kicking up plumes of red sand. A chipmunk let loose a startled scream before scurrying under the fence.

Alex traded her dark brown shorts for dark brown pants, called Koko inside, and hooked her leash. "Come on. Let's go show our visitors the park's nightlife." She ruffled the dog's ears and locked the door behind them.

****

The next few days passed much like the ones before. Everyone scrambled to get their work done before the Hollywood elite showed up and started filming. Thankfully, the construction crew finished the set on time. After they left, Alex inspected it closely. They had built on an old riverbed, which would look like a compacted dirt road in the movie.

Wooden stairs led to a saloon with swinging doors that squeaked when she pushed inside. While the building appeared to be finished, it was just a shell with a makeshift roof and walls. Three stools waited just inside; other than that, the room was empty. Outside, she followed the wooden walkway to the next building, and peeked into the general store window. That's all it was, a wall with a window. It didn't even have a floor. The door didn't open. Neither did any of the others. Main Street consisted of a row of two-dimensional buildings and a place to tie up horses. It didn't look like much, but it didn't have to. Not when you have movie magic.

She and Maggie had met with the pre-scout group weeks before, and the first assistant producer, Steve Frederick, had told them the construction crew would build everything they would need for filming external shots. That's why it looked so weird. Why construct a whole building when you only need the outside?

When Thursday night arrived, Alex couldn't wait to tell Maggie about the set. They always left that night free so they could hang out, watch a classic movie, and drink beers, except during the last year. Maggie had begrudgingly given up alcohol when she had begun the journey of trying to get pregnant. Movie night had become a tradition both of them needed. Living inside the park, fifty miles from town, meant neither of them had much of a social life. Not that Alex wanted more. Having one good friend was enough for her.

Koko barked before Maggie knocked and when Alex opened the door, Maggie's dog Pelli pushed through. Koko and Pelli tumbled on the floor in a tangle of skinny legs and open mouths, playing as only siblings could. Shortly after Alex had accepted the job, she and Maggie had adopted mutt puppies from a family in town, and their friendship grew out of their love for their dogs.

"Simmer down, girls. It's movie time." Maggie waved the movie back and forth. "We've seen this a million times," she said. "One of these days you need to see something new. Jim could get something from town. Dembi Brewing is right next to the movie rental place."

Alex scrunched up her nose. "I don't really like new movies. They're all action. I like meaningful glances and well-developed dialogue."

Maggie laughed. "The next two weeks might kill you. They're filming the next Hollywood blockbuster here. You know that, right? *Saddles of Glory* or something. It's going to have a ton of CGI and special effects."

"It won't be that bad, will it?" The dread she had been fighting for weeks solidified into a tight ball in the pit of her stomach. Filming would start tomorrow and she would be in charge.

"Depends. But don't worry, I'll be a phone call away." Maggie put the movie in and eased down on the couch. "You've never worked with a crew before?" she asked with an air of sophistication.

Alex shook her head. "My last job was at a federal park in Oregon, remember? The location manager who came out a few weeks ago said film crews typically work with state parks because they're cheaper."

"Makes sense. The last time we had a crew working here was when Rick the Dick was still manager. What a douche. I'm just sorry my timing is leaving you high and dry." Maggie popped open the beer with the bottle opener attached to her keys, inhaled deeply, and handed it to Alex. "I miss it."

"I know." Maggie's moving belly made her smile. "He's worth it though, right?"

"Right." Maggie smiled and caressed the little life inside her.

Alex settled onto the couch next to her friend, and their dogs eventually tired themselves out and fell asleep together. After the movie, they talked about the baby, work, the dogs, and Maggie's husband, Jim.

"He really doesn't mind the commute into town every day?" Alex asked.

Maggie shrugged. "He says he's used to it. Anyway, it's a pretty drive, and you can't beat not having a mortgage or rent."

"That's true. In Oregon, we didn't have housing. We were too close to the city. I like it here. It's peaceful." Alex sipped the last of her beer. "Tell Jim thanks for the beer. It's good."

"Will do. One of the perks of being the brewmaster's wife." Maggie yawned. "I better push off before I fall asleep on your couch again."

"Are you too tired to walk next door?" she joked.

"Pelli will keep me awake." She winked and then

stroked the dog's sleeping face to wake her for their walk home. "See you tomorrow."

"Tomorrow," Alex repeated; the tight knot reforming in her stomach. No matter how hard she tried, she couldn't shake her case of nerves.

When she woke the next morning, every muscle in her body tensed. Koko tried to help her relax with her daily dose of slobbery kisses before she left home, but even that didn't work.

The walk to the entrance gate eased a little of the stress from of her shoulders as she watched thin clouds skirt across the pale sky. By the time she unlocked the gate booth, she had convinced herself the movie crew wouldn't be as bad as she assumed.

A long, straight road extended away from the entrance gate in two directions, giving the ranger on duty a view of the Visitor Center and oncoming traffic at the same time. That's how she first saw the convoy of vans—bright white blobs snaking through the serene landscape, one after another. As they neared, she could clearly see the same design printed on the sides of each van with the words *DEMBI WILDERNESS RENTALS* above a rosy pile of picturesque boulders. A string of trailers followed clearly marked for costumes, makeup, and food services.

The first van stopped at the gate, and the window eased down with an electronic whir. The driver didn't say anything beyond a greeting because the man sitting next to him interrupted.

"Good to see you again, Alex." Steve's silvery head appeared along with a wide smile.

"Nice to see you, Steve. I wasn't sure what time you'd be here." She smiled. "Is this the whole group?"

Steve nodded. "For today. Are you ready for us?"

After taking a deep breath, her smile tightened just like her stomach. "I think so." She turned her attention to the man behind the wheel. "Have the drivers park in the overflow parking lot," she said, showing him a park map. "I'll meet you guys there once my replacement arrives."

"You got it, ma'am." The driver nodded. Steve waved and then they drove away.

Unhooking her walkie-talkie from her waistband, she spoke, hoping someone in the Visitor Center would answer. "The movie crew is here. I need someone to come to the gate and relieve me."

Twenty minutes later, Alex waved at the seasonal ranger who took over for her as she slipped outside. The bright morning sun warmed her shoulders and the black asphalt under her feet. Taking one deep breath after another, she tried to calm her jangly nerves. It was time to pretend to be in charge.

As she passed the Visitor Center, Maggie came up alongside her. She slowed down—Maggie didn't walk so much as waddle those days.

"It's going to be fine," Maggie said, patting Alex's shoulder lightly, sending a wave of calm through Alex.

When they reached the worn road to the overflow parking area, there were dozens of people milling around. The sheer size of the crew made Alex and Maggie stop in their tracks. A craft service truck blocked the entrance to the parking lot, offering a variety of snack foods as well as a formidable barrier between the movie crew and the rest of the park visitors.

Alex swallowed hard and searched for Steve, the

only person from the crew she knew. Her anxiety ratcheted up a notch, and she had to remind herself she had promised to do her best, for her friend. It was almost impossible to ignore the pounding of her heart.

Alex and Maggie wove through the throngs of people and finally located their target.

"Good. You're here. Now we can get started," Steve said, giving Alex a meaningful nod.

"Started," she repeated, forcing the word out of her tight diaphragm as her mind went blank.

"With your introduction and guidelines," Maggie offered helpfully, nudging Alex's arm lightly.

"Right." Alex chewed on the edge of her thumbnail. Even though she had been preparing for her speech for weeks, the words swirled around in her head like papers blowing in the wind. "Where should I..." She swallowed hard and wrung her hands.

Steve's eyes crinkled as he smiled and then he picked up a megaphone. "People, attention on the set." Speaking away from the amplifier, he said to Alex, "Why don't you stand up on the costume trailer steps so everyone can see you."

Maggie leaned close and whispered, "You'll be great," before finding a place in the crowd.

Alex nodded and walked slowly toward the trailer.

As soon as she was in position, Steve thrust the megaphone into her hands. When she pushed the button and cleared her throat, a magnified squeal made the crowd jump. "Sorry," she mumbled. Glancing out at the sea of faces, she found encouragement from Maggie. After taking a deep breath, she said, "Hi, my name is Alex Mitchell. I'm the assistant manager at Twisted Juniper. Welcome to our park. There are a few guidelines you need to follow while you're here. Please stay on the paths as much as possible; the earth is very fragile. Cairns, the little stacks of rocks, will mark the borders." She pointed to a tiny tower of stone nearby. "When you're hauling equipment, it must be carried by hand. Twisted Juniper is home to a variety of protected plants and animals, and I can't stress enough how important it is you minimize your impact on them. My job is to make sure you can do your work safely without harming the environment. There will be a number of rangers working with you, so please feel free to ask questions. We're easy to spot since we're all dressed the same." She pointed to Maggie, who raised her hand and gestured down at her matching outfit. A quiet laugh worked through the crowd. "Any questions?" She didn't try too hard to find one and stepped down, handing the megaphone back to Steve before anyone else could talk to her.

"Are the horses here yet?" she asked him.

"No. They'll come in a few days," he answered.

"I'll need to discuss the disposal of manure. It's full of seeds that aren't native to this area. We can't afford to have any more noxious weeds here, so it'll need to be picked up immediately."

"I'll send the wrangler to you when he gets here. Is there anything else I need to know?"

"Not that I can think of. I'll get out of your way so you can get to it." The sooner they started, the sooner they would leave, which was just fine by her.

Steve nodded, turned away from her, and started barking orders through the megaphone.

"Maggie, will you please ask Neal and Robyn to help supervise today? They'll need walkies." She touched the walkie-talkie on her belt. "The others will need some instructions. Oh, and can you let Koko out for me at lunch?"

"You bet," Maggie said as cheerfully as ever before lumbering away.

Alex watched as the camera and sound crews began the time-consuming task of carrying their heavy equipment from the vans to the set. Pity tugged at her as she watched them abandon their hand trucks at the end of the paved parking lot and struggle with the thick cables and huge black boxes. It took several hours to get their gear in place, and when the crew stopped for the day, she thanked them and finished a few small tasks at the Visitor Center before her shift ended.

When she poked her head into Maggie's office she couldn't help but smile. "You were right. It wasn't so bad."

"I told you." Maggie grinned.

"Thanks for helping me today. I'll see you tomorrow, right?"

"Unless Henry decides to come tonight, which would be totally fine," Maggie said to her swollen stomach. "I'm too old for this," she said.

"You are not. Thirty-five is perfect." Maggie was only four years older than Alex, so she wasn't about to let her friend think she was too old.

"My back is killing me." She rubbed along her spine.

"I don't think age has anything to do with that. My mom was almost forty when she had my little brother and she said her back hurt the worst with me, but she likes to blame me for everything."

"Troublemaker," Maggie said and then got back to

the project on her desk.

On the short walk to her house, Alex hummed. Everything really *was* fine. One day down, thirteen more to go. The typical duties she had would be disrupted a little, but she was sure she could handle it.

She'd never been so wrong in her life.

Chapter Two

"This place is a shit hole," Blaze mumbled as he ducked his head out of the commuter plane. The landing strip looked like a long-forgotten highway with weeds growing in the abundant cracks. A row of boxy fluorescent lights illuminated the desolate landscape, including a tiny air control tower, which doubled as a car rental. Three cars were parked outside. Three.

Nate cleared his throat, so Blaze stepped out onto the rickety stairs leading away from the aircraft. The metal frame creaked under his feet, making him grip the handrail a little tighter.

No one greeted them. No fans, no cameras, nothing, just a uniformed man strolling back to the lone structure after delivering the rolling stairs.

Blaze stopped on the last step, making Nate bump into him. "Where are we?"

"The Dembi airport. I already told you," Nate snapped and gave him a shove.

Blaze shrugged but refused to move. Nate probably had told him, but he didn't care enough to listen. Plus, he'd helped himself to a few drinks on the short trip, which always made time with Nate more tolerable. "I thought we were going to a hotel." The dark night that surrounded them didn't show any signs of civilization. "There's nothing around here for miles."

"It's a thirty-minute drive." Nate sighed. "I don't

know why I let you drink. At least one of us is sober."

"Let me?" Blaze mocked and then finished descending the stairs. "How are we getting there?"

"A driver is supposed to be meeting us here." Nate came up alongside him, checked his phone, and then scanned the empty parking lot.

Blaze dropped his duffle bag on the worn asphalt. "Did you request an invisible van?"

Nate had already started dialing and had his back to Blaze. "Where's our van?" He listened to the response. "What are we supposed to do? You expect us to wait another hour? Out here?" A groan accompanied the disconnection before he stalked toward the building.

"What's going on?" Blaze asked as he ran after him.

Nate didn't respond; he just kept walking.

By the time they reached the tower, the aircraft had moved to the end of the runway and its engine whined as it prepared to take off. Blaze considered running after the plane to head home, but his agent would kill him. It might be worth it. Too late. The wheels lifted off the ground and the plane blasted him with grit as it took off.

"Come on," Nate grumbled as he held the door open to the passenger waiting room. It looked more like a doctor's office. Half a dozen chairs lined the walls and a man stood behind the solitary counter.

The man had been watching a rerun of an old sitcom on the ancient TV mounted on the wall across from him. "Welcome to Dembi Airport." He narrowed his eyes. "Are you two Hollywood types?"

"What does it look like?" Blaze asked as he straightened his back.

"If I could figure that out, I wouldn't have asked, would I?" the man replied. "You missed your van. They left about..." He paused to look at his watch for more than thirty seconds. "Twenty minutes ago."

"They were supposed to wait for us," Nate ground out.

"I can call into town if you'd like," he offered as he slowly pointed to an olive green corded phone attached to the wall.

"I already called." Nate slumped into one of the dumpy chairs and dropped his bag on the floor.

"We're not staying, are we?" Blaze was tired and had no intention of waiting another hour and a half before he could get to bed.

"Do you have any better ideas, genius?" Nate snapped.

"Let's rent a car." Blaze nodded to the parking lot. "They're for rent, right?" he asked loud enough that the man behind the counter could hear him.

"One of them is mine, but the other two are fair game. Which one are you interested in?" The man pulled out a stack of papers from behind the counter.

Blaze went to the window and sneered as he sized up the two worn cars. "Neither."

The man must not have heard him, because he added, "The white one is a little nicer. It has a heater that works."

Blaze's shoulders sagged. "We'll take the white one."

"What do you mean, we?" Nate asked. "You can't rent a car."

Blaze turned to face him. "Would you rather sit here and wait for a van to come get us? Maybe you're interested in watching the rest of this episode." He pointed a thumb at the TV, which had developed a gray band that flickered across the screen and distorted the image. "Or maybe you want to spend more quality time with me? Is that it? You want to bond?"

Nate rolled his eyes.

"We could braid each other's hair and talk about boys," he added with a fake smile. "Isn't that what best friends do?" Blaze sat in the chair right next to Nate and leaned his head close. "Do me first."

Nate sighed and walked to the counter. "We'll take the white one." He pulled two wallets out of his luggage, one Nate's the other Blaze's. "You're paying for this." To prove his point, he removed one of Blaze's credit cards.

"Fine by me." Blaze watched TV for a few minutes while Nate filled out the paperwork and called to cancel the van.

With keys in hand, Nate went to the car, and Blaze followed immediately. They put their bags in the trunk and then Nate got behind the wheel. "Here's a map of the area."

Blaze turned the overhead light on and looked at the folded paper as Nate started the car. There was one road that led to Dembi. "Turn right and drive until you reach the interstate. Pretty straightforward." His eyes followed the lines on the map all the way to Twisted Juniper State Park. It would be a long drive for filming every day. Why had he taken the job?

After switching the tiny light off, he leaned his seat back as far as it would go, and closed his eyes.

Nate drove in silence for a while and then said, "Here's the interstate."

"Turn the heater on, will you? It's a little chilly."

Nate complied as Blaze put his seat back up.

"Now we're really living it up, huh?" Blaze smiled.

Nate shook his head.

The fabric on the ceiling was peeling from the corners and the faux leather dashboard was cracking, but at least the heater worked.

As they approached the city, the sky began to glow. Nate drove toward a massive new building overlooking the small town. It was a little after midnight and they were all alone on the roads. In California, the roads were never empty.

"Here we are," Nate announced as he pulled up next to a row of white vans with a rental logo painted on the side. "I'll go check us in."

Blaze nodded and waited in the car. A sidewalk wound around the perimeter of the parking lot and disappeared into the night.

"You're in room 212. I'm in 215." Nate gave Blaze a keycard.

Blaze scanned the parking lot before getting out. "Where is everyone?"

Nate shrugged and shouldered his bag. "Sleeping? It was empty in the lobby, too. You're safe."

Blaze couldn't remember the last time he'd gone to a hotel without a paparazzi accompaniment. "Cool." With the bag over his shoulder, he followed Nate inside. The man behind the lobby desk nodded to acknowledge them but immediately went back to work.

The hotel seemed pretty upscale for such a small town. From the lobby, signs were posted for the pool, gym, and restaurant and bar. Fresh flowers were positioned in massive vases throughout the spacious room.

Once they were in the elevator, Nate said, "He assured me they are very discreet here. They're probably getting paid double to keep their mouths shut." The doors slid open and they walked down the hall together in silence. "Night."

"Night," Blaze echoed as he pushed his key into the slot and stepped into his room. It was smaller than the suites he was used to, but the bed was clean and comfortable, which was all that mattered. He kicked off his shoes, pulled back the comforter, and fell asleep.

****

The room phone woke Blaze several hours later. Nate had arranged a wake-up call, of course. Couldn't be late for work. He stretched and pushed the curtain open. From his window, he had a view of the entire sleepy town. The hotel sat on a ridge overlooking Dembi; it was small but beautiful. The sun had started to lighten the sky, but sunrise was still a ways off.

He smoothed his rumpled clothes, tied his running shoes, and pushed out into the hall, stopping at Nate's door so he could return the favor. "Wakey, wakey," he said as he pounded on the thin door.

"Asshole," Nate grumbled.

Blaze smiled and yanked the door to the stairway open, following them down, past the lobby, and outside to the sidewalk. What had appeared dismal and gray when they'd arrived, turned out to be a dusty red landscape as far as the eye could see. The sidewalk he had eyed the night before gave way to a dirt path that cut into the side of the ridge. He dug his shoes into the red soil and followed the trail onto a rocky rim that spanned a mile to the east. As the sun approached, it turned the dull sky a cheery blue and painted the ground bright red. Stunned by the beauty, Blaze stopped in his tracks and stored the images of his surroundings in his memory. Never before had he seen such a contrast of colors: blue, red, and pale green dotted the landscape.

The sun warmed him while he stretched every muscle in his body. Push-ups came next and then he started running.

The invigorating breeze was perfect. He breathed deep, savoring the fresh air as he rounded the edge of the cliff and looped back toward the hotel. By the time he returned, the caravan of vehicles was loading up.

"Where have you been?" Nate demanded.

Blaze pointed over his shoulder. "I went for a run. I thought that's why you woke me up so early."

"We need to go and you need a shower. Hurry." Nate wrinkled his nose and pointed to the sweat marks under Blaze's arms and around his neck.

"Last time I checked, I'm the star. We'll go when I'm ready." Once Blaze was out of sight he hustled to his room, showered in record time, and returned to the parking lot to get into the last van. A few of the extras offered their seats to him, but he declined and squeezed into the very back. Nate followed, naturally.

With the van loaded the driver headed out of town, straight into the heart of the desert. Blaze tried to sleep on the hour-long trip to the park, but Nate filled the time with idle prattle.

"Steve said the assistant park manager would be waiting for us." The screen on Nate's phone displayed a paragraph of text. "Alex Mitchell."

"Whatever." Blaze couldn't care less what the ranger's name was. As long as the guy didn't get in his way, things would work out fine. Of course things never worked out just fine. They always wanted something from him: autographs, pictures, or an hour-long chat. "Did you get me anything to eat?"

"I'll get you something on set." Nate looked out the window. "It's pretty here. I didn't think it would be." Blaze followed his gaze and nodded before Nate went on, "We need to be on set earlier tomorrow. You'll have to plan your run accordingly."

"Fine." Blaze propped his foot on his bent knee. Tiny red rocks were wedged into the bottom of his shoes. He smiled and could almost feel the wind on his face again.

They passed through the entrance gate and finally pulled into a parking lot next to the other vans. Blaze waited patiently while everyone got out and then grinned when murmurs went through the crowd.

"I have arrived," he announced as he strutted toward the waiting cast. While he had enjoyed the solitude and anonymity, there was nothing quite like a sea of adoring fans. A few faces were familiar, but most were extras he hadn't worked with before. One of the women was already in costume and smiled at him. By the cut of her dress, she was probably playing a prostitute. "Hot damn," he said before introducing himself. She was the kind of woman who had gotten him in trouble in the past.

"Blaze. Costume is waiting," Nate reminded him.

"In a minute. I'm getting to know—what did you say your name was?"

"Caitlin," she said.

"Caitlin." They shook hands slowly. "Pleased to make your acquaintance."

"Likewise."

"See you on set," he said and winked.

She blushed.

"Costume waits for no man." Blaze laughed and then followed Nate to the costume trailer. "I was just being friendly."

"With the prettiest woman on set," Nate added. "I bet she'd look even better on her knees. You'll have to let me know," he said with a nudge.

Blaze nodded and stepped into the costume trailer. It was the same wardrobe he'd been wearing for months, but he'd never worn it outside. So far, everything had been shot in a studio. Mr. Reid, the director, had insisted on filming the action sequences on location, which meant everyone and everything had to be transported to the middle of the Utah desert.

Javier handed him a pile of neatly folded clothes and motioned to a tiny dressing room. "Carol will get your props when you're dressed."

"Nice to see you, too, Javier."

Javier smiled and pushed him into a dressing room.

Blaze changed quickly and then got his gun and holster from Carol. It felt real around his waist, and his scuffed up cowboy boots and hat were the final touch. When he left the trailer, he truly felt like Buck, the Wild West outlaw he was playing.

Nate waited outside with a packaged muffin. "Where are your clothes?"

"In the dressing room." Blaze snatched his breakfast out of Nate's hand.

Nate grunted and pushed past him. "Don't worry, I'll clean up after you, as per usual."

"Isn't that what you're paid for?" Blaze didn't get

far before the seam of his pants rubbed against his boot. He put his muffin down just in front of him on a flat red rock as he squatted to adjust his costume. Within seconds, something swooped in and stole it. "Hey," he shouted.

A big black bird croaked from a branch near his face.

"That's mine," he said as if the stupid animal could understand him.

The bird tilted its head and croaked again.

"I thought you were hungry," Nate said. "Why did you give your muffin to that bird?"

"I didn't give it to the bird," Blaze shouted.

An audience grew and so did the laughter. Heat crept up Blaze's neck. All he needed was the perfect rock.

Chapter Three

Alex made a quick stop in her office and was heading to the set when Beth, one of the perkier seasonals, came running up to her.

"I saw him," Beth squealed, her face flushed.

"Who?"

"Blaze Johnson," Beth screeched.

Alex shrugged and shook her head. "Who?"

"Blaze Johnson," she repeated as if saying his name again would somehow enlighten Alex. "The hottest star in Hollywood. And I mean hot." She fanned her face for emphasis. "I heard he was making a new movie. I can't believe it's going to be here. Did you see his last one? Good Lord."

"Can't say I have."

Beth's mouth hung open. "You really don't know who he is?"

"Nope. I know Steve, the first assistant producer. I'll be dealing with him the most, so he's my main concern."

Beth tilted her head and frowned.

"Will you cover the entrance gate today?" Alex asked, making a mental note to keep Beth busy while the film crew worked. Mr. Howard's advice ran through her mind—keep the star-struck staff and visitors away from the actors.

"Sure, I guess." Beth's smile fell.

"Thanks. Time to get to work." She nodded, giving Beth an encouraging pat before continuing along the path toward the overflow parking lot.

The crowd had doubled from the previous day with over a hundred people already on set. Her anxiety set in, stealing her breath and muting all the sounds around her. The rough edge of her thumbnail became the focus of her worry as she picked at the flap of skin she had chewed the previous day. You can do this, she reminded herself. One small cluster of people stood out from the rest because they were shouting at a juniper tree, which didn't make any sense.

She pushed into the circle of people in time to see a man chuck a rock at the branches. A raven croaked and hopped higher, clutching a shiny bag with its feet.

A tall, muscular man bent over, picked up another rock, and raised his arm.

Alex lunged forward, gripped his wrist, and said, "What are you doing?"

"That little bastard stole my muffin," the man shouted, turning his attention from the bird to Alex while he twisted free from her grasp, his steely blue eyes boring into hers.

"Ravens are protected by The Migratory Bird Treaty Act," she stated. "They also mate for life, so if you hurt it, you'll be hurting its partner, too."

He smirked. "Who gives a shit? It's just a stupid bird."

"I do." Forgetting her worry for a moment, she glared at him. This asshole needed to be put in his place. "So stupid it managed to steal your muffin?" Alex lifted her eyebrows and stared into his eyes, challenging him. "If I see you assaulting another living thing inside this park, I'll fine you."

"Don't you know who I am?" the man replied before puffing his impressive chest. "Of course you do. Is this your way of asking for an autograph?" After looking her up and down, he glanced at the man standing closest to him. "Nate, get me another muffin."

Without a word, the sandy-haired man scurried away, making a hole in the group.

"Excuse me?" Alex said.

"There you are," Maggie said, clutching Alex's elbow and pulling her out of the crowd toward the craft service truck. Maggie leaned in and asked in a whisper, "Do you know who that is?"

"A dick, with a capital D," Alex shouted. "You should've heard what he said."

"That's Blaze Johnson. *The* Blaze Johnson."

Alex flinched. The hottest star in Hollywood. Shit. No wonder he was so ripped.

"Remember the whole conversation you had with the regional manager? About glowing recommendations, a donation to the park, and us getting raises? We need that letter and that's an important guy to have on our side."

"I don't want him on my side. He's a dick," she shouted.

The sandy-haired man chuckled and made eye contact with Alex before disappearing into the crowd.

"Oh shit. Do you think he heard me?" Alex struggled to breathe.

Maggie grimaced. "Probably. You shouted *he's a dick* loud enough everyone in a fifty-mile radius could hear you."

She buried her face in her hands. "Just shoot me

now. See? I can't do this. Day two and I've already insulted the most important actor on set. Save me. Please? Don't have your baby. Ever. Okay?"

Maggie laughed and tugged on her arm. "Come on. We have work to do."

****

Some of the actors clustered around Mr. Reid, the director, while others visited the trailers set up for costuming, hair, and makeup.

From her vantage point near the set, Alex watched Blaze walk around in his tight-fitting cowboy costume. Nothing like the classic attire worn by the stars of spaghetti westerns, his clothes were meant to show off his body. And what a body it was. A gun hung low on one side, tugging down his pants to reveal the carved hollow above his hip and the muscles that flexed when he walked. The smooth planes of his tan chest were visible under his loose vest. With a perfectly sculpted hat tucked on his head, he strutted toward her.

A dense fog settled in her brain, and her mouth went dry.

"Like what you see?" Wiggling eyebrows accompanied a cocky smile. Without giving her a chance to answer, he went on. "You know, I thought you were a dude. You have a man's name. Two, actually. Alex. Mitchell. Your parents must have really wanted a son."

A frown tugged down the corners of her mouth. "I don't have a man's name," she said finally. "And I wasn't watching you," she lied, making a note to wear sunglasses in the future.

"Yes, you were," he said as he hooked his thumbs over the waistband of his tight pants, drawing her eyes to the golden trail of hairs running down the center of his abs. "It's okay, I'm used to the attention. I can handle it, little darlin'."

Swallowing hard and crossing her arms over her chest, she said, "I'm not your *darlin'*. What's wrong with you?"

"Oh, you're feisty. I love a challenge." Confidence oozed out of him and his stupid, sexy smile.

"I'm trying to work and you're in my way." Her words had the effect she hoped for and his arrogant smile faltered. She shooed him away with her hands. "Don't you have something to do?"

"That's still in the works," he said before winking and swaggering away. In spite of herself, she watched him join the other actors gathered around the director. The view of his backside was just as good as the front.

After hours of supervising cameramen, everyone took a break for lunch. Alex found a secluded spot in the shade while Neal, Robyn, and Dana got in line with everyone else at the food truck. Neal had been the park's naturalist for years and, like Maggie, had loads of experience with movie crews. Robyn and Dana were the only experienced seasonals, having returned for another summer at the park. At the moment Maggie was instructing Beth, Todd, and Brandon on what was expected of them during filming, a task Alex was glad to delegate and even happier to know Maggie was still there. Just in case.

Neal wandered over to her with a plate in his hands. "You should get some food. It's good," he said before taking a bite of his burrito and nodding.

"I already ate," she replied showing him an empty wrapper.

"A granola bar? It's not really about the food. It's about getting to know these people. We'll be working side by side with them for the next two weeks. You should reach out, make a good impression," he added, reminding her of Mr. Howard's stern lecture.

Blaze lounged at a cluster of tables around the food truck, laughing and eating with his friends. Reaching out to him filled her with equal parts of disgust and curiosity. "I don't feel like getting to know them."

Neal followed her line of sight and nodded. "I'm not a fan, either. They're not all like him."

Alex had worked closely with Neal over the past year improving the naturalist programs in the park, so she trusted him. "Okay, but I hope I don't regret this," she called out before wandering over to the food truck to order lunch. "Do you mind if I sit here?" she asked Steve.

"Not at all. Sit, please." Steve smiled at her. "How do you like it so far?"

"It's noisy," she said, glancing at Blaze's raucous group before taking a bite of her delicious lunch.

"He's not always like that," Steve said.

"I'll have to take your word for it." The last thing she wanted to talk about was Blaze. "How do you like the park so far?"

Steve smiled widely and squinted up at the bright blue sky.

In that unguarded moment, she realized why she liked him so much: he reminded her of her dad. It had been years since she'd been home, and she missed him.

"It's spectacular. I've never been here before and I can't figure out why. I've always loved being outdoors. We spent every summer at Live Oak Canyon above

Beverly Hills at my grandparent's estate. My sister and I just inherited it."

She let out a low whistle. "I bet that's prime real estate."

"I could never turn it into a neighborhood."

"A neighborhood? How much land are you talking about?"

"Fifty-seven acres. My sister doesn't want to develop it either. Neither of us has kids, so I'm not sure what we're going to do."

"Why not protect it? Have you thought about turning it into a nature reserve?"

"I wouldn't know the first thing about that." Steve shrugged. "I can tell people what to do all day long on a set, but I don't know anything about taking care of a piece of property."

"All you need to do is contact your local wildlife trust. They could get you started."

"You know, that's not a bad idea. I'm going to talk to my sister about it. Thanks, Alex."

"No problem." The conversation shifted to his plans for the rest of the day before everyone was called back to the set.

While she stood around watching everyone and everything, she thought of a million things she could've been working on: the rocks marking the edge of the trail needed to be tidied, cairns had been tipped over, and weeds needed to be pulled. But she couldn't do any of it. Being on the film crew's clock almost every day for the next two weeks meant everything else would have to wait. She hated it.

When they wrapped up that night, Alex walked down the road toward her house. As the crew packed up and drove out, a peaceful calm settled over the desert as if it had been waiting for them to leave, too.

Koko smashed her nose against the window and then wiggled to the front door to greet Alex.

"Hey, did Maggie give you lots of love today? I bet she did," she said in a singsong voice to her dog as she rubbed her ears. "Let's get you some dinner."

Maggie knocked on the window before she had a chance to close the door.

"How was it? Tell me everything," Maggie said as Pelli pushed past them. Maggie held her hands behind her back, clasping a long tube of white paper.

"What's that?"

"A gift." Maggie pressed her lips together, smothering a smile.

"A gift?"

"To help you during the filming." Maggie unrolled the tube, revealing a full-size glossy picture of Blaze Johnson: shirtless, sweaty, and smiling.

Just like earlier, he had his thumbs hooked on the waistband of his jeans, but this time, they happened to be unbuttoned. It was an even better view than the one Alex got earlier that day.

"How is *that* supposed to help me?" Her cheeks burned. Had Maggie seen her ogling him earlier?

"So you remember who he is," she answered sweetly. "Also, he's hot. I kind of want to lick him." She wiggled her tongue near Blaze's shiny abs.

"Stop," Alex protested with a groan.

"I asked Jim to pick it up in town with the intention of giving it to you as a gift."

"Jim won't let you keep it, will he?" Alex arched her eyebrows, waiting for the answer.

"Hell no. Blaze is paid to look good. I think Jim's a little intimidated by him, which is ridiculous."

Alex chuckled. "Especially if Jim knew him. Blaze is a disgusting pig." The events of the day replayed in her mind, and she rolled her eyes. "You're not leaving it here, so you might as well go put it in the fire pit."

"I'm not going to burn him. He's too pretty to burn. He's so hot he might spontaneously combust, but that's beside the point. I'll find something else to do with him." Maggie spoke to the glossy face, "Can you believe she wants to throw you in the fire? Me either."

"You've lost your mind. Get that out of here." She shook her head and walked into the kitchen. "Pelli, are you hungry?"

Maggie called out, "I need to use your bathroom."

"You know where it is." Alex turned her attention to Koko and Pelli who sat together waiting for dinner. She filled Koko's bowl with extra kibble and put it between them. "Share please."

By the time Alex got back to the living room, Maggie was waiting on her couch with an exaggerated pouty lip.

"I'm sad you didn't like my gift."

"It's the thought that counts," Alex said, soothing Maggie's fake hurt pride.

"Okay. Tell me everything."

****

Blaze pulled his hat down to hide his face. It didn't matter how discreet the staff at the hotel was supposed to be, it was still embarrassing to have to use the computer in the lobby. Yet again, he wished he had his phone. It had been confiscated on the plane along with his wallet.

That was the deal. Blaze promised to stay out of trouble and his agent made sure he kept his promise by removing the temptation. He didn't like it. At all. As an adult, he should be able to do whatever he pleased. Should be. In the past, he had done plenty of things that nearly ruined him, which meant his agent had reasons not to trust him. But a lot had changed. Blaze had changed. None of it mattered. The only thing that mattered was work. Without work, he was nothing.

"Birds of prey," he said as he typed. The screen filled with images of all kinds of birds. "What did she call it?" He searched his brain for the answer. "Bird protection act. Bingo. The Migratory Bird Treaty Act of 1918 is a United States federal law... I guess she wasn't lying about that." He skimmed the article. "Makes it illegal to possess, import, export, transport, sell, purchase, barter... It doesn't say anything in here about throwing rocks at them. They mate for life," he mocked Alex's high voice. "You'll hurt its partner."

The next search focused on ravens. "Like I'm supposed to care about some stupid bird," he muttered as he read pages of information about the common raven. "They are intelligent, graceful, confident, and inquisitive." The articles backed up everything she said and more. "The parents both care for their young for several months. Aw that's nice."

"What are you doing?" Nate asked from behind him.

Blaze flinched. "How long have you been there?"

"Long enough to hear you say something was nice." Nate frowned. "What's all that?"

"Nothing." Blaze shrugged. "Just doing a little research. Remember the bird this morning?"

Nate nodded.

"They're one of the smartest birds. They remember faces and can solve complex puzzles."

"Are you trying to tell me ravens are smarter than you?" Nate laughed. "Not surprising."

Blaze shook his head and closed the browser. "You're an asshole, you know that?"

"Takes one to know one."

"Real mature." Just like that, Blaze was thirteen again, being teased by the school bully.

It didn't matter how much fame or money Blaze had, he still had to deal with pricks like Nate. It was actually the opposite. Fame and money put him directly in Nate's path. "I'm going to my room."

"What are you doing tonight?"

"None of your business," Blaze snapped.

"Cathy, or whatever her name is. From this morning," Nate asked as he nudged Blaze's shoulder.

"Caitlin," he corrected.

"Right. Caitlin's been waiting for you all this time while you've been doing research?" Nate asked.

"Something like that." Blaze slid into his larger than life persona, the one with a thick skin Nate couldn't bother. "I had to give her a chance to catch her breath before round two." He winked and strutted toward the stairs. Nate didn't follow.

As soon as he was alone, he eased out of his exaggerated walk and jogged up the stairs to his room. The door clicked behind him.

He stripped, dropped his clothes on the floor outside the bathroom, and then stepped into the shower and turned the water on. "Looks like it's just you and me again," he said to his hand as he closed his eyes and touched himself. Even though he tried to keep his mind blank and focus on the physical pleasure, his brain had other plans. Like a movie playing in his head, dozens of pretty women flashed before his eyes. And then Alex's face appeared—glossy brown hair, chocolate eyes, soft lips parted. In the moment he'd walk toward her, her face was totally unguarded and he had seen desire. When he had tugged on his pants, her eyes had followed. His dick hardened and he pumped it hard and fast, holding onto the memory of Alex—her eyes glazed over, her breasts heaving inside her brown uniform as she denied watching him.

It was obvious she wanted him, but she wasn't like the others. He would have to work to charm her, and he loved a good challenge.

"Don't you have something to do?" she had asked.

"You," he said. In his mind, he was inside her while she kissed him with those luscious lips. Euphoria spread through his entire body when he came.

He was already looking forward to work the next day.

Chapter Four

Alex woke when the first rays of sun crept over the horizon and pushed through her windows, surrounding her with dim light. Koko stirred next to her, her body vibrating as she stretched. Early September air spilled in through her open window, carrying the scent of rain with it. Alex rolled onto her stomach and peered out the window. Sure enough, water had carved tiny valleys in her sandy backyard.

The morning was cool and her bedroom had developed a chill. Fall was approaching and the vast Utah desert seemed to sigh with relief. The end of summer was her favorite because of the spectacular monsoons that brought life back to the parched land. The potholes that dotted the rocky eastern trail had begun to fill in August and teemed with triops and fairy shrimp, in a rush to grow and mate before the water evaporated.

Koko enjoyed walking in the wet sand after a stormy night, and wiggled with anticipation next to Alex. "Sorry, baby. I can't take you out today; I need to be on the set." With her face buried in her pillow, she groaned.

A minute later, her phone rang. Jim's anxious voice said, "It's happening."

"The baby? Is Maggie in labor?" She wanted nothing more than to be with her friend but knew she couldn't leave.

"We're at the hospital. I'll call when I have news. I gotta go. The doctor just came in." Jim's words gushed out of his mouth.

"Give her a hug. I'll talk to you—"

The line disconnected.

"Later," she finished. Koko looked up at her with an expectant face. "You're going to be a big sister. I hope you're ready. Come on, let's go get Pelli; she'll be staying with us for a few days."

Locking two rambunctious dogs in her house all day didn't seem like the best plan, but she didn't have much choice. The bin full of toys would have to keep them busy for the day.

Alex's mood didn't improve when she found Blaze waiting for her at the edge of the overflow parking lot.

"I've been waiting twenty minutes for you," he said. A stupid smile tugged up the corners of his mouth.

"It's seven fifty-five. I'm five minutes early," she snapped.

"We can't do anything without you on the set," he said.

"That's right. It's part of the contract I signed. I have to be here to make sure you don't harm the park. I know how much you enjoy taunting birds." That got the response she was after, but he looked even better when he was embarrassed. Life just wasn't fair. She pulled her wet hair into a low ponytail and tugged her hat over her head, not because the sun bothered her, but because he did.

"You have a weird attachment to this place."

She glared at him. "No, I don't." A snappy comeback got stuck in her throat and then her phone chimed in her back pocket, announcing the beginning of her workday. "Time to work. Are you coming?"

He slid his hands down his bare chest. "Not yet."

Instead of slapping the smug, suggestive smile right off his face, she shook her head and walked away.

All day long, she stood like a statue in the background; staying out of the way yet close enough to supervise every movement in and around her area of the set. No news about Maggie came, despite how many times she checked her phone. It was the perfect distraction from her anxious mind. Worrying about Maggie was much less stressful than worrying about screwing up without her. As the day wore on, it didn't distract her enough. A guy holding a boom mic slipped and almost fell off a fifteen-foot cliff, making her heart nearly stop. In her first month at the park a tourist had fallen off a much bigger overhang, ignoring warning signs and trying to get the perfect selfie. Alex had never been afraid of heights before, but after she and Maggie found the woman's mangled body, cliff edges made her nervous. After his close call, her shirt was saturated with sweat.

Beth handled a large group of extras being outfitted in the costume trailer while Todd and Brandon watched over the stunt team practicing a fight sequence farther away.

When everyone took a break for lunch, Alex lined up behind a group of extras, her mouth salivating when she got a whiff of the aroma coming from the makeshift restaurant. Blaze flirted with the women at the head of the line and she rolled her eyes. It was easy to assume he was the kind of guy who had sex with a different woman every night since he hit on anything with boobs.

The woman ordered a sandwich with everything, and Blaze replied, "I like a woman who can take it all."

"Oh, Blaze," she said, putting her hand on his chest.

Alex's stomach churned, but not out of hunger. "Pig," she muttered.

Blaze's public display of disgusting behavior continued as he found a seat with the woman.

With her sandwich tucked safely in one hand, she slipped through the crowd toward her house. After changing into a clean, sweat-free shirt, she let Koko and Pelli out for a bathroom break and sat in the shade of her house while she ate. The furry sisters sat patiently at her feet, waiting for their share of her lunch.

With a few minutes of her break remaining, she walked back toward the set. En route she stopped at a cluster of weeds: Russian thistle, the bane of her existence.

The sharp barbs on the stems dug into her fingers as she yanked them up, making her wince as the pile of weedy remains grew.

"I thought we weren't supposed to *harm the park*," Blaze said.

Alex tilted the brim of her hat up and found him leaning over her. She sighed. "This is an invasive species. Part of my job is monitoring invasives to make sure they don't get out of hand."

"They're not as important as stupid birds?" He sneered.

"No." Why wouldn't he just go away? Instead, he stood there, looming over her while she worked. Eventually, her inner ranger took over and she began to explain the process while she gripped a spiny plant and tugged, grimacing as it bit into her palm. "The trick is, you have to grip it by the base and pull."

"Do you twist, too?" he asked.

"Sometimes," she started, preparing to launch into an explanation of how you have to get the whole plant, roots and all when she looked at him again. A stupid, sexy smile played at the corner of his mouth. "That may work on your fangirls, but it won't work on me."

"What?" he asked innocently, his eyes sparkling.

She stood, squared her shoulders, and squinted at him. "You know *what*."

"No need to get angry," he teased.

"Listen, buddy," she said, poking his chest in the little section covered by his vest. "I'm trying to work. If you want to get laid, you could ask any one of those women." She nodded toward the set. "They seem more than happy to oblige, but you need to leave me alone before I report you."

"*You're* going to report *me*?" He puffed out his chest and stared down at her.

"Just because you're a movie star doesn't give you the right to harass your coworkers."

"Coworker?" He let out a sharp laugh. "You work for us." He paused, letting his words sink in. "We're your bread and butter and you're threatening me."

"I didn't—" her reply got lodged in her throat.

"Twice. You've threatened me twice." His jaw tightened into a firm line before he turned and walked back to the set. After a few stunned seconds, she jogged after him but stopped short when she found him deep in conversation with his lackey, Nate.

While Blaze spoke, Nate stared at Alex, his face impossible to read. Her heart sank. Why didn't she tell someone about his comments? Now it would be her word against his.

****

"Who does she think she is?" Blaze said. "Talking to me like that. You'd think she would be more careful. After what you said about the donation and letter and all that shit."

Nate nodded and glanced at Alex where she stood nearby.

"She said she was going to report me," Blaze said scornfully.

"What would you like me to do about it?"

"I don't know. Take care of it."

"Okay." Nate typed something into his phone. "By the way, the director wants to see you."

Blaze took a deep breath. Getting Alex out of his head was hard since she stood glaring at him a few feet away. Why was she so being difficult? That's not how it was supposed to go. Teasing shouldn't end with threats. What was he supposed to do? Stand there and take it?

He made his way to Mr. Reid. "You asked to see me?"

Mr. Reid looked over the top of his glasses. "You missed the meeting I called after lunch. Where were you?"

"I took a walk," he said.

"Listen, we've been working together for months now. I know you're a good kid, but you can't miss any more meetings. What you do on your time is your business, but don't waste mine. Understood?"

"Yes, sir." Blaze looked at his dusty boots. It felt like he had been sent to the principal's office, half expecting his mom to show up so Mr. Reid could explain all the trouble he had been causing. But who needed a mom when Nate was standing there, waiting to remind him what a screw up he was?

****

The earlier dread had solidified into a knot in Alex's stomach. Disaster loomed around every corner, which left her exhausted. At the end of the day, she barely had the energy to drag herself off her couch to answer her land line. The number wasn't one she recognized, but she answered anyway because it might be news from the hospital.

"Miss Mitchell?" A harsh voice squawked through the phone.

Her stomach lurched. "Mr. Howard, how can I help you?" She sat up straight and gripped the phone. He had never called her at home.

"I received a complaint today."

"A complaint?" Alex asked, her hands shaking.

"Yes. I received a call from," his voice trailed off as he rifled through papers, "Blaze Johnson said you have been very difficult to work with."

"I can assure you I'm doing my job." The meager dinner she had eaten earlier threatened to evacuate at any moment. "I… He…" It was too late to tell him about the sexual comments and the way he followed her around trying to get a rise out of her. Now it would seem like a distraction from Blaze's complaints.

"He said you threatened him."

"I threatened to *fine* him," she replied quickly. "He was throwing rocks at a protected bird. My job is to protect the park and make sure no one gets injured." That was the truth.

Mr. Howard didn't respond. The phone creaked in her hand as she strained to listen. He exhaled slowly before finally saying, "This needs to be a slam dunk, remember?"

"Yes, sir."

"The next time I hear from the crew it better be to schedule their next film. I have no intention of letting someone remain in their position if they can't do their job. I've made that mistake before and I don't intend to repeat it. Are we clear?"

"Yes, sir," she repeated in a whisper.

"Good," he said before disconnecting.

When she dropped the phone, it clattered against the counter. Hot tears filled her eyes and spilled down her cheeks. Koko and Pelli nudged her legs and whined.

She sank to her knees and put her arms around the dogs, comforted for the moment knowing someone loved her, no matter what. They licked her face while she nuzzled Koko's soft fur. "Thanks, girls. It's been a shitty day. How am I going to survive the next twelve days? It doesn't matter what I do. It's never good enough. *I'm* never good enough." A sob shook her body.

On her first solo day, she had screwed up. Maggie shouldn't have trusted her with such a large responsibility. Alex was supposed to charm the movie crew, but she ended up getting reported. The worst part was she would have to tell Maggie all about it…eventually.

****

"Remember last winter in New York?" Blaze asked Travis, his stunt double. A bunch of the crew sat around sharing drinks and stories in the bar attached to the

43

hotel. It doubled as a restaurant and had been the go-to destination for everyone involved in filming.

Travis was among the crowd at the bar in the hotel that night. They had worked together for years. Good stunt doubles were hard to come by. Travis laughed and the rowdy group that filled the bar laughed with him. "When we raced on set and both ended up on our asses? That was a hell of a storm."

Blaze rubbed his butt. "It still hurts." Tailbone bruises took forever to heal.

"What about Seattle?" Travis said. "Earlier last year, we had been filming near an open market and during a break, we decided it would be fun to lend a hand at the fish shop."

"They made it look so easy," Blaze added. "I smelled like halibut for days."

"What happened?" a woman asked as she leaned closer to Blaze. Before he could answer, Travis piped in.

"Have you ever been?" Travis waited for the woman to respond with a shake of her head. "It's a great place. Right on the water. There's one of the most famous fish markets in the states. If you want something, they shout your order, get into position, and proceed to throw the fish back and forth. Blaze and I decide to give it a shot after watching for a few minutes."

"I duck into the middle," Blaze said, taking over. All eyes swiveled toward him, everyone waiting for the rest of the story; everyone except Nate. Nate had heard it before and didn't hide his boredom. Blaze ignored him. "Travis grabs this big ass halibut. It must've been fifteen pounds."

"A fifteen-pound slimy, cold torpedo," Travis added.

"Right." Blaze put his hands up. "I shout, I'm open, and Travis throws."

Travis held his right hand up like he was about to throw an imaginary football. "I let go a little too early," he admitted.

"Bam," Blaze shouts as he mimes getting hit on the chin. "Halibut to the face."

"Oh," the woman said, worry creasing her forehead. "That must've hurt."

"Nah, just smelly."

Everyone laughed again. Nate yawned as Travis started a new story. Blaze didn't have many friends, but he always had a good time with Travis. Shooting the shit with him had taken the edge off his humiliating encounter with Mr. Reid.

Nate had overheard the whole thing and then lorded it over Blaze all day. Just like he always did. No matter how much he protested his agent wouldn't fire Nate. Nate was a safeguard. A babysitter. That gave Nate power.

Luckily, Blaze had discovered the key to distracting his guardian: women. And he was up to his eyeballs in women. Fans, coworkers, you name it. The only way he would be able to spend time alone was if he found someone to entertain Nate.

While Travis recounted another adventure, Blaze leaned toward the woman sitting between him and Nate. "Have you met Nate?" he asked.

She followed his line of sight and then shook her head. As much as he knew he would enjoy her company, he had a strict rule against dating in

Hollywood. If his career had taught him anything, it was to keep his dick in his pants. Working with someone after a failed affair was always uncomfortable.

"Nate and I went to Paris earlier this year," Blaze said. Nate perked up at the mention of his name.

"Really?" Her face brightened. "I've always wanted to go."

"Nate speaks French."

"I don't, not really—" Nate began to protest.

"He's being modest," Blaze added. "French is such a beautiful language, don't you think?"

The woman nodded and turned from Blaze to Nate and pushed her hand toward his. "Charlotte."

"Bonsoir, Charlotte," Nate said in a thick accent and then he kissed the back of her hand.

Charlotte swooned and Blaze congratulated himself. After another half hour, he would be as good as free. He jumped back into the conversation with Travis, keeping a careful eye on the blooming romance to his left. Just as planned, Nate forgot all about Blaze.

When he was sure the coast was clear, Blaze excused himself from the table and slipped away. Instead of going back to his room, he walked outside.

With his hoodie pulled tight around his face, he followed the road down into town, walking into the first restaurant he found. He waited for the recognition, but none came, so he ordered and ate in peace. That was one good thing about being in a small town.

It had been a while since he'd been able to infiltrate the public. Listening to conversations around him was a luxury. They talked about their kids, work, and everything in between. No one mentioned agents or publicists or rehab. No one talked to him besides his server, who only asked if he wanted a refill on his drink and how his meal tasted. Feeling like a regular person would change when he went back to work. In the spotlight, he was a star and no one let him forget that.

Chapter Five

Alex didn't want to get out of bed. Work had never conjured dread like it did now. Nothing cheered her up—not a hot shower or either of the sweet dogs that greeted her. Maggie and Jim didn't answer their phones, either.

She lingered outside her house as long as possible before making the short journey to the set. Just like the day before, Blaze waited for her, but instead of giving him the confrontation he wanted, she stopped to talk to Travis, his stunt double, who was standing with the rest of the stunt team.

Blaze strutted over and inserted himself into the conversation, and as soon as they started talking shop, she excused herself and got in position at the edge of the set. Before too much longer, the crew filtered in around her. The actors rehearsed their lines while the set decorators worked tirelessly to prepare for the long day of filming.

An hour later, when Blaze sidled up next to her, she had to turn away. It was impossible to be nice to him, which was the most important part of her job. Mr. Howard wouldn't let her forget that. Maggie had been wrong to trust her with so much responsibility.

Before she said something she would regret, she walked toward Dana, who was on stunt duty for the day.

All she had to do was concentrate on her breathing. In. Out. In. Out. If she let him see how much his complaint had upset her, he would win.

"Are you okay?" Dana asked.

She nodded. "I need to head over to the entrance gate for a while. Some sort of emergency. Can you cover for me here?"

"Sure."

"I'll be back after lunch," Alex said and then she started walking, making a point not to look back at Blaze. Her eyes, still swollen from the previous night, filled with tears. Everything was her fault. Maggie said she would be fine, but she wasn't cut out for a job like this. If the other day was any indication, she was facing a demotion. Mr. Howard's angry words bubbled to the surface, sending tears down her cheeks.

How could she admit her temper had gotten her in trouble, or that Blaze's relentless teasing was more than she could handle? Being the acting park manager meant she was supposed to be professional, courteous, and polite. Not a failure.

She blew her nose, wiped her eyes, and took several deep breaths when she closed in on the booth.

Robyn smiled from the stool in front of the cash register and removed the headphones from her ears. "What are you doing out here?"

"I wanted to, um…check the brochures. Make sure we have enough."

"I guess we are getting kind of low." Robyn slid off the chair and opened the cabinet under the desk, pulling out a huge stack of glossy papers.

"I'll fold them. You take care of customers." Alex nodded to the car slowing down outside. "Pretend like

I'm not here."

"Okay," Robyn said, frowning. "Hey, are you okay?"

"Yeah, just a little overwhelmed by the crowd."

"I hear ya."

Alex sat on the floor and leaned against the wall. Robyn greeted the visitor and then put her headphones back in, humming along with the music while Alex folded. Hours passed like that, until she had folded every brochure in the cupboard.

"Thanks for letting me hide out," Alex said when she left to go home for lunch. "Don't mention it, okay?"

"I won't. I totally get it."

As much as she wished she could spend every day in the entrance booth, she knew everyone was relying on her to handle things. Hiding wasn't an option.

****

Blaze frowned as he watched Alex disappearing down the long road to the entrance gate. A woman in a matching brown uniform stood in Alex's usual place. Something had just happened, but before he could get to the bottom of it, Mr. Reid called him to the set by name.

Heat flushed his cheeks and he ran to get back to work. With one strike against him, he went through his lines and followed directions. He couldn't afford to screw up again.

When they stopped for lunch, he ate quickly and made his way over to Alex's replacement.

"Hey, where's Alex?" The apology he had planned still waited in his brain. Telling her they were her bread and butter was overstepping. Even if it was true.

"Entrance gate. There was an emergency," the

woman replied as her cheeks flushed pink.

"Emergency? What kind of emergency?"

"Beats me. I'm just following orders. Alex seemed kind of stressed out. I'm glad I'm not the acting park manager." In a much quieter voice she said, "I know I'm not supposed to ask because we're professionals and all that, but could I have your autograph?"

"It's not a big deal," Blaze said.

The ranger pulled a tiny notepad and a pen out of her pocket and handed it to him as she said, "Please don't tell Alex."

"Who should I make it out to?"

"Dana," she said and then laughed nervously after she spelled it out.

With the tip of the pen against the paper, he paused. "Why would she be stressed out?"

Dana frowned.

"You just said Alex seemed stressed out."

"Oh, right. Yeah, it's a lot to take on. Her regular job is already pretty intense, and to have all these responsibilities added would be more than I could handle."

Blaze nodded as the words rattled out of her mouth. It was the kind of nervous chatter he was used to. As he thought about the extra responsibilities Alex had he couldn't help but feel sorry for her.

"I'm just a seasonal. I'll be gone at the end of next month. I hope I get hired next season, too. I love Twisted Juniper. It's a great park because of the management." Her smile faltered as she looked at the little notepad still in his hands. "I would hate to get in trouble."

Blaze scrawled his name across her paper and then

handed it back to her. "I won't mention it."

"Thanks." Dana's shoulders relaxed.

"While we're here, when is there time to do your regular jobs?"

"There isn't," Dana responded automatically. "I should be out burning pines. There's a huge infestation of pine engraver beetles this year. That's what Alex and I were working on last week," she said as she rubbed her upper arms. "To be honest, I'm kind of glad for a break."

"Speaking of breaks, I think ours is over." Blaze had been watching Mr. Reid very carefully to be sure he didn't miss anything.

"Thanks for the..." she trailed off and patted her pocket.

He nodded and got back to work. Alex didn't reappear until much later, and despite his best efforts, he couldn't sneak away to talk to her. When filming ended, she seemed to vanish. The apology would have to wait for another time.

****

That night, Alex looked up from her couch in time to see the headlights from Jim's car sweep across her front porch as he parked in their adjoining driveway. It had been days since she'd seen them and practically bounded out to greet them, followed closely by the girls.

"Welcome home." Alex grinned despite everything.

"Alex, meet Henry." Jim opened the back door and showed off the brand new car seat containing a tiny pink person.

"Hi, Henry," Alex cooed. Pelli licked Jim's hand

and then sniffed the back seat of the car. "Look, it's your little brother," she said to the dog.

Maggie laughed as Jim helped her out of the passenger seat. "How has Pelli been?"

"Missing you. We all have."

Maggie put her arms around Alex and gave her a gentle squeeze. "Thanks for taking care of her. I owe you one."

"No, you don't." Taking care of Pelli didn't add much work to Alex's life. If anything, it had been a great distraction. Unwilling to leave, she supported her friend's elbow all the way into their house. "Can I help you with anything?"

"You just did." Maggie sighed and sank into her couch. "Walking is still a bit tricky. My joints are all floppy."

Jim came in with the car seat hooked over his elbow. Squeaky cries came from within. "Damn. I woke him up. I hope I'll get the hang of this thing eventually."

"I'm sure it'll take some getting used to." Maggie reached for the baby and fumbled with a tiny diaper and a giant box of wipes. "Changing diapers is way harder than it looks, by the way."

Alex nodded and tried to keep the dogs from getting onto the couch. "How was it? Everything okay? No complications?"

Jim grimaced. "I thought she was dying. Turns out labor is really noisy."

Maggie shrugged. "I hemorrhaged a little, but I stabilized last night. So, no problems other than that."

"Yeah, just a little excessive blood loss," Jim added, shaking his head.

"I'm fine. How has it been? I missed two whole days. What happened?" Maggie unsnapped the tiny pajamas and unhooked the wet diaper.

Alex stalled. "You gave birth. That beats any stupid thing that happened on a movie set."

"I really did it." Maggie beamed. "I wasn't sure I could do it, but then I did."

"He's precious." Alex admired the new addition.

Jim stroked Henry's little head. "He's got my chin."

"It's a wonderful chin," Maggie said before kissing Jim.

"I'm going to give you a little privacy. You just got home. I should get out of your hair."

"But we didn't get to talk," Maggie protested.

"Tomorrow. We'll talk tomorrow." That was her cue to leave, grateful to avoid the unpleasant conversation that waited for her. But she knew she wouldn't be able to dodge questions for long.

****

Alex returned to the set early the next morning. Everything was riding on her performance, and she couldn't afford to screw up again. Mr. Howard wouldn't let her forget. It was more important than ever that she did exactly what he asked of her.

The first thing she did was talk to Steve about his plans so she would know where to stand to be the most efficient. Their discussion made her job easier and took some of the dread out of her day. It wasn't clear if he did it intentionally, but he always made her feel like she was doing her best. It was nice to have that reassurance after what happened. "Hey, is it okay if I check in with you every morning so we're on the same page?"

Steve smiled. "That would be perfect. You're the best." Alex started backing away, but he spoke again, "I talked to my sister about the nature reserve."

"Oh? What did she think?"

"That it's a great idea. We're going to meet with a representative from the wildlife trust when I get home."

"That's awesome." A little surge of happiness bubbled up inside her. At least she hadn't screwed up everything. "Okay, until tomorrow." It was easy to watch Blaze from her position, to see him scan the area, probably so he could remind her of all the ways she had failed at her job. The alarm on her phone had chimed while she and Steve were talking, marking the beginning of her workday and another successful attempt at avoiding Blaze. That seemed to be the best option. If she couldn't be nice when she interacted with him, it was best to avoid contact.

The director started shouting to the actors, putting them to work. As everyone spilled onto the set, Blaze meandered toward Alex. Trying to find an escape route, she backed away from him and bumped into a boulder. Trapped.

Lacking his usual cocky smile, he asked, "What exactly *is* an entrance gate emergency?"

"Sorry?" A real question was the last thing she expected from him and she couldn't keep her mouth shut.

"You disappeared yesterday and Dana said something about an entrance gate emergency. What happened?" He furrowed his brow and seemed genuinely concerned.

Thankfully, Mr. Reid called everyone to the set. How was she supposed to talk to him when he was nice?

"Gotta go." Before taking off, he smiled and winked.

Alex wondered if Blaze had some sort of eye condition that made him wink so much. Unless he thought he was charming. It wouldn't work on her.

By the time noon rolled around, she was more than ready for a break. The line moved quickly, everyone shuffling forward, getting closer to the delicious smells wafting over the crowd.

"Are you going to tell me?" Blaze said in her ear.

She squealed, clutched her chest, and spun to face him. "Where did you come from?"

The corner of his mouth tugged into a crooked smile. "Well, when a man and a woman love each other very much—"

Of course, he would bring up sex as often as possible. "How did you get right behind me in line?" Words would have to be chosen very carefully around him.

He shrugged and pointed over his shoulder with his thumb. "Oh, these guys all know me, and I figured I'd grace you with my presence."

"You think it's okay to cut in line?" The question came out before she could stop herself.

"It wasn't like that..." he trailed off and looked down.

"Wasn't it? I've been waiting for ten minutes, and so has everyone else."

Just then, the line moved, so she stepped ahead. When she glanced behind her, Blaze had ducked out of line and gone to the very back where it curved. She almost felt sorry for him, but then went back to hating him for making her life miserable. Why did he act like he didn't know how difficult he'd made things for her? More like didn't care. The only person he cared about was himself.

"Blaze, it's so big," a woman said loud enough to reach the front of the line.

"You've heard?" Even from her spot in line, Alex could see his million-dollar smile.

"I didn't think it would be so heavy." The woman passed his prop gun from one hand to the other.

Alex wanted to slap them both, but instead, she ordered her lunch, put him out of her mind, and found a place to sit alone.

Just when she'd taken her first bite, her phone chimed as an incoming video message came through. Great, it was her mother. From experience, she knew if she didn't answer, the phone would ring ten more times. Of course, she had chosen to sit in only one of a handful of places where her cell actually got signal.

"Hey, Mom," she said with a mouthful of food.

"Hi, Ally. I've been trying you all day. Are you eating?"

"Yep, that's what I do at twelve-thirty."

"I always forget it's so much earlier there. I ate two hours ago."

"That's nice." Waiting in line had already taken too much time, so she took another bite.

"Don't be rude," her mother scolded before clearing her throat. "Anyway, I'm calling to see which day you're arriving for your brother's birthday. It's next week."

If she hadn't been chewing, she probably would've laughed. For two month, she had always managed to change the subject, no matter how much her mom badgered her, but this time she had to come clean. "Mom, I'm not going to be able to make it."

"Matty is going to be sad you can't come."

"I'm sure he'll be fine. He wouldn't even notice if I were there."

"Don't say that."

"It's true." When she'd gone home for Thanksgiving three years ago, she had endured a torturously long layover and noisy flight only to be harangued by her brothers. Junior had started in on her and Matt came to his aid, going on about how they had real jobs and maybe one day she would join them. Just like they always had. "I'm sure you'll manage without me."

"You haven't even looked into flights, have you?"

"I can't get away from work right now."

"You work at a campground in the middle of the desert. I'm sure you can be spared. Besides, work isn't the most important thing in life."

Alex rolled her eyes and anger propelled her words out of her mouth before she could censor them, "Matt's an expert at that part, isn't he?"

"What's that supposed to mean?"

"Nothing," she muttered.

"No, go on, tell me what you mean," her mom said leaning closer to her camera, her angry eyes filling Alex's screen.

"When was the last time he had a job?" Alex asked even though she knew. It was a part-time job at a fast food place two years ago.

"You know the economy's been bad here." There was always an excuse. Anything to justify her favorite kid.

"Sure, whatever." Matt never left home. After high school, he'd taken a few college classes, but never been serious. Within a year he dropped out and dedicated his every waking moment to online gaming and mooching off their parents. Why couldn't her mom see what a loser he was?

"Junior's hours have been cut back at the plant, too. He tried to get Matty a job, but then they started making cuts. Poor Junior, he's—"

Before her mom could get into all the grim details of her brothers' pathetic lives, she interrupted. "Sorry Mom, but I need to go. The director just called everyone back to the set."

"Director?"

"You know, the movie crew filming here at the park."

"Movie crew? I would've remembered that," her mom said.

"I told you a few weeks ago when I met with the pre-scout group. Ring any bells?"

"Honestly, Ally, I can't recall every boring detail about your job. Why didn't you just say you were going to be working with movie stars?"

"Anyway, I have to get back to work. They're waiting for me to start filming," she lied. Their lunch break still had twenty minutes left, but she couldn't stand to talk to her mom for another minute.

"I think it's great you're *finally* doing something worthwhile out there. What's the movie?"

Alex's cheeks burned and her stomach clenched. "We're not allowed to discuss it with the public," she said. "I need to go." With that, she ended the call before her mom could respond and turned her phone off so it wouldn't ring if she called back.

The food on her plate had lost its appeal, or maybe it was just her appetite that had vanished along with her meager confidence. Dumping her plate into the garbage, she took off toward the trail on the eastern rim where she knew she could be alone. Each step away from the noisy group helped clear her mind. The storm from the previous day had refilled the potholes and the wind had brought a fair amount of garbage with it. All she had to do was step a few feet off the trail, and onto a giant slab of rock dotted with depressions that varied in size with some as small as her shoe, others like shallow bathtubs. Squatting next to a particularly lively little pool, she used a stick to fish out a candy wrapper.

"Stupid people leaving their stupid garbage all over the place," she grumbled. As she skimmed the surface with the stick, cleaning other scraps away, fairy shrimp scuttled away from her shadow. Their delicate legs fluttering through the water made her smile.

"What are you doing?" Blaze asked, his big head blocking the sun.

Alex tossed the stick away, picked up her pile of garbage, and glared at him. While she had been trying to actively avoid him so she wouldn't get in trouble again, he seemed to go out of his way to find her. Why wouldn't he just leave her alone? "Cleaning up litter."

"How can you see it in that murky water?" He crouched next to her and squinted at the pool. "What the fuck is in there?" When he recoiled, he did it so fast he fell backward, his ass connecting squarely with the bedrock.

Trying not to laugh, she pressed her lips together. It

turned out nothing helped her forget her anger faster than him getting hurt. "Fairy shrimp."

Back on his feet, he bent over the water slowly with a worried look on his face.

"They're not going to bite you." People who came from cities, who never went outside and interacted with the natural world, had reactions like that. Fear of an animal less than an inch long made her want to laugh. Blaze looked like he'd just seen a three-headed monster.

"They're creepy."

"I think they're pretty." As she waved her hand over the pool, the tiny creatures darted this way and that. "They only live for sixteen days."

"That's not very long. Doesn't seem like they could accomplish much." He sounded like her mom.

"Life is short and then you die." Their conversation began to take a turn toward catastrophe, so she stood, tucked the garbage in her back pocket, and walked back to the trail. She'd gotten around the bend before he called out to her.

"Hey, wait up," he shouted.

Why should she wait for him? By the time he caught up with her, they were approaching the edge of the set.

"I said," he paused to breathe, "wait up."

"Do you always get what you want?"

A cocky smile reappeared on his lips. "Yeah."

Did he know how cute he was when he smiled like that? Why was she even thinking that?

"You know a lot of stuff about the desert."

"It's my job," she said. "We lead tours all the time. They're very informative. You should sign up for one if you're interested."

"Are you offering to teach me? It would get you that autograph you've been after." His smile grew.

"No, Neal is our naturalist. You should talk to him."

"Oh." Hurt flashed across his face.

It was easy to revel in his disappointment. It didn't matter how nice or charming he was, he deserved it. Didn't he? A hint of guilt tugged at her for being so rude to him, but it didn't last long.

As she walked away from him, she felt she did a fine job of hiding her pleasure at finally putting him in his place, but her smile faltered when she decided it was time to admit the truth to Maggie.

Chapter Six

Blaze stood long after Alex was out of sight. It was no use following her since she didn't seem like she was willing to listen to an apology. Not right then, anyway.

Before following her onto the trail, he had ten minutes of lunch left. Without his phone, he had no way of knowing how much time had passed and decided to play it safe and head back. It wasn't the first time he wished he had his phone, but he wouldn't get it or his wallet until filming was over. It was part of the deal he had made with his agent, Alan.

"You're walking on thin ice," Alan had said. "After that shit you pulled over Christmas. No one will hire you if it happens again. It's just a precaution."

Blaze hadn't responded. How could he? That was when he'd met Nate.

"Fucking Nate," Blaze mumbled as he followed the trail back to the set. How had his life gotten so far off track? Of course, he knew the answer and so did anyone who read the news.

"Nice of you to join us," Nate chided when Blaze returned.

The blood drained out of Blaze's face. "Oh shit, am I late again?"

Nate cracked a smile. "No, I'm just fucking with you."

Blaze balled his hands into fists. "Asshole." Instead

of punching Nate, he turned to the closest group of people and immersed himself in their conversation. They were talking about scorpions. Anything was better than Nate.

The lead actress, Jennifer Roman, stood nearby, her makeup and costume impeccable. But she didn't seem to be following the discussion. She didn't seem to be following anything. All dressed up with nowhere to go and motionless as a doll, she seemed asleep on her feet.

"Hey, Jennifer," he said as he approached her.

"Hiya, Blaze," she said after she blinked and focused on his face.

"How do you like it so far? The location," he added to clarify.

"It's dirty." She scrunched up her nose. "Everything I own is covered with red dirt. I feel like we're filming on Mars. I don't know why we couldn't just stay at the studio."

"Mr. Reid said the sky never looks right in the studio."

Jennifer tilted her head. "How are you?"

"I'm fine," he responded habitually. He didn't want to complain about the dirt because he happened to like it. It made everything more real. When the director shouted action, he didn't have to act like a cowboy, he just was. "You look amazing."

A smile made her cheeks dimple. "Why thank you, Buck."

He slipped into character and tipped his hat and drawled, "May I escort you onto the set, miss?"

"I would be honored," she replied. When she took his arm, she dug her nails into his skin as she struggled to walk on the uneven path with her teetering heels. If he had been inclined, he would've enjoyed the view down the front of her dress because she practically spilled out of it, so it was hard to miss. While he had enjoyed flirting with her throughout the filming, their conversations weren't exactly sparkling. Plus, he had that rule against dating actresses.

When they arrived at the steps leading up to the saloon, he held her hand while she mounted them. At one point, her ass was right in front of his face.

"Enjoying the view?" she asked.

"Always."

"Scoundrel," she exclaimed.

He laughed and then joined her on the platform. "I think this is where Mr. Reid wants us," he said in his normal voice.

Jennifer nodded. "I think so, too."

"Would you like to sit? There's a stool inside," he offered.

"I can't sit. If I did I wouldn't be able to breathe." She spread her fingers across her tiny waist. "Corset."

Blaze grimaced. That one word embodied a world of pain he could only imagine. The women from his world sacrificed everything for their looks, even their ability to breathe. It was insane, but he understood why they did it. To some degree, he felt the same pressure, but was grateful it wasn't as intense.

Jennifer spread out her fan and leaned against the outside of the saloon while Blaze spun his prop gun in his hand. They were about to film the villain's death scene, so his gun-slinging skills were about to pay off.

Extras joined them on the platform, some inside the saloon, some standing near Jennifer, all of them waiting for the director to shout, "Action!"

The villain, played by Blaze's acquaintance Jake, waited a few yards away. When Mr. Reid gave the signal, Jake strolled up to the saloon, tied his horse to the post, and pulled his weapon. The women standing outside screamed. Blaze cocked his gun and shot Jake.

On cue, Blaze ran to Jennifer and cradled her body while giving her a charming one-liner.

"Cut," Mr. Reid said through a megaphone. "Jake's charge didn't go off."

Everyone stood and got back into position while the crew investigated Jake's blood bag and the mechanism that had failed to go off at the right time.

As they waited, Blaze made jokes. Jennifer laughed at all of them. Even the ones that weren't funny.

When they finished for the day, the sky began to transform. An ominous layer of clouds blotted out the sun and filled the air with the promise of rain. Everyone loaded into the vans in a rush to beat the storm.

"Hang on a second, okay?" Blaze didn't wait for Nate to respond, instead he bolted for the Visitor Center intent on apologizing to Alex, but he stopped when he spotted her walking the opposite direction, down a worn road on the other side of the park.

"Blaze, we're leaving," Nate called out.

Blaze growled. He would have to wait. Again.

****

Dark clouds gathered overhead when Alex approached the row of modest ranger houses. Maggie, holding Henry close against her chest, came out to greet her. Her hair hung around her face and her clothes were covered with stains, but she smiled anyway.

"How was work?" Maggie said.

"Long," Alex replied, unlocking her front door and greeting Koko.

The baby started to fuss and Maggie bounced him in her arms. After a quick diaper check she said, "He's wet again. Hang on, I'm going to hand him over to Jim." A few minutes later, she reappeared at Alex's door.

"My baby pees more than anyone I've ever met."

Alex laughed. "How has your first day home been?"

"Crazy. I don't know what I'm going to do when Jim goes back to work." Maggie wiped her forehead, smearing something chalky white across her skin. "Tell me about you. It's been forever since we've talked. How are things with Blaze? Any better?"

Alex's confidence began to crumble. "Not exactly…"

"Why? What happened? Did someone get hurt?"

"No. No one got hurt. He won't leave me alone. I can't get away from him and his stupid comments, and…"

Maggie shook her head and sighed. "I remember a guy like that from junior high. Ryan. Oh, how I hated Ryan. He made my life a living hell. Come to find out, he liked me. What's wrong with asking a girl out? It's a lot more effective than calling me peckerhead. Blaze seems like that kind of guy."

A laugh escaped her lips. "Are you saying he has the emotional maturity of a thirteen-year-old?"

Maggie shrugged. "Sounds about right. Some men never grow up. Others, like my husband, have been groomed for so long they've learned how to behave. It takes a lot of work, but it's worth it." She smiled and patted Alex's leg. "Also, he's probably intimidated by you."

Alex snorted. "I intimidate him, right. Whatever."

"I'm serious. Just imagine the women he usually deals with. You're not like them."

"Because I'm not falling all over him?"

"Exactly."

"It's more than that." Alex's shoulders fell. Time for the truth. "Blaze reported me," she whispered. Each word hurt.

"Oh, no."

She nodded. "Mr. Howard called me the other night."

"And?" Maggie urged her on.

"Well, he's not happy." The rest would have to wait for another time. "So, what did you do? About Ryan?"

Maggie answered solemnly, "I kicked him in the balls. I got detention for a week."

Another laugh bubbled out of Alex. "Are you suggesting I kick Blaze in the balls?"

"No, I'm certainly not. If it got me a week of detention, just imagine what would happen to you. Don't let him get to you."

"Easy for you to say."

Maggie shook her head. "No, it's not. I know how hard it is and so do you, but he's trying to get a rise out of you. Don't give him the satisfaction."

Alex sighed. "I'll do my best." The promotion had been much harder than she anticipated, not just because of Blaze, but because of everything. Maggie never should've trusted her with the job, and she wished Neal was acting manager instead. Sharing that information wouldn't make the problem go away, so she kept her mouth shut.

Maggie pressed her arms against her breasts and grimaced. "Um, I need to leave. Now. Apparently, I need to nurse Henry. My milk came in this morning." She gave a pathetic smile. "Sorry. I really do want to talk to you, but I'm leaking."

"You're fine. Don't worry about it. You helped more than you know. Believe me." Truth be told, she was happy for the interruption and opened the door just as a few fat drops fell from the sky. "I'll talk to you tomorrow."

"Tomorrow," Maggie called back.

The clouds opened and a torrent of rain spilled down on the arid sand. The drops tapped against the windows and drummed on the roof for the rest of the night. When Alex slept, she dreamed of kicking Blaze as hard as she could right in the balls...over and over again. For the first time in a while, she woke with a smile on her face.

****

Rain dripped off the rim of Alex's hat as she made her way to the overflow parking lot. The smile she had woken with grew when she noticed the lot was empty. No extras, no cameras, no Blaze. She tried to check the time on her phone but realized she hadn't turned it back on yet. Two messages.

"I can't believe you hung up on me," her mother screeched. "You need to—"

Alex pulled the phone away from her head, her mother's voice trailing off, and erased the rest of the message.

"Alex, hi, it's Steve. Listen, it's been raining all

night and the forecast isn't great, so we're going to postpone filming for a day. The storm is supposed to blow over tonight, so I'll see you tomorrow morning. Call me when you get this."

Alex grinned and returned his call to confirm that postponing a day would be great, fantastic even. In the Visitor Center, she smiled at Lynn who was standing behind the gift shop register.

"Hey, I just got a message from the assistant director. They're not going to film today. Will you let everyone know?"

"Sure thing." Lynn picked up a walkie-talkie and spread the word. "I took Maggie dinner last night. Isn't Henry the cutest?"

Alex nodded. "He is. Maggie seems really happy, doesn't she?"

"Yeah."

"Hey, would it be okay if I head into Dembi for a bit? I haven't been in town for a couple of weeks and I'd like to get Maggie something." Unable to cook to save her life, she had to rely on the best restaurants and bakeries in town.

"You're the boss. Anyway, I think we have things covered. We never get many visitors during storms anyway and without the movie crew here, we're going to be hard-pressed to find ways to keep busy."

Boss didn't seem like the right word for her. It never did. Couldn't everyone see that? "I'll have my phone with me if you need something. I'll be back soon. Thanks, Lynn."

At her house, she grabbed Koko's leash and then they got in her dark green SUV. "We're going to town," she announced. Koko responded by panting and thumping her tail against the passenger seat. Town meant treats. Koko loved going to town.

The damp landscape passed in a blur outside the windows as they drove the long road out of the park. Thankfully the rain subsided slightly, which meant the dip was still passable. During heavy rain, it filled like a river and she would have to wait for it to drain before she could cross. She didn't want to wait. Not today— her first day off in weeks.

****

Blaze had gone to bed and awoken to the sound of rain. He loved the rain. News spread fast about the delay, which would mean an extra day on location. Most of the cast and crew were unhappy with the news, but not him.

"Why do you look so happy?" Nate asked when he plopped down at the table where Blaze was eating breakfast in the restaurant attached to the hotel.

Blaze shrugged. "No reason." Having a day off was more than enough to make his day and he intended to keep their conversations as brief as possible. "How are things with Charlotte?" he asked, saying her name in a French accent.

"Fantastic." Nate smiled.

"Good." Blaze didn't want details. Far from it. "Okay, I'm taking off." The rest of his breakfast filled his mouth in one final bite.

"Where?"

"I'm going for a run," he said.

"In the rain?"

"I'll have the trails to myself."

"You know there's a gym down the hall, right?" Nate flagged down a server and ordered coffee.

"Why would I run on a treadmill when I can be outside?" He inhaled deeply and grimaced. "It smells like chlorine in here."

"There's a pool. Of course it smells like chlorine." Nate shook his head. "Suit yourself. Just don't complain when you get pneumonia."

"You sound like a grandma. *You're going to catch your death*," Blaze added in his best old lady voice.

"Shut up."

"*Don't spill your coffee, sonny*," he said in the same creaky voice.

"Asshole."

Blaze charged his breakfast to his room and pulled the hood of his rain jacket tight around his face before stepping outside. The trail into the hills above the hotel waited for him. The saturated sand slid under his shoes with each step and then flattened under the incessant rain. Without anything planned for the rest of the day, his run turned into a leisurely walk into town. Busy with work, he hadn't had a chance to explore much of Dembi. As he walked down the deserted sidewalks, he passed a rock shop, a bakery, a few restaurants, and ATV rentals. It was perfectly peaceful.

It didn't seem like his day could get any better, but he was wrong.

Chapter Seven

Surrounded by cars spraying up muddy water, Alex had a hard time seeing as the windshield wipers worked double time. Red rock cliffs gave way to flat land with a giant freeway cutting through its center. The exit for Dembi would be visible in ten miles.

Most of the cars exited together, slowing as the town engulfed them. The majority of buildings had been there for years, long before Dembi became a resort for outdoor enthusiasts. Only a few businesses, like the new monstrous hotel, seemed out of place. The rest fit right in. Little ruddy shops lined Main Street advertising souvenirs for sale or ATVs for rent, camouflaging into the red rocks that surrounded them. Alex drove away from the tourist traps and toward the local grocery store and the very best hole-in-the-wall restaurants.

She parked outside the grocery store, hooked Koko to her leash, and walked her toward the front door. They stopped just outside in a covered area the store called The Barking Lot. A row of dog beds and water dishes lined a fence where Alex tied Koko's leash. She gave Koko fresh water and told her to lie down.

Koko curled into the bed, crossed her paws, and wagged her tail as she waited for her treat.

"I'll be right back," Alex said before ducking into the store. Once inside, she took her hat off and headed straight for the bakery. An entire corner of the display was dedicated to dog treats. The bag bulged with goodies, and she planned on sharing them with Pelli when she got home. After she paid for it, she returned to her patiently waiting pup.

"Two now and two for later, okay?" Alex pulled out two pumpkin treats and put them in the dog bed. Before going back inside, she ruffled Koko's ears and said, "I'm going shopping. Behave yourself."

Koko ignored her completely and set to work on one of the treats.

Alex hummed along with the music playing on the overhead speaker and took her time shopping, walking every aisle. Before she left, she bought a dozen muffins: blueberry for Maggie, poppy seed for her. With a cart full of groceries, she made her way to Koko. The rain had picked up again so she tugged her hat back onto her head. Someone in a rain jacket squatted next to Koko, rubbing her favorite spot on her shoulder.

Koko loved people and always had a happy face to offer visitors, which meant she had them often.

"She's a good girl," Alex shouted to the stranger over the thrumming rain.

"Yes, she is." The man stood to face Alex and smiled that stupid, sexy smile. "Is she yours?"

The smile fell from her face. Even here, at her store, with her dog, in her town, she couldn't escape Blaze. "Yeah."

"What kind of dog is she?" he asked.

"The brown kind." Alex shrugged. "She's a mutt."

"How old is she? Is she still a puppy?"

"She's one," Alex replied keeping her answers as

short and brisk as possible.

"I thought so," he replied, in a sweet singsong voice. Crouched in front of Koko again, he said, "You're just a baby, aren't you? You like that, huh?" He dug his fingers into the thick fur around her neck and massaged her skin. Koko tilted her head up and closed her eyes.

Alex's grip on her shopping cart tightened. "We should probably be going."

"I'll help you," he offered, motioning to the bags of groceries as he untied Koko's leash.

When he started walking out into the parking lot, she couldn't protest.

"Which one is yours?"

Alex took a deep breath then jogged her cart over to her car so she could unlock the passenger door for Koko. Blaze placed the dog's leash inside and then used the towel covering the seat to dry her fur. Alex frowned as she watched his careful hands move across Koko's face and ears.

"Your groceries are getting wet," he said, snapping her out of her haze.

"Yeah." Once she opened the hatchback, he squeezed next to her, his wet shoulder brushing hers. Frozen, she watched him lift bag after bag. Why was he being so nice? What was going on?

The box of muffins had suffered worse than the rest, the lid soggy and limp. But when she peeled the lid away so the muffins inside wouldn't get wet, too, she sighed. They were still perfect.

"Are those lemon poppy seed? Mm," he hummed.

"Yeah. I know it's just a grocery store, but they have the best bakery. Lemon poppy seed is my favorite.

The blueberry muffins are for Maggie."

"Maggie? Your dog?"

Alex laughed. "No. Maggie my friend. That's Koko and she doesn't get people muffins. She gets her own pup treats." The crumpled bag was still wedged in her jacket pocket, so she pulled it out to show him. "Pumpkin."

His smile made her melt.

"I'll take it back for you," he said as he started pushing the empty cart.

"Do you...need a ride somewhere?" she asked, regretting her words as soon as they left her mouth.

"No. I was just out for a walk," he said as he looked over his shoulder at the ugly hotel looming over half the town. "I'm tired of being cooped up in there. I want to be like everyone else, you know?"

"No one else is taking a stroll in the rain."

His deep, warm laugh took the chill out of the air around them. "I guess that's true."

"Thanks for helping me," she said, smiling a little. It was hard to hate him when he laughed like that.

****

Blaze blinked and then stared at her, struggling to find the words to apologize now that he finally had a chance.

It was her smile that threw him off. It would've been easier if she had told him to fuck off. But she didn't and it only made it that much harder to figure her out.

"I wanted to apologize for being such a dick," he blurted out.

A frown creased her perfect forehead. "Which time?"

"Fair enough." Maybe he shouldn't have said anything because now she wasn't smiling, and he didn't like that. A water drop made its way down Alex's face and lingered on her jaw, so he swiped at it with his thumb. "Your face is wet," he mumbled. It was the first time he had touched her, and he wanted to do it again. He also wanted to kiss her.

"It's raining."

"Rain," he repeated stupidly.

"Are you sure you don't need a ride somewhere?"

Why was she being so nice? Did she forgive him? "I spaced out for a second. I really am sorry."

The frown on her face deepened as she nodded but didn't say anything. It was obvious he had blown it again. Even his apology came out wrong.

"See you tomorrow." What had he expected? That she would accept his apology? "I'm so stupid," he muttered to himself as he steered the cart away from her car.

****

"See you tomorrow," Alex mumbled. Blaze didn't hurry across the parking lot; he meandered toward the cart return and then continued on his way to the deserted sidewalk.

After she closed the trunk and got behind the wheel, she sighed. Koko wagged and leaned across the cup holder separating their seats, sticking her nose in Alex's treat pocket. "Those are for later." Koko sat upright and tilted her head when Alex went on, "What just happened? He was so…nice."

Koko's mouth hung open in a happy doggie smile as if she agreed.

Alex made two more stops and chided herself for

trying to find Blaze roaming the streets—rain jacket drawn tight around his handsome face and tight sweatpants damp and clinging to his powerful legs. Just what she needed. One nice encounter and she was obsessed. Great.

Their interaction filled her head the rest of the day and even managed to infiltrate her dreams once more. They were in the parking lot again, but the rain was warmer and he wasn't wearing a shirt. Summer rain trickled down his chest and soaked the waistband of his jeans.

Smiling that smile, he didn't say a word before he kissed her. Pressed against the back of her car, his tongue thrust into her mouth while his hands tugged up the hem of her shirt. When he kissed down the side of her neck and trailed his fingers up her ribs, her head swam and delicious tingles spread through her body.

"Yes," she murmured as she responded to his touch. He ran his thumbs across her nipples, making her gasp for air and then he kissed her breasts with his perfect lips.

She woke with a start, her sheets wrapped around her legs, an echo of orgasmic bliss still pulsing through her.

Koko observed her from the doorway, tilting her head from side to side.

Alex buried her face in her pillow. "I'm in trouble."

****

Before leaving the hotel for the day, Blaze pulled a lily out of the flower arrangement in the lobby, holding the delicate stem carefully as he boarded a van.

"Is that for Caitlin?" Nate asked.

Blaze smiled. "No."

"You're such a player."

Blaze didn't argue. Everyone expected him to be a certain way and who was he to disagree? Hollywood had put him in a role he had to play no matter what.

He had no idea if Alex liked lilies, but if it redeemed his stupid, bumbling apology then it was worth it. Even though he stared out the window and showed no interest, Nate still went through Blaze's schedule for the day, making comments about what he would do if he were Blaze, but he didn't fill the entire ride with small talk. And for that, Blaze was grateful.

When they got off the van, Blaze made his way to the costume and makeup trailers and then he went straight to the set. By the time he found Alex in the sea of faces, he lost his nerve. What if she thought he was stupid? What if she hadn't forgiven him?

"Blaze," Jennifer called out.

It had been a dumb idea. The gnawing feeling in his stomach should've tipped him off. Why did Alex unnerve him?

"Is that for me?" Jennifer asked, smiling widely.

"Of course it is," he replied.

****

When Alex left for work, she tucked not one but two lemon poppy seed muffins in her jacket pocket. After his help yesterday, she needed to thank Blaze properly and to acknowledge she appreciated his apology, even if she wasn't sure what he was apologizing for. When she stopped to think about it, she frowned. Giving him a muffin wasn't much compared to what he'd done, besides he could probably get every flavor from the food truck. They probably weren't as good as the ones in her pocket, though. The decision to share with him went back and forth in her mind. Should she? Shouldn't she? When she arrived at the overflow parking lot, she found Steve and discussed the details for the day's shoot. It was going to be a good day because it would be easy to be nice to Blaze.

Already in position outside the saloon, all she had to do was wait. Extras filled the set around her, and then the main actors appeared. The lead actress, Jennifer something-or-other, stood waving at her pretty face with a white lacy fan. A few moments later, Blaze sauntered onto the set holding a single flower. It looked like he was going to talk to Alex, but that changed when Jennifer said something to him.

Alex almost waved at him but didn't. Thankfully. Unable to look away, she watched him leap up the saloon stairs and offer the flower to his leading lady. Like a train wreck unfolding, Jennifer blushed all over, and there was plenty of skin to see.

"Little missy," he said, bowing deeply.

"Blaze, you shouldn't have." With one quick movement, she snatched the flower out of his hands, snapped the stem, and tucked it into the folds of her elaborate hairdo.

"Please, call me Buck. And might I add, you're looking as lovely as a flower," he drawled while he kissed the back of her hand.

When she dipped her shoulders, she gave him and everyone else a better view down her neckline. "Thank you, Buck."

Alex wanted to scream, or throw something, anything to make them stop. How could she have been so stupid? Their encounter in town had been an act.

Everything was with him. The sooner she realized that the better off she would be.

The day went downhill from there.

****

Determined to keep on the good side of Mr. Reid, Blaze focused on work. Everything was perfect. He smiled, recited his lines, and stood on his mark. Between takes, he tried to work up the courage to talk to Alex.

The first time, he turned away before he got too close because she looked furious. Maybe someone had said something that pissed her off, and she needed time to cool down.

Once he figured the coast was clear, he stepped up behind her and said, "Hey."

She exhaled loudly and turned to face him. "What do you want?"

Uh-oh. He hadn't given her enough time. "Nothing," he said. "I should probably get back to work."

"Good idea," she said.

Too sick to move, he stood awkwardly for a minute.

"Alex, we need you by the costume trailer, pronto," a voice squawked through her walkie-talkie.

"Copy that," Alex responded and then bolted up the trail toward the overflow parking lot.

"Fuck," Blaze said. It was clear from her response that her anger was directed at him for some reason.

Chapter Eight

Alex filed the first injury report before lunch, an extra with a twisted ankle. Just what she needed. While she was in her office finishing the paperwork, her desk phone rang. When she answered it, she wished she hadn't.

"What are you doing in your office?" Mr. Howard barked.

"I um…I'm doing some paperwork. Injury report," she added and then squeezed her eyes shut. She shouldn't have told him about that.

"What's going on out there?" he asked.

"It was a costume malfunction," she said. The shoes the actresses had to wear weren't designed for rugged terrain. "Can I help you with anything?" she asked in an attempt to keep the conversation on point before she admitted how rocky things were with Blaze.

"I'm calling to check in. I thought I'd be leaving a message since you should be occupied during the day. You're on *their* clock."

"I understand, sir. I needed to submit this report. The medic on staff is helping her. Everything is fine," she said trying to reassure herself more than him. "I'm meeting with the wranglers today. It's all coming along nicely."

"Hmm. Well, I'll be in touch," he grumbled before hanging up.

If she had learned anything in the last few minutes it was that she wouldn't answer her phone at work for the remainder of filming. She sighed and slumped into her chair for a minute before returning to her position on the set. Long after her shift should've ended, she waited for the horse wrangler. Mercifully, Joe, a seasoned professional, knew all about collecting the manure to prevent the spread of invasive plants. Even still, they discussed the minutiae of horse digestion and seed dispersal for close to an hour.

By the time she got home, she barely had enough energy to eat. She unloaded both muffins from her pocket, squished and stuck to the wax paper she had wrapped them in. The urge to scream and then eat them both was stronger than she could resist.

While she had fought the temptation to research Blaze before, Alex couldn't any longer. After entering his name into her Internet browser, she read headline after headline:

BLAZE AND RUBY, THE NEW POWER COUPLE?
BLAZE SAYS MODEL'S SEX AND PREGNANCY CLAIMS ARE LIES
LIFE OF THE PARTY BLAZE JOHNSON BRINGS IN THE NEW YEAR

The image search was worse; a thousand thumbnail pictures filled her screen. Each one featured Blaze standing with a different woman, sometimes multiple women. He seemed to love the camera almost as much as it loved him.

It was obvious by the constantly rotating girlfriend pictures he didn't care about anyone but himself, probably not even Jennifer. Nothing personal, just typical dickish behavior.

She transferred Maggie's blueberry muffins to a plate, added Koko and Pelli's pumpkin treats, grabbed the to-go boxes from the restaurants she had visited, and walked with her dog the short distance to her friend's house.

Tiny cries came from inside, so she figured it was probably safe to knock. Jim answered a few seconds later.

"Hey, Henry is grumpy about something. Must be a Thursday," he joked. "Did you come over for movie night? Can I get you a beer?"

"That would be awesome," she replied. When she saw Maggie she smiled and held up the plate and boxes. "No movie, but I brought you guys dinner."

Maggie grinned around the fussing baby. "You're an angel. I've been craving blueberry muffins. I'm so hungry I could eat all of them."

"You're eating for two, so I think that's probably okay." Alex thanked Jim for the beer, handed him the packaged meals, and pulled up a chair near where Maggie sat.

"I have to warn you," Maggie started, her face dead serious. "I need to nurse Henry again. I'm like a sprinkler. If I spray you with milk, I'm really sorry."

Alex smiled. "I can go if you want me to."

"No, I'd like you to stay, I just can't guarantee I can feed him discreetly yet."

"I don't care. Go on, feed that little fella." Alex wasn't fazed by a little milk. Her aunt had nursed all three of her children well into their toddler years very openly at all their family parties. While Maggie got the baby situated, she and Jim talked about the weather, yard work, and the dogs. Anything but the movie.

"This is delicious," Alex said, holding up the bottle to Jim. She glanced at her friend and hung her head. "Sorry, I'm not trying to rub it in."

"It's summer ale. Do you want to take the last few bottles home? My palate has moved on and it won't keep long enough for Mags." He turned to his wife. "Don't worry, honey, I'll make another batch next summer."

"You're so kind." Maggie pouted.

"Hey, I appreciate your sacrifice, and so does he," Jim said, pointing to their baby.

"I know." She put her thumb in Henry's tiny palm and he wrapped his fingers around hers.

"Now that he's content, I'll let you two catch up and go check emails and that sort of thing." Jim kissed Maggie on the forehead and ducked out of the room.

"Sorry I didn't come over yesterday," Maggie said. "I told you we would talk more, and then I tried to bathe Henry. It was a disaster."

"Don't worry about it. The movie crew didn't come yesterday, so I spent the day in town, which is where I got these," she said, holding the muffins toward her. Koko and Pelli waited patiently at her feet for their treats, eating one and then the other before snuggling together.

"You seem like you needed the break."

Alex frowned. "I didn't really get a break from work."

"What do you mean?" Maggie mumbled around a mouthful of blueberry muffin.

"Blaze was there. At the grocery store."

"Ugh. I'm sorry. I know that must've been awful."

"It wasn't." Trying to explain what happened was

difficult since it seemed so surreal. "He was nice and helpful. I don't understand."

"See?" Maggie beamed. "I told you he likes you."

"He doesn't. I thought he did, and then he was flirting with what's her face, the blond with the big boobs. If he liked me he wouldn't do that, would he? Everything is an act with him."

"I'm sorry." Maggie reached toward Alex, bumping her nearly sleeping infant, making him stir.

"I'm fine. Don't worry about me, I can wallow later."

"Is there anything I can do?"

"I need to stop having unrealistic expectations of people. I just can't figure him out. One minute he's nice and the next he's a dick."

"With a capital D."

"Right." Alex laughed. "I dreamt about him," she added in a whisper.

Maggie waggled her eyebrows. "Oh yeah?"

"Yeah, it was…interesting." She was sure by the heat in her cheeks she had turned bright red. "I'm not sharing anything else, so tell me how you've been." The admission had done the trick. Maggie didn't press anymore about work, and Mr. Howard's call didn't come up.

They talked about Henry for a while, but the later it got, the more difficult it became for Maggie to stifle her yawns. When her eyes began to droop, Alex said goodnight and headed for the door. Jim handed her a milk crate nearly full of beer bottles.

"This is too—"

Jim put his finger to his lips and shushed her. "You need to take it. It's killing Maggie to have it around. It's her favorite," he whispered.

"It really won't keep?"

He shrugged. "It's better fresh. Besides, I'll make her another batch when she can enjoy it."

"Thanks, Jim. Night."

"Goodnight."

A gentle chorus of crickets serenaded her and the waning moon illuminated the path between their houses. She inhaled the sharp scent of juniper and rain and vowed to put Blaze out of her mind.

She ran into trouble that night when the vow-making part of her brain was overridden by the dream-making one.

That time, she was the one waiting for him outside the saloon in an elaborate costume. He flew up the steps, not stopping until his face was inches away from hers. "This is for you," he said, brushing her exposed chest with the delicate petals of a lily. When she took it from him, he kissed her and his hands migrated south, stopping only to navigate through the piles of fabric. He trailed his fingertips across the top of her stockings where he followed the taut elastic of the garter. She moaned and opened her legs, inviting him to keep going, which he did. He slid one long finger against her slit.

"Come for me," he said, his lips brushing hers as he pushed inside her in one fluid movement.

She came hard, jerking awake with her hand buried between her legs. The residual pleasure washed over her and she sighed. "Damn it," she ground out.

****

As Friday afternoon approached, Alex realized she had almost survived her first week with the movie crew.

Almost.

It had been rocky in the beginning, but with each passing day, she had moments of confidence. Despite the pressure from Mr. Howard and her struggle to be kind to Blaze, she had lots of support. And with the first week coming to an end she wanted to celebrate.

Alex surveyed the action sequence from a distance, watching the movement of the horses and the people.

"What are you doing?" Blaze asked from behind her, entirely too close for her comfort.

She wheeled around and faced him. "Why do you always sneak up on me?"

The vest he wore opened when he shrugged, showing a little more skin than usual. "It's easy. You're always so focused." In a pose that mirrored hers, he repeated, "So, what are you doing?" He seemed comfortable like he had been in town.

"My job."

"Making sure no one harms the park. That sort of thing?" he asked without a hint of sarcasm. "I've never seen anyone take their job so seriously before. You manage to take care of everything and make it look effortless."

Trying to figure out if he was mocking her or not, she frowned. Was he complimenting her? If that was really how he felt, why had he filed a complaint with Mr. Howard? Now she really didn't know what to think of him. All she could do was change the subject. She lifted her arm and pointed to a patch of shadowy earth around the base of the plants on either side of the arroyo where the horses trotted back and forth. "See that black stuff?"

He squinted and nodded.

"It's cryptobiotic crust. It's a living mat that prevents erosion and stabilizes the entire ecosystem. It takes centuries to grow. If one of those horses strays too far, or if one of those stunt guys takes a step up that slope, it could devastate the area."

"Did you tell Travis?" he asked, pointing to his stunt double.

"Yes. I told them all, but I still need to be here watching, just in case. There are signs posted all over the place at the Visitor Center, but that doesn't stop people from walking wherever they want." It frustrated her to no end. "People are so entitled, you know?" A laugh erupted out of her. She expected outrage from the most entitled person she'd ever met.

"What's so funny?"

She stared at him. Because he was so blissfully unaware, she wished she could educate him, just a little, about what a self-involved prick he was, but she couldn't risk another call to Mr. Howard. It could cost her job. "Nothing."

"Do you live in Dembi?" he asked.

"What?"

"I never see you drive anywhere, except when I saw you in town a couple of days ago, so you either live close or leave for work really early."

"The park provides housing for all the rangers. We're too far from the city."

"You get to live here?" His eyes widened.

"Yep."

"I have to be honest. I didn't think much of the desert when we landed at the Dembi airport, but it's kind of growing on me." He shielded his eyes as he took in the sights near and far, his face completely open.

Alex looked at him closely, his sharp jawline covered with the perfect amount of scruff, the tiny scar on his eyebrow, and his beautiful blue eyes. As soon as he turned his attention back to her, she looked away. "It's my favorite location so far."

"Do you move a lot?" he asked.

"I guess." Avoiding the climb up the federal jobs ladder meant moving to different locations, which meant never becoming too attached to any one place. "Do you live in California?" She leaned against a boulder, the cool rock helping diffuse a little of the heat that had crept up her back.

He nodded. "It's noisy and crowded."

"Must be beautiful, too," she added as she looked across the desert and imagined trading junipers for palm trees.

"I guess. Everything is so perfect and fake, just like the people. Not like here."

When she turned to look at him, he was staring at her so intently it made her fidget. A wisp of something tickled her forehead. She froze. "What? Do I have something on my face? Is it a spider?" Pushing away from the rock, she brushed her skin instinctively, her pulse pounding in her ears. "Widows love the desert." She swiped at her face repeatedly before feeling satisfied that she wasn't about to be bitten by a venomous spider. "There's one that lives inside the frame of my front window. I've never been able to catch her. It makes me nervous since Koko is too curious for her own good."

"You have a black widow living at your house?"

Alex nodded. "At least they stay off the ground. I

can't say the same for scorpions."

"Can't you call an exterminator?"

"To come spray poison in a state park?" she asked. "No. So I just keep an eye out and make sure they stay outside while I'm inside."

He shivered. "I don't like spiders."

The idea of a macho movie star, rippling muscles and all, crouched on a chair screaming for help made her chuckle. "Looks like they're finishing up for the day." She motioned to the cast and crew as they started packing up.

"I guess I'll see you tomorrow." He gave her one last smile. In that moment she actually believed he sought her out, maybe even enjoyed her company. Something along the lines of what Maggie had said. And then he rejoined the cast and just like that, he shifted to his usual noisy, obnoxious self, mentioning how boring that day's shoot had been. He had obviously been using Alex to pass the time.

It made her hate him a little bit more.

****

On Saturday afternoon, Alex stood in an area where she had at least one bar but could still see the set so she could keep a constant eye on the weather forecast—thundershowers moving in with a hundred percent chance of rain. Clouds rolled across the sky, bumping into each other as they blotted out the sun, but the film crew continued working anyway, much to her dismay. Steve, trying to reassure her, stated that the shots would be easier without the direct sun, that it was, in fact, a perfect day for shooting. She didn't want to file another injury report; especially one where lightning killed someone.

Travis and Blaze took turns on the same horse as they filmed parts that would be spliced together later, each with identical costumes and props. They laughed and joked around the whole time, engaged in a game of "anything you can do I can do better." The villain in the movie, an actor named Jake, and his stunt double rode on another horse, but they didn't seem to be having any fun. The fight sequence seemed choppy with carefully placed punches and perfect positioning of arms and legs. Nothing like the fluid scene she imagined. It was beyond her how the crew would turn fragments of dialogue and bits of movement into thrilling action.

When the sky rumbled, the horses danced in place, but Steve and Mr. Reid needed a little longer. The clouds hung heavy overhead.

Alex paced back and forth in her spot where she could see everything. She wanted to call it quits for the day, but that would mean going against the director *and* putting them even further behind schedule. Neither sounded appealing, so she waited.

When the first drops fell, it was easy to make her decision. If the storm was bad enough, the riverbed could flood.

"We need to be done for the day," she called out as she approached the crew. Mr. Reid looked up from his seat behind the camera and reluctantly nodded in agreement.

The call went out and people scurried in every direction, packing equipment and starting the trek back to the overflow parking lot. Everyone moved except Blaze and Travis, who continued to goof around despite the storm gaining momentum by the second. Travis stood on the back of the horse, balancing carefully on the saddle before dismounting. Blaze repeated his movements, perching on the rear end of the horse, but just as he was about to stand up, lightning streaked through the sky followed by a clap of thunder. The horse whinnied and surged forward, launching Blaze into the air. He fell, arms flailing, and landed hard on the dense sand.

The wrangler rushed over and took control of the horses, leading them to the trailer.

A group of people closed in on Blaze and backed away just as quickly. Alex joined them and discovered immediately what had happened. When the horse got spooked, it also voided its bowels, and as luck would have it, Blaze landed in the fresh pile of shit.

Chapter Nine

"Joe?" Alex hollered loud enough for her voice to travel over the storm.

The wrangler stopped and looked back at her.

"This waste needs to be cleaned up."

He nodded. "I'll send Mark to take care of it while I get these girls taken care of."

The rain would make things messier, so when Blaze tried to get up, Alex stopped him. "Wait. Please. You're shielding it with your body. If it gets wet, it'll be that much harder to clean up."

He glared at her and his friends who couldn't stifle their laughter. "You want me to hang out in horse shit until Mark gets here?"

"Yes. That's exactly what I'm asking."

"It's still warm," he growled.

"Horses don't digest all the seeds they eat. The last thing I need is an invasion of noxious weeds. Please?"

He glowered but didn't move.

Mark arrived with a shovel a minute later and asked, "Where is it?"

"Under me," Blaze spat.

"Good thinking keeping it covered." He offered a hand to Blaze and when he got to his feet, Mark scraped Blaze's clothes with the side of the shovel, smearing it into his vest and pants.

"Glad I could help," he mumbled.

Alex supervised the cleanup while Blaze tried to keep his disgusting costume off his skin. They were the last ones to leave the set, and as they walked into the parking lot, only one van remained.

The driver looked Blaze up and down and said, "No offense, but you smell like shit. You're not getting on here like that."

"Javier is gone, so I can't change. Do I have to walk back to town?" he said, throwing his hands up in the air.

"I'll take you," Alex offered, not looking at him. The driver nodded, Mark got onboard, and they took off.

The rain drummed against her hat as she started walking toward her house. "You did me a favor, now let me do one for you. Are you coming?"

He grumbled but finally followed her.

"You need to shower."

"I will as soon as I get back to the hotel."

"No, at my house. You're not getting in my car without cleaning up first." She turned down the walk and unlocked the front door. Koko came out to greet them, paying particular attention to the fresh scent coming from Blaze. "Get inside," she said to her dog, but Blaze moved past her.

"Not you. You reek. Koko get inside. Blaze get undressed."

"If you want to see me naked, just say so." He smiled, exuding sex and confidence.

It wasn't easy, but she had to pretend his words didn't shake her. "Give it a rest, cowboy. Hang on, I'll go get you a robe or something."

"For what?"

"To change into."

He shrugged and stepped out of his boots, dropping them against the house. Next came the vest, which he draped over the stone wall that lined the walkway. "Carol, the prop mistress, will kill me if these get ruined," he said as he handed her his gun and holster.

"Okay," she said, her voice a little wobbly. When he peeled his skin-tight pants off and arranged them on the wall with his vest, her heart raced. He stood in front of her in boxer briefs that didn't leave much to the imagination. The words written across the front read: *#1 JOHNSON.*

"What? They're from a fan."

"Your fans send you underwear?"

"Among other things." He grinned again. "Can I come in now? I'm getting cold."

"Sure. Yeah. Come on in." She stepped inside, hung her hat on the doorknob, and scanned the living room quickly to make sure it wasn't too messy. "Can I get you something to drink, coffee, tea, or—"

"A beer would be great."

"I thought you said you were cold."

"A little."

Who was she kidding? A beer sounded amazing. "I'll be right back." In the kitchen, she pulled two summer ales out of the fridge, lingering long enough to cool her heated skin. When she returned to the front room, Blaze was squatting and talking to Koko. The light near the door made his skin glow and his face lit up when Koko licked him. "Here you go," she said, opening it before handing it to him.

"Thanks," he replied as he stood. His muscular legs drew her attention to the curve of his perfect ass.

Alex opened her beer, took a long draw, and gripped the bottle tight to keep her hands from shaking.

"What is this? It doesn't have a label." He smacked his lips together. "Damn, that's tasty."

"Summer ale. Jim is the brewmaster for the pub in town. I get to sample all the goods."

"Who's Jim?"

"Maggie's husband. They just had a baby and this is Maggie's favorite, so he asked me to take it home so it wouldn't make her sad anymore."

"Score." He clinked his bottle against hers and smiled before taking another drink. Even though she was beginning to sweat, he seemed completely at ease standing in her living room in only his underwear. He stretched from side to side and then rubbed his low back.

"Are you okay?" she asked.

"Yeah, a little sore, but nothing that won't heal on its own. I have an old injury." He slid his hand down toward his ass. Her eyes followed.

The thought of filing another injury report made her want to die. Were there always that many accidents during filming or was it because of her negligence? "Do you need to see the medic? I should've asked before. Sorry I didn't. I'm new at this."

"Don't worry about it," he said and smiled. When he stepped toward her, the smell came with him.

"The bathroom is down the hall," she said, hoping he would take the hint.

"Right. Can I take this in with me?" He motioned to the beer.

"Sure. Follow me." They walked down the hall, through her bedroom, and stopped in the bathroom doorway. Because she'd never had company before she didn't even think about how weird it was that he would have to go through her room to use the shower. But it was too late to back out since he was standing right behind her, looking around. "There's body wash and shampoo. I could get you a fresh bar of soap if you want."

When he slid past her their bodies were inches apart. "I'll use whatever is in there. I'm not picky." He put the beer down on the sink and then hooked his thumbs over the waistband of his boxer briefs. "Are you going to join me, or..."

"Sorry." She squeezed her eyes shut and backed out of the room, closing the bathroom door behind her. The water turned on and she sighed. "Shit. I forgot to get him a fresh towel."

After a quick trip to the linen closet, she knocked on the bathroom door. "Blaze?"

"Yeah?" he called, his voice wet and warm.

"I'm putting a towel on the sink for you, okay?"

"Okay."

With the door cracked just enough for her to reach inside, she averted her eyes from the shower since the curtain wasn't closed all the way. "Here's your towel," she mumbled. The mirror hadn't fogged over yet so as she put the towel on the sink, she got a spectacular view of his ass. It was better than her dreams. "Damn," she whispered.

"What?"

"Nothing," she said and then she ran, slamming her bedroom door behind her. Under no circumstances should she go back in there. It was far too dangerous. Maybe she should've locked it, too. She took a swig from her beer and then put it down. If she was going to take him to town, she shouldn't drink anymore. The bottle was more than half full and would keep until she got home.

All she had to do was wait. From her seat on the couch, she noticed Blaze's disgusting clothes draped on the wall outside, getting even wetter. She grabbed a plastic grocery bag from the kitchen, ducked out into the storm, and stuffed them inside, leaving it against her house with his boots. Once she was in her house again, she washed her hands vigorously.

The shower still ran.

Koko wagged and followed Alex as she paced back and forth. "I have to sit in a car with him," she explained. Koko wiggled. "Maybe you should come with us. That's a great idea. You can sit on his lap. His scantily clad lap." She cradled her head in her hands and sighed. All her clothes were in her bedroom, which was definitely off limits, and besides, what did she own that would fit him? Nothing, which is exactly what he would be wearing unless she came up with something better. An apron hung on the side of the fridge, the one Maggie had given her for Christmas as a joke stating: *WORLD'S GREATEST COOK.*

That wouldn't work. That's when an idea struck her. Jim probably had clothes that would fit Blaze, which would make the fifty-mile ride much better.

"Koko, stay here. I'll be right back." Alex ran out the front door, through the pouring rain, to Maggie's. Koko whined from the window. Alex knocked and smiled when Jim answered the door. "Just the person I wanted to see."

"What can I do for you?"

"Blaze is at my house. Showering. He fell in manure, so he doesn't have anything to wear back into town." Pelli nudged Alex's fingers and looked expectantly at the door.

Jim nodded along.

"Can I borrow a pair of sweatpants and a T-shirt? And maybe a pair of flip-flops?"

"What size does he wear?" Jim asked

"I don't know." She narrowed her eyes as she sized up Jim's shoulders and waist. "He's a little bigger in the chest than you, but you probably have the same waist size."

"Shoe size?"

She shrugged. "Big?"

Jim laughed and walked into their bedroom.

"Alex, is that you?" Maggie called. "I'm in bed with the baby, come see me."

Alex walked down the hall and smiled at her friend. "Hey, Maggie. I can't stay."

"Why? What's going on? Why is Jim sorting through his closet?"

"I need to borrow clothes. Blaze is at my house. Showering."

Maggie's eyes widened. "Really? And why is that?"

"He slipped on the set. Messed up his clothes."

"And you're just helping out?" Maggie lifted her eyebrows. "Because you're so nice."

"I am nice," she protested.

"There's no other reason?" Maggie tilted her head. "Nothing *dreamy* happening over there?"

Alex flushed and shook her head. "Shh. No. He's showering. I'm driving him to town. End of story."

"Ah," Jim said, finally pulling his head out of the recesses of his closet. "We had these T-shirts printed last year for a promotion, but I never got around to wearing this one. You can tell him to keep it. It's too big for me anyway. But, I'll need the other stuff back." He arranged a pair of sweats on top and then crowned the stack with a pair of neon yellow flip-flops. "I hope those fit."

"If not, he can suck it," Alex said.

Maggie pursed her lips. "I think I'd be more careful about your choice of words if I were you." A laugh erupted out of her, waking the sleeping baby in her arms.

"You're a jerk," Alex said to her friend. "You, on the other hand," she said pointing to Jim, "are the best. Thanks. See you later."

"I expect a full report," Maggie called out between giggles.

Alex clutched the clothes to her chest and ran to her house where Koko waited, her nose smashed against the window.

"Hi, baby. Did I miss anything? Is he done?" Even from the living room she could hear the water running, just like it had been before, only now Blaze was humming. She was worried she'd been gone too long, but apparently, she hadn't been gone long enough. "I guess we'll just wait for him, huh?"

Waiting turned out to be harder than she anticipated. Pacing helped for a while, then she tried to read her book, but gave up and turned on the TV. The longer he showered, the more irritated she became. When the water finally turned off, she stalked down the hall and waited with Jim's clothes pressed against her chest, glaring at the closed door.

****

Blaze dried off and then wiped the corner of the mirror and tousled his hair to style it. Alex's bathroom smelled amazing. He'd never used rosemary mint shampoo before and suspected he'd never use anything else once he bought some for himself. The tiny bathroom didn't have a medicine cabinet, so the counter was lined with toothpaste, moisturizer, sunblock, and deodorant. It was a first for him since he'd never been in a woman's bathroom that didn't have makeup in it. He finished his beer in one long swallow and smiled.

With the towel held in place around his waist, he carried the empty bottle into her bedroom. Without prying too much, he glanced at her unmade bed, the cluttered nightstand, a pile of laundry stacked against the wall, and the massive bookshelf that took up more than half the wall. He put the bottle on one of the shelves as he read the titles displayed there. As his eyes traveled from spine to spine, he walked toward the door and stopped when he noticed the full-sized poster taped to the back. His smile grew and he couldn't stifle a laugh.

"I thought you weren't a fan," he said.

"A fan of what?" she answered, her words muffled through the door.

"Me," he replied when he turned the knob.

"What are you talking about?" she asked. The anger that had been firmly planted on her face started to slip away.

The truth was out, she was a fan. The proof hung on her door. "That."

She followed him into the room and looked around,

still not looking at the poster. "What?"

Once he pushed the door closed and pointed to the poster he repeated, "That."

"Maggie." A blush crept up her neck. "She thinks she's so funny. I never close my door. I didn't see that until just now."

It was too funny not to laugh. "Don't be embarrassed, I'll autograph it for you."

"Maggie brought it over here a few days ago. I told her to get rid of it."

He walked over to her nightstand, picked up a pen and scrawled across the middle of his chest: *TO MY FAVORITE RANGER, BLAZE JOHNSON.* "There." It was true. Every word of it.

"I don't want your autograph. I didn't...I'm not..." she stammered.

That old saying about protesting too much fit her to a 'T'. Maybe she really did want him as much as he wanted her. Only one way to find out. In a bold move, he put his finger to her lips. "It's okay." They were so soft, and all he wanted to do was to kiss her, but he hesitated, too afraid to screw up again.

Her chest heaved as she took each breath. "We need to leave."

"Do we? I'm all relaxed after that nice long shower, maybe you could relax, too." He took a step closer to her and smiled when her breath warmed his chest.

Just like that, her anger came back. "Yeah, about that. Did you know our water is brought in by truck? Fifty miles. Fifty," she shouted, stepping away from him. "Your *nice long shower* just consumed more water than I use in a week."

"It felt so good. Come on, don't be angry," he cooed, but it was too late.

She thrust a pile of clothes into his hands. Instinctively, he reached for them, releasing his grip on the towel, sending it falling to the floor in a puddle around his feet.

"Holy shit," she whispered, before clamping her eyes shut, turning around, and slamming the door behind her. "I'll be waiting in the car," she shouted to her closed door. "Koko, come on, let's go."

He glanced down. The promise of a kiss had worked its magic on his dick. "False alarm. She hates me."

Thinking about sitting next to her in the car was more than he could handle, and it took five minutes to force his erection to go away. No need to rush out to her in the mood she was in. On the other hand, the longer he made her wait, the madder she would be.

****

Alex took a deep breath of the cool evening air, savoring the aroma of wet earth. Some of her frustration slipped away. The rain fell lightly for the moment, a mere drizzle compared to the downpour earlier. When she got in her car, Koko followed, sitting in her spot on the passenger seat. The idea of Blaze sitting behind her, doing who knows what the whole ride, unnerved her. "We should probably make room for him," Alex said. "Get in the back." Koko hopped over the cup holder between the front seats and landed effortlessly in the back seat. Alex twisted and spread her towel out. "Lie down," she told Koko, but Koko pressed her nose to the window and beat her tail rhythmically against the seat the moment Blaze came out the front door. His flip-flops glowed against the ground, but the rest of his outfit seemed perfectly suited for him. The T-shirt stretched across his broad chest and the sweats hugged him. "Honestly, I thought you were a better judge of character," she mumbled to her dog before he opened the door.

Without a word, Alex started the car and backed out of the driveway. She began the long drive out of the park, and after a few miles she asked, "Did you lock my front door?"

"No. Why would I?"

"Because the park is full of strangers? People have stolen from us before." She slowed down and pulled over to call Maggie.

"Hi. What's up? Did you tell him to suck it and you're calling to tell me I'm right and know everything?" Maggie said in an extra cheery voice.

"Shh. I'm mad at you." Alex's cheeks burned.

"Why?" Maggie giggled.

"Because of your gift on the back of my door."

Maggie's giggles turned into a full-on fit.

"Will you lock my door, please? I'll be home in a couple of hours."

Maggie didn't respond with words, only more laughter.

"Thanks." As soon as she hung up, she put the pedal to the metal, making everyone in the car slam back into their seats.

"I'm sorry, I—" Blaze started.

"I don't want to hear it." The rain picked up again, adding to the sound of windshield wipers squeaking and Koko panting. They traveled that way for another fifteen minutes. She groaned as they came down the hill. The dip overflowed with a river of water. She slammed on the breaks, threw the car into park, and growled. "Damn it."

"What?" He squinted through the smudged windshield.

"We're stuck."

"What do you mean? Why are we stuck?"

"See that dip? It's full of water. I'm not driving a submarine," she pointed out, just in case he hadn't noticed. "We have to wait it out." Great. Sitting next to Blaze and his number one Johnson for who knows how long.

A slow smiled tugged up the corners of his mouth. "I know something we could do to pass the time."

"Ugh." She twisted in her seat to face him. "Don't you ever give up?"

"What? I meant we could play a game on your phone," he said innocently.

"I'm so frustrated. I don't get you. Sometimes you're the worst person I've ever met and other times you're totally nice."

"The *worst* person you've ever met? That seems a bit harsh."

"You tried to get me fired. That makes you pretty bad in my book." Her heart pounded wildly and her breath was erratic. "I've been trying so hard to be nice to you so it won't happen again."

"Fired? I didn't—"

"I. Don't. Want. To. Hear. It," she ground out before getting out of the car. The rain pelted her head, mixing with the tears that spilled out of her eyes. The other door slammed and Blaze made his way to her side, his shoes slapping the pavement. "Just leave me alone," she said, trying to turn away from him.

He held her shoulders and ducked his face in front of hers, forcing her to look at him. "I didn't try to get you fired."

"Yes, you did," she shouted. "This isn't even supposed to be my job. I'm only doing it because Maggie is on maternity leave. You reported me to the director. He said—"

"No, I didn't."

"He called me and said you reported me because I *threatened* you. Remember? The day you put me in my place and told me I wasn't valuable enough to be your coworker. When you reminded me I need a letter and all that stupid shit so I can prove I didn't fuck this job up. Remember?" She took a deep ragged breath, pulling salty tears and cool rain onto her tongue.

"I didn't report you. Nate must've." His shoulders fell. "I told him to take care of it. I didn't think he'd… I didn't think about what he would do. I was frustrated." He sighed. "I'm sorry. I didn't mean for that to happen. Why didn't you say something?"

"How could I? How could I admit I screwed up my *one* chance to prove myself? If I blow it, no one gets raises. The other rangers are counting on me, and I fucked up." She rested her chin on her chest and sobbed.

"You didn't fuck anything up," he said soothingly, running his hands down her arms. "Let's talk about this inside the car."

Sitting inside the car with him didn't sound appealing at all, so she stood there and cried and, to her surprise, he hugged her. As she leaned against his chest, he patted her back and told her it was going to be okay.

And she believed him. She ran out of tears at about the same time the sky ran out of rain.

"Are you done?" he said.

Instead of answering, she pulled away from him and returned to her seat. Leaving his arms turned out to be harder than she imagined and relief filled her when he joined her a few seconds later. Koko stood in the spot between them, licking and nuzzling while Alex dabbed at her eyes and nose with a tissue.

"Thanks, baby." Koko was always there when she needed her. Eventually, Alex's breathing evened out and Koko receded. Water dripped from Blaze's short hair, and after a quick glance in the mirror, she laughed. "I'm a mess." Strands of soggy hair hung limp around her face.

"No, you're not," he answered.

She wiped her eyes and laughed. "Have you seen me?"

"I'm looking right at you," he said, stroking her cheek. And then he kissed her. Soft, warm, and gentle.

Chapter Ten

Alex moaned and leaned into Blaze's hand, parting her lips and pushing her tongue into his mouth. He wound his fingers into her hair and pulled her closer. The cup holder dug into her side as she bent toward him. Why hadn't she kissed him before? Oh, right. It would be unethical for her to get involved with a coworker. Despite the ugly truth, tingles spread through her entire body, a thousand times more powerful than her dreams. Just because it felt good didn't mean she should keep doing it, so she pulled away from him. "I shouldn't have…"

"Stopped? I agree," Blaze said, leaning toward her again for another kiss.

"No. Kissed you. I'm sorry, but I can't…" If kissing felt that good, she could only imagine what the rest would be like. No. That couldn't happen. What would people think? That she was using him to get the letter the park needed. And what about him? Why was he even interested in her? The answer to that question was one she didn't want to know. She took a deep breath, faced forward, and buckled her seat belt.

"What just happened?" he asked, touching her arm lightly.

Pulling away from him, she said, "I turned you down." The more she thought about it, the more she questioned his motivation. It might be an elaborate prank, proving that he could get her, too. That she had succumbed to him like everyone else.

The river had subsided to a small creek, which wouldn't be a problem for her car. Water arced on either side of the windows as she pushed ahead into the dark night, leaving her moment of weakness behind. When she sucked her lip into her mouth, a jolt of pleasure shot through her; it still tasted like him. Screaming was definitely not an option, but she wanted to anyway. More than anything, she wanted to kiss him again. Her grip tightened on the steering wheel as she merged onto the highway that would take them to town.

****

Blaze shifted in his seat. What had happened? The moment he had been waiting for had finally arrived. After all the time they had spent together, they kissed. Not just any kiss, the kind that took his breath away. But she stopped. Why? Didn't she want him? Of course she didn't. Not after he got her in trouble. As if she would forget all of that with one kiss. Sure, she seemed to accept his apology, and when he kissed her, she kissed him back, but then everything changed. The moment had passed, and he needed to accept it.

As she wound through the quiet streets of Dembi toward the hotel, he stared at her stony face, her cheeks still flushed from crying and her lips swollen from their kiss. She wouldn't look at him.

"It's not real," he said.

"What?" she asked, looking at him out of the corner of her eye.

"Me, my persona. Blaze Johnson." He sighed. "People expect things. So why not play the part?"

Outside the entrance to his hotel, she turned off her

car and looked at him. "You're telling me all that swagger and confidence isn't really you?"

He shook his head. Why couldn't she see it?

"I don't know what to think of you," she replied.

It didn't matter what he said, he was getting nowhere fast. "Thank you for driving me all the way out here. I hope you have a safe drive back. Thanks for the clothes, too," he added.

"Thank Jim. He needs the pants and shoes back but said you could keep the T-shirt if you want. It's too big for him."

"Okay. Goodnight, Koko." He twisted in his seat to pet her. "Tell your mom I like her, okay?" With one last glance at Alex, he got out.

****

Alex jumped when the car door slammed. Maybe she was wrong about him. Blaze seemed so…honest.

The lobby doors opened and he walked in without looking back.

Koko jumped to the front seat and licked Alex's cheek.

"Is that your way of sharing his message?" she asked. "We need to get home before Maggie organizes a search party."

Sure enough, when Alex pulled into her driveway an hour later, Maggie was waiting outside, bouncing her tiny bundled baby in the harness strapped to her chest.

"You said you'd be home in two hours. It's been three," Maggie started.

"I should've called. We got stuck at the wash and had to wait the storm out." Alex looked at her shoes.

"And?"

"He kissed me," she admitted.

Maggie squealed and hugged her, squishing the baby between them. "Oh sorry, Henry. Tell me everything."

That night, as Alex fell asleep, she stared at her closed door. She didn't mind the picture of Blaze so much anymore because it reminded her everything had been real. Even though she couldn't have him, she could relish the tiny moment they shared. No one would ever believe it had really happened. No one but Maggie, of course.

When she dreamed, he took center stage. Well, him and his number one Johnson.

****

Alex arrived early at work the next morning, her stomach fluttered with a thousand butterflies. Blaze didn't seem to be anywhere in the crowd.

"Looking for me?" he asked with a laugh.

A squeak of surprise escaped her lips and then she breathed deeply. "You have to stop doing that."

"But it's so much fun," he teased. "Hey, I brought you breakfast." At that, he held up a bag from her favorite grocery store.

She peered inside and grinned when she saw the perfect golden top of poppy seed heaven. "Thank you," she said.

"I bought some for Jim, too." In his other hand, he had a dry-cleaning bag and a box full of muffins. "To thank him."

"Do you want to take them to him now? I'm sure they're up. Their baby doesn't sleep in."

"Sure. I have a few minutes before I need to be in costume. Can you go with me so we can get my clothes off your porch?"

"I'm sorry I forgot them last night. I put them in a bag and everything, but didn't put them in the car." She pulled her walkie-talkie off her hip and called out, "Neal, I'll be back in a few minutes."

"Sure thing."

"Come on," she said, taking her muffin out of her bag. "Do you want some?" She held it out to him.

"I already ate mine. Like, in two bites." He smiled. "They're really good."

Alex laughed and ate hers on the short walk to the small neighborhood. "That's where Maggie and Jim live," she said, pointing to their house. "I'm going to see Koko while you talk to him. It'll drive her crazy if she knows I'm here and I don't say hi to her."

****

Blaze straightened his back and walked over to the house next to Alex's and knocked twice.

A woman began talking as she opened the door, "Did you for… Never mind. You're not Alex."

"You must be Maggie." Blaze pushed his hand toward her. "Alex talks about you a lot."

"Likewise," Maggie said, shaking his hand.

Blaze grinned. Alex talked about him. A lot. "Is Jim home? I had these cleaned and I wanted to thank him." He put the box of muffins in her hand.

"Jim, honey," she called.

"I got a variety," Blaze pointed out.

"That's nice of you. You didn't have to go to all this trouble," she said as Jim joined her with a tiny baby nestled against his shoulder.

"It's no trouble. I appreciate the clothes." Blaze shook Jim's free hand. "Nice to meet you, Jim. I'm

Blaze."

Jim laughed. "Did you get my sweats dry cleaned?"

Blaze nodded. "The hotel has a laundry service. They couldn't do anything with the shoes, so I washed them with hand soap. I'm glad I don't have to clean the costume I was wearing." Just the thought of it made him scrunch up his face.

"Alex mentioned you slipped on set," Maggie said.

Blaze laughed. "That's putting it mildly. I fell off the horse right into a fresh pile of shit." He covered his mouth immediately and apologized.

Jim glanced down at the baby and chuckled. "He's only a few days old, he doesn't understand swear words yet. I figure we have a few months before we have to start filtering." The baby started to fuss, so Jim bounced him up and down.

"Anyway, it was pretty disgusting." Blaze grimaced.

"Did they get it all? Horses don't digest—" Maggie started.

"I know, Alex told me all about it. I stayed put until the cleanup crew could get to me. I wouldn't want to spread weeds."

Maggie nodded. "Good."

"I better get back. I can't be late. Thanks again for helping out, and for the shirt. It's cool."

"Glad I could help. Thanks for the treats," Jim said before taking the baby inside.

Maggie touched Blaze's shoulder before he could leave. "Alex is like a little sister to me. I don't want her to get hurt."

"I'm not going to hurt her."

"Good," Maggie replied.

Blaze turned back toward Alex's house and thought about what Maggie said. They had obviously talked about the previous night, and Maggie was worried about her friend. That's what any good friend would do. If he were in Maggie's situation, he would want to protect Alex, too. Everyone assumed they knew what kind of man he was, and it was up to him to change their minds.

He knocked on Alex's window and then let himself in when she waved. "Hi, Koko," he sang, putting his arms around her. "I miss my baby. It's hard being gone for so long."

"You have a dog? That explains so much," Alex said.

"Yep, a little fluffy mutt I rescued a few years back. Ozzie has to stay at doggy daycare while I'm filming. It sucks."

"Yeah, it would suck," she said.

When he stood to face her, his heart raced. "I guess we should get back to—"

She quieted him with a kiss, her body crashing into his. After a second, he relaxed and put his arms around her. While their tongues dueled, his fingers spread out across her ass and dug in, dragging her soft, warm body closer to his. Holding her was even better than kissing her.

****

Alex tightened her hold on him and moaned as a shiver of pleasure washed over her. Everything felt so good: his hands, lips, and broad chest. What if no one found out about them? Why couldn't she keep him all to herself? That wouldn't hurt anyone. And then reality set in. Of course they would find out. "I'm sorry," she mumbled, covering her face with her hand.

"Quit apologizing," he said.

"We need to get back to the set." And she needed to practice self-control and be a professional. Professionals didn't go around kissing their coworkers. Unfortunately. "They're waiting for us." Being alone in her house with him wasn't a good idea, because she couldn't look at him without thinking of his sublime chest and the way her body tingled when he touched her. "Before we go, you forgot these last night." The underwear he'd left in her bathroom had been in her pocket all morning. Not that he needed to know that. It was more proof that they had a moment, but now she had to hand them over.

"Shit, I'm sorry. Nate usually cleans up after me."

"Must be nice."

"Not really."

"Don't forget your costume," she said, pointing to the soggy clothes waiting outside.

While he bent over to pick them up, she locked her house and got a head start.

"Can we talk about this?" he asked.

"Not right now," she said, nodding toward the set. "You need to get into costume and I need to get back into position."

"Later." He gave her a meaningful glance and jogged toward the costume trailer.

When she approached the set, she called Neal and let him know she had returned. She spent the rest of the morning watching the cast and crew work but found her mind wandering more often than not. They had kissed. Twice. The line had been crossed, and she wasn't sure she wanted to go back. When Mr. Reid called lunch, Alex got her food and found a secluded spot half-hoping Blaze wouldn't find her. When he did, she couldn't help but smile.

In a low voice he asked, "Can we talk now?"

"What is there to talk about?" she asked casually, trying to eat as quickly as possible.

He lifted his eyebrows. "The fact that we can't keep our hands off each other."

With her hands in front of her, she said, "I don't seem to have that problem. See? I'm keeping my hands to myself." Never mind she wanted to jump him right then and there.

"So am I, but I don't want to. Why does it have to be complicated?"

"Because it is. Because you're you and I'm me. You're a star and my job is to make sure you have a good experience at the park so we get money for raises. Conflict of interest. And I'm not supposed to interfere with filming."

"This has nothing to do with the movie."

"You're…" As if on cue, her phone chimed, interrupting them. She groaned. "It's my mom." Even though she knew it wouldn't make a difference, she declined the video call. Four seconds later it began chiming again. "She knows I'm at lunch right now, and she won't stop calling. I should probably take this."

"Fine, but I'm not going anywhere. We're not done talking."

What was worse—video chatting with her mom or talking to Blaze about something that could never happen? "Hi, Mom," she said as the image of her mother filled her screen.

"You have some nerve, Ally."

Alex glared at her phone. "Is this why you called me? To yell at me again?"

"I left you a voicemail and you didn't return the call."

"Why would I call you back?" A blush crept up her neck as Blaze listened to the humiliating conversation. "I told you I'm not coming home for Matt's birthday."

"Because work is more important," her mom added. "I'm not sure I even believe you. A movie? I can't see hide nor hair of anything except the same ugly desert."

Alex clenched her jaw. "Why would I lie about my job?"

"Oh, I don't know, to get out of helping your brother feel special, or to make yourself seem more important."

Alex opened her mouth to respond, her venomous reply on the tip of her tongue when Blaze touched her shoulder. He held his hand out and motioned for her to give the phone to him. Pressing her fingers over the microphone and camera, she whispered, "What?"

"Let me talk to her," he whispered back.

"Fine." She pushed the phone into his hand and held her breath as she watched over his shoulder.

"Ma'am, I'm sorry to interrupt," Blaze drawled, turning into his character Buck, "but we need Ms. Mitchell back on the set."

Her mom squinted at the screen and tilted her head. "Are you...?"

"Your daughter is the most important ranger in the park." Laying on the charm, he smiled that dazzling smile. "Which means we need her for every aspect of our work here. I hope you understand," he finished.

"Well, yes, of course," her mother stammered.

Alex took the phone away from him and said, "Bye, Mom."

"Was that Blaze Johnson? You're working with *him*?"

"Bye, Mom," she repeated a little louder before ending the call. Alex sighed and tucked her phone into her pocket. "Thank you for that, she can be…"

"Difficult?" he offered.

"That's not the word I would choose, but sure."

"My mom is so great, I'm always surprised when I meet women like her. I like spending time with my family, but I bet you don't."

Alex snorted. "That's for sure. I owe you."

His smile widened. "Really?"

For a moment, she had forgotten to be careful with her choice of words. "You didn't have to say all that stuff about my job."

"Why not? It's true. It blows me away you can't see how amazing you are. I've told you before. You're managing all the other rangers, maintaining the park, and dealing with assholes like me, and you do it effortlessly. Now, back to our conversation. You were about to say something about me. Please go on."

She took a deep breath and said, "You're Blaze Johnson. The whole world knows who you are."

"Except you," he reminded her.

"Right. I found out the hard way." Looking him up on the Internet wasn't her proudest moment, and she still couldn't forget the headlines and pictures. Especially the ones with his latest love interest. "Who's Ruby?"

"The lead actress in the last movie I filmed," he answered. "How do you know her name?"

"Um, I looked you up on the Internet."

He laughed. "I'm sure you read some very interesting things."

"About you and Ruby, Hollywood's new power couple."

"We were never together, not that it matters. I have a rule of not dating in the industry. Not anymore. It's too messy and too dangerous. Wait, is that why you're so hesitant around me? Because you think I'm already with someone?"

"You're out of my league. I'm nothing. No one," she said.

He touched her chin and turned her face toward his. "You're not nothing, you're real. You call me out on all my shit. No one does that. Except you."

Drawn to him like a magnet to steel, she started leaning toward him and then growled with frustration. "Damn. Why do you have to be charming?"

"So you'll kiss me again?"

Alex scanned the area, acutely aware of the presence of each and every person on the set. "People will see."

"Who cares?"

"I do," she stated. The headline popped into her mind, *THE RANGER WHO SLEPT HER WAY TO GETTING A RAISE.* No thank you. "Thanks again for your help with my mom. I really appreciate it." She stood and started walking away from him but stopped after two steps. Keeping her back to him she said, "I'm not sure if you're free, but I'm leading a nature walk tonight: Things with Wings. I thought I'd let you know in case you were interested."

"When and where?"

"Seven thirty at the Visitor Center," she replied, smiling so hard her cheeks hurt.

****

Blaze tried to focus on his work, but after his conversation with Alex, all he could think about was how he was going to show up at the Visitor Center that night at seven thirty. He could probably get a ride with someone at the hotel or even ask the front desk to call him a cab, but either way, he would be stranded. And then it hit him: Nate had a car, but because Blaze had paid for it, it was practically his.

The problem was how.

Before the end of the day, he found Charlotte standing on the sidelines waiting to be excused for the day. "How are things with Nate?"

A blush shone through her makeup. "Great. Thanks for introducing us."

"That's what friends are for, right?"

"I'm going to see him tonight," she said.

Blaze checked over his shoulder to be sure Nate was still occupied in the conversation across the parking lot. "Can I tell you something?"

"Sure," she said with a shrug.

"I've known him for a while. You know what he's into? Champagne, roses, and dinner for two. The works. He's a hopeless romantic."

"Really?" She grinned. "Thank you so much for telling me. I know what I'm doing tonight."

Blaze winked and walked toward the costume trailer to swap out his clothes. "Hey, Javier, what time is it?"

"Almost five," Javier replied as he tidied Blaze's costume.

"Thanks. And thanks again for cleaning everything from yesterday."

"That shit was ground in there. What were you doing? Rolling around in it?" Javier laughed.

"I fell in it and then had to stay put so the wranglers could collect it all. The ranger, Alex, was worried about weed seeds spreading."

Javier's mouth hung open. "You just sat there and protected a big pile of horse shit so seeds wouldn't spread?"

"Alex asked me to."

"She did, huh?" Javier lifted an eyebrow. "Are you sweet on her?"

Blaze's smile turned into a grin. While he didn't know what to expect from her, she had invited him to spend time with her. No movie crew, no Nate. Just two people getting to know each other. If he thought about what that meant, he might fuck things up again.

****

Blaze's leg bounced the whole way back to Dembi. The plan was fully formed in his mind, but the list of ways it could go wrong was long. Nate chattered for more than half the trip back to the hotel. Blaze did his best to tune him out.

"Do you want to get something to eat," Blaze asked him as they walked into the lobby of the hotel, hoping like hell that at least this part of his plan worked.

"Nah. Charlotte's got something planned. She was all excited. Sounds like I'm going to get some tonight," Nate said. "I'm heading there in a bit."

"See you tomorrow," Blaze went to the restaurant and ordered a sandwich to go. Keeping an eye on Nate as he headed for the elevator, Blaze tried to play it cool. Inside he was dancing. With a clamshell container in hand, he ran up the stairs to the second floor and pressed his ear against Nate's door long enough to hear the shower running. Blaze groaned and walked to his room, propped the door open, and ate his dinner. He must've checked the clock on the bedside a hundred times, the minutes slipping away.

"Come on, Nate. You're going to make me late," he whispered. The clock read *6:15*.

A bit later, Nate strolled by and headed to the elevator. Blaze figured it would take a few minutes for Nate to get to the main floor and walk to Charlotte's room.

Blaze watched the clock and waited for *6:20*. When he was sure it was safe, he picked up his room phone and called down to the front desk. "Hey, my friend is up here trying to get into his room, but the key won't work. Can you send someone up to help? Two-fifteen. Thanks."

Blaze rushed out of his room and slumped against Nate's door. Every noise in the hallway made him twitchy. The elevator dinged and his stomach dropped. What if Nate had forgotten something?

A faint squeaking sound met his ears and then the housekeeping cart rolled toward him. The woman pushing the cart smiled at him. Blaze shrugged as he slid his keycard into the slot and showed her the red light.

"These are so finicky." When she inserted the master keycard, the door clicked and the green light flashed. "If you continue to have problems, take your key to the lobby and they'll get you a new one."

"Will do. Thank you. I'm so sorry to bother you," he added.

"No bother." She smiled and backed out of the room.

After waiting a few seconds, he started searching. "Damn it, Nate, where did you put my stuff?" The bathroom drawers, closet shelves, and dresser were all empty. Finally, he found the keys to the rental car in the nightstand drawer. With phase two complete, he still needed to find his wallet and phone. Before handing them over on the plane, he had taken out a wad of cash, but was almost out. "The plane," he said as he ran back to the closet where Nate's lone piece of luggage sat in the corner. There, in the outside pocket, still in the same place Nate had put it, were his phone and wallet. Phase three complete. Things were starting to look up.

He put everything back where it had been and hoped like hell Nate wouldn't notice the missing keys. The clock read *6:32*.

"Fuck." Phase four involved getting gas, and he was running out of time. With his ear to the door, he listened for a minute before making a break for the stairs. His heart hammered in his chest all the way down to the main floor and nearly deafened him in the silent parking lot. Only a few more seconds and he would be free. Free to spend his time the way he wanted away from Nate. With one more glance around the deserted parking lot, he unlocked the car, started it, and headed into town.

At the gas station, he prepaid at the window. While the attendant was entering the information for his pump number, Blaze spotted a display of condoms and pointed to them. "Will you add a three-pack of those, too?"

"Sure thing, buddy," the guy replied with a knowing smile and slid the box through the tiny slit in the window that separated them. "You're all set."

Blaze dialed Ozzie's dog daycare center while he waited for the gas tank to fill. It had been a week since he'd been able to check in and it was driving him crazy. When the woman on the line explained that his dog was having fun and making friends, he smiled. Just like Blaze.

The box of condoms wouldn't fit comfortably into his jeans, so he opened the package, chucked the box in the garbage can, and stashed the flexible packets in his pocket. It was too much to consider if he was going to get to use them, but he could hope, couldn't he?

The minutes ticked away on the dash clock as he drove into the desert. Out of habit, he practiced his lines. Not the ones written for him, but the ones he would say to Alex. It was crucial that he get it right. She wasn't like most women. The lines that typically worked made her roll her eyes. Maybe the best choice would be to keep his mouth shut and hope for the best.

Chapter Eleven

Alex paced the length of her house. "What if he's not there?" The evening rays of sun spilled through her living room window. She groaned. "What if he *is* there?"

Maggie laughed. "Then you can count your blessings."

"What am I doing?" she stopped and faced her friend.

"I don't know, but I've never seen you this excited." Maggie smiled and bounced Henry on her knee.

"He drives me crazy. I feel an ulcer coming on." Alex rubbed her stomach. "I really like him, but I shouldn't be doing this."

"Why not? You only live once." Maggie laughed again. "You'll be fine. If nothing else, you can educate him and the other visitors about the abundant wildlife that lives in our park."

"Right. I can do that. Thanks, Maggie." She hooked Koko's leash to her collar and they all walked out together. "I promise I'm not letting this—whatever it is—interfere with my job. I'm not using him. I swear. Also, I couldn't stand to disappoint Mr. Howard again, or you," she added.

"I know, which is why I support you one hundred percent." As Maggie headed toward her house, she called out, "Live in the moment. Enjoy yourself."

Alex laughed nervously.

Before she left, her mom started a video call. There was no use ignoring it. "Was that Blaze Johnson?" her mom asked immediately.

"Hi, Mom."

"Don't *hi mom* me. Answer my question. Was that Blaze Johnson?"

Alex sighed. "I'm not allowed to discuss details of filming with the public," she repeated.

"I know what I saw," her mom screeched.

"Then why are you asking me when you know I can't answer? I signed a confidentiality contract."

"When are you allowed to talk about it?" The question came out as a whine.

"When the movie is released. Until then," Alex finished by squeezing her lips shut. "Work is crazy right now, so it's best if you wait for me to call you. In fact, I'm leading an interpretive program in a few minutes so I have to go."

Another whine. "You mean I have to wait for months until you can tell me all the juicy details?"

"Yes." The only thing she could do at that point was placate her mother. "I'll call you next week when we're done so we can talk about Matt's party."

Her mom smiled a little. "I'll let him know you're thinking of him."

"Sure. Talk to you next week," she said before touching the red button that would end their call, hoping her mom would stop calling. There was already enough going on and she didn't need her mom piling on.

Alex and Koko walked together on the main road

leading toward the Visitor Center. A small group of guests waited under the light outside the locked doors. Blaze wasn't one of them. Devastated, she wondered if he was really going to show up. Maybe he got hung up in town. Whatever the case, it became very clear that she wanted to see him more than anything. "We'll wait a few more minutes before we begin." From her position, she could see a lone car coming down the long road from the entrance gate and hoped with all her might he was in that car.

While she waited, Alex filled the next few minutes with some light cleaning in the area outside the Visitor Center. A car door slammed and she couldn't help but look. Blaze stepped out from behind the wheel, pulled a hood over his head, shoved his hands into his hoodie pockets, and joined the group of visitors without drawing any attention.

It was time to begin. "Welcome to Things with Wings, I'm Alex Mitchell, your ranger for tonight, and this is my dog, Koko. Thank you for joining us."

When he smiled at her it made her heart beat sideways.

"If you'll follow me, we'll go see burrowing owls," she said, starting down the path that wound around the west side of the park. "Please stay on the trail and let me know if you have any questions."

"I have a question," Blaze said when he caught up with her. "Are you happy to see me?"

"Maybe," she replied.

He bumped her shoulder with his, but they walked together in silence.

As they approached a rock outcropping, she slowed and the group gathered around her.

"Burrowing owls live in our park from April to October each year. They live in ground burrows made by other animals and can be found near dusk and dawn hunting insects and small mammals," she said. "The prairie habitat just around the corner has a few families still living together before they migrate south for the winter. We'll need to be quiet and hold really still. They're small birds, so when I see one I'll point it out, okay?"

A little girl, clinging to her mother asked, "Do they have any babies?"

"Their babies are all grown by now, but they're still really cute." Alex smiled and then held her finger to her lips and crept around the corner.

When they got near the owl nesting area, Alex and Koko both crouched down. The other seven people mimicked her and waited. After everyone got settled, Alex held her hands to her mouth and called to the owls. The first attempt was a little off, so she cleared her throat and tried again. That time, she got an answer.

A tiny round head popped up out of the ground and hooted back to her.

"Do you guys see it?" she whispered.

The visitors nodded in unison.

"The best part of being on this side of the park is that there aren't as many scorpions. Owls *love* scorpions. Owls are excellent hunters," she said, trying to reassure everyone. "Let's see if we can get more to come out." She hooted again.

The girl smiled at her and whispered, "You sound just like them."

Alex shrugged. "I have lots of practice. My friend Neal taught me."

After another hoot, two more heads popped up from different burrows. The owls didn't seem to be bothered by their presence after a while, which meant the small group of visitors got to see them hunt and interact.

Thirty minutes passed before Alex said, "Would you like to see bats now?"

"Yes," everyone said at the same time.

"I'll lead the way back to the Visitor Center," Alex announced. The sky had darkened in the last forty minutes, so she tried to retrieve a flashlight from her jacket pocket, but couldn't get it with Koko's leash in her hands. "Will you hold her for a minute?" she asked Blaze.

"Sure," he said, smiling.

With both hands free, she pulled her flashlight out and switched on the black light filter. "This will give us a little light and help us spot scorpions. They glow bright green under this light."

It was obvious by how close Blaze got that scorpions were on the list with spiders. All he needed was a little comfort and she was more than happy to provide that by patting his hand. When he turned his palm up and laced his fingers through hers, she almost pulled away but then looked behind them. No one seemed to notice or care that they were holding hands. The other visitors were too busy talking about burrowing owls.

Heat radiated from his palm, spreading through Alex's hand and up her arm. Koko walked alongside, wagging and smiling up at them. When Alex swept along the side of the trail and spotted a scorpion, she pointed it out to everyone. His grip tightened.

"Scorpions live underground, too. Sometimes their homes flood during rainstorms, which means you're more likely to see them after a storm. Their sting is very painful, so stay in the middle of the path, okay?"

The group behind her tightened up and shuffled past the tiny creature, picking up the pace.

Reluctantly, Alex pulled away from Blaze as they approached the brightly lit Visitor Center. "Twisted Juniper is home to a handful of species of bats. They can eat their body weight in insects in a single night. Bats live in caves, hollowed trees, cliffs, mines, and sometimes buildings. They're nocturnal, which means they're active at night. They have excellent vision and also use echolocation to find their prey. Follow me," she said before leading them to a set of benches that lined the front of the building. "Once we get settled, they'll come back."

Blaze sat down next to her, near the end of the bench and Koko napped under their feet. Waiting for bats was totally underwhelming for a dog. "Hold still and watch the light." With everyone looking at the exposed bulb overhead, she reached down between their bodies and gripped his hand again.

Dozens of moths fluttered around the light, tapping the glass with their wings and bumping into each other. A tiny blur of brown darted through the air.

"There, did you see it?" Alex asked. Another bat swooped above them, doing an acrobatic maneuver that illuminated its paper-thin wings for a split-second.

A chorus of delighted sounds came from the group as they watched one bat after another soar gracefully above them. At the end of the program, Alex stood and asked if anyone had any questions.

The girl asked, "Is it true they're making a movie here?"

"Yep, that's true," Alex confirmed. Blaze tensed and tilted his face toward the ground, hiding behind the fabric of the hood he hadn't removed.

"Are there movie stars around here?" the girl asked, looking out across the peaceful desert.

Alex laughed. "Not right now. They're in town, getting ready for bed like everyone else."

"Really?"

"Yep. They're just like the burrowing owls. They keep to themselves, but once you learn how to speak their language, they're pretty nice if you get to know them." Experience had taught her that. "Thank you for joining me tonight."

After the visitors thanked her, the small group headed back to the campsite and dispersed, leaving Blaze and Alex alone.

"Thank *you* for joining me." Alex nudged his shoulder as they started walking toward the parking lot.

"I'm glad I came. I learned a lot," he said. "I was already impressed by your knowledge, but now I'm blown away. You're a natural at this."

Heat crept up her cheeks. There he was, complimenting her again. "I studied biology in college. My mom said it was a waste of time, that I should focus on something more practical, like finding a husband." She rolled her eyes.

He laughed and pulled his keys out of his pocket.

"Have you looked up? You can see the Milky Way." It was too early for him to leave, so she stalled and pointed overhead at the creamy streak in the sky.

"Wow."

"Dembi puts off a little light pollution, but out here the sky is so dark you can see satellites. There," she said as she pointed to the tiny speck moving much faster than anything else.

"Where?"

"I'll show you. Squat down a little, you're too tall." Once he got down, she stood next to him, cheek-to-cheek and pointed again, holding her hand up between them. "Do you see it?"

"Uh-huh." He turned his face until his lips brushed her cheek.

The urge to kiss him was almost too much to resist, but they were out in the open where anyone could see them. They had to get somewhere a little more private. "Do you want to come over and have a beer?"

"Mm-hmm," he hummed.

"We should do that then. Come on, Koko, let's go home." She laced her fingers through his and dragged him away from the rental car. Once they got into her house, Alex shrugged out of her jacket and unclipped Koko.

Blaze tugged his hoodie off and closed the gap between them.

"I should probably get those beers," she said, breathing heavily.

"I have a better idea," he said, draping his arms around her waist and kissing her.

With her arms wrapped around his neck she deepened the kiss and moaned when he lifted her off the ground and tucked his hands under her ass. They were barreling across the line they couldn't come back from. Was it ethical to sleep with your coworker? No. But they wouldn't be working together for much longer. On the other hand, if things went sideways she would be in all kinds of trouble. The war raged for another few seconds until she bumped against the growing bulge in his jeans. "Bedroom," she said, and then he kissed down the side of her neck.

"Mm-hmm." In her room, he kicked the door closed and pressed her against it.

She giggled. "I'm the center of a Blaze sandwich."

"I'm not interested in sharing," he said, spinning and placing Alex gently on the edge of her bed then kneeling on the floor between her legs.

His mouth never stopped moving, kissing and licking down the opening of her shirt, making her moan again. "I love that noise."

When she reached between them and unbuttoned her brown uniform shirt, he watched every movement, his eyes wide. She hesitated when she reached the bottom, so he took over, sliding the last button through the hole and pulling the shirt off her shoulders.

"Is this okay?" he asked with his face inches from hers.

"Yes." More than okay. "Is this what you want?"

"Yes," he said with such certainty that her apprehension vanished.

With that, his mouth descended again, kissing her breasts through the thin material of her bra, and then his fingers unclasped the band, releasing the garment. He sighed and cupped her soft flesh with his hands, rolling her nipples between his fingers and thumbs.

Next, he sucked one of her nipples into his mouth. Unable to keep her eyes open, she straightened her arms and leaned backward on the bed, digging her fingers into the sheets. His mouth moved down, leaving a trail of kisses across her belly while his fingers moved to the button holding her pants closed. She gasped for breath and stilled his hands.

"You need to catch up," she said, and just like in her dream, he stood in front of her and stripped. First his shirt, which he pulled off slowly to reveal his perfectly chiseled abs and muscly shoulders; his *world-famous* muscles. Next, he unbuttoned his jeans, smiling as he wiggled out of them.

"Now *you* need to catch up," he said, pushing her backward so he could unbutton and unzip her pants and then tugged them and her shoes off. All that remained were her panties, which he caressed, bringing one little detail to the forefront of her mind.

"Shit," she said.

"What?"

"I don't have any condoms. I'm sorry. I don't usually…"

"I do," Blaze said, kissing along her waistband.

"That's presumptuous, don't you think?" she teased.

"No. Hopeful." He grinned and retrieved a three-pack folded neatly in his back pocket, which he placed on the small table next to the head of her bed.

"I'm glad you're prepared," she admitted.

"Me too," he said, rubbing her clit with his thumb, drawing a mewling sound out of her mouth. "Fuck. You make the best noises."

"I'm trying to be quiet," she said. "Neighbors and all."

"Fuck being quiet." It wouldn't be easy if he kept yanking at her panties with his teeth. "I want to hear you come."

Déjà vu. "Just like my dream," she mumbled.

He kissed along her waistband and stroked her through the thin material. "What dream?"

"I've been dreaming of you," she confessed. "In the most recent one, you told me to come for you."

"Sounds like me. You know me better than you think you do," he said, smiling. He planted a kiss on top of her clit and slid her panties to the side, breathing against her pussy.

"Ugh," she grunted because she wanted him to touch her more than anything in the world. "Please," she begged.

Blaze circled her clit, rubbing and sucking until her grunts turned into cries. At the brink of release, he thrust his tongue inside her and pushed her over.

Alex clamped her mouth shut and filled her cheeks with a scream. Her pulse pounded in her ears, and she gulped air. When she focused on him, he was smiling up at her and tugging her panties off her hips. "Please. More."

As he stood, he peeled his boxer briefs off allowing his cock to jut up toward the ceiling.

Fumbling with the strip of condoms on the table, she finally managed to rip one off and open it. "Come here," she said, sliding up to the head of the bed and beckoning him to get closer. Which he did while she dipped her hand between her legs, coating her fingers with cum. His hips jerked when her slippery hand encased his length and started twisting, forcing a groan out of his lips. Every time the tip of his dick pushed through the circle of her thumb and finger, tingles spread through her body as anticipation built. "I need you," she said between breaths for air.

"Now."

She rolled the condom onto him and cupped his balls before lying down and pulling him between her legs. Guiding him into her, she closed her eyes and held her breath.

"Are you okay?" he asked.

"Yes." It would take a little getting used to, that's all. The key was to relax.

The muscles in his arms flexed as he kissed her, but he kept pushing into her slowly, stretching and filling her. It was a perfect fit. They shared a moan and she arched off the bed, needing to feel him deeper.

Nothing else in the world mattered. Their bodies, the room, his breath, his touch. That was the whole world to her and she'd never been happier. She sucked on his tongue with each thrust trying to muffle her cries as another orgasm ripped through her.

While she quaked around him, he held perfectly still, his face pinched with pain.

"Are *you* okay?" she asked, touching his creased forehead.

"Trying to hold on a little longer. You're not making it easy. You feel so good."

"What, this?" Arching again, she gripped his ass and slammed against him. Hard.

The next time she did it, he growled and met her thrust, crushing her clit against his pelvis. With one final union, his cock swelled inside her and another yell escaped her lips. The sounds of pleasure echoed off the walls, deafening her.

He collapsed onto his elbow, panting.

"Holy shit," Alex said finally.

"I'll be right back," he said before rolling away

from her.

The loss of him was more than she could handle and her body shook in protest. Watching him wobble toward the bathroom made her happy she didn't have to get up because she was pretty sure her legs wouldn't work right for a while. A few seconds later, he sat on the edge of the bed.

Alex wound her arms around him and pulled him next to her, where she nuzzled his chest and draped her limbs across him. Even though he stretched out next to her, he remained tense. "Do you need to leave?"

"Do you want me to?" he asked.

"No. Don't go," she said.

Only then did he relax and put his arm around her. Tracing random patterns on her back, he said, "Okay. I won't." They cuddled in silence for a few minutes.

"That was way better than my dreams."

"Oh?"

"Yeah." She laughed. "Because it really happened."

"Why don't you tell me about your dreams?" he replied, cupping her ass.

"There's not much to tell. Just little snippets of you kissing me or touching me."

"Touching you how?"

Alex smiled. "The first time, you sucked on my nipples. I like that a lot."

"I can tell," he replied.

"The next dream was a little more explicit. We were on the set, both of us in costume. You put your hand up my dress."

Following directions, he slid his fingers between her legs, exploring her swollen lips.

She moaned and twisted her body so she was straddling one of his legs, giving him greater access. "And then you pushed a finger inside me," she said, struggling to breathe again.

"Like this?" he asked, plunging into her.

To her delight, his cock stirred to life against her hip. "Yes. Just like that."

"Come for me," he said again, twisting his wrist and rotating his finger inside her. Thrashing against his leg, she came hard.

When he pulled his hand away, she quivered but she wasn't done. She needed more.

Chapter Twelve

Blaze wanted her again but waited to follow Alex's lead. Thankfully, he didn't have to wait long.

Vibrations of pleasure were still pulsing through her when she shimmied across his body and reached for another condom. Keeping her preferences in mind, he caught one of her breasts in his mouth, rolling her nipple around with the tip of his tongue while she struggled to open the package.

The sounds coming out of her mouth drove him crazy. It was impossible to determine which he liked better, the moans, whimpers, or screams. Just thinking about it made his cock jump. When he pulled away to breathe, she focused her attention on him, straddled his legs, and put the condom on his dick.

He held her hips as she aligned their bodies and then she eased down onto him, taking him in with one fluid movement, surrounding him with her wet heat. It was almost enough to finish him, but he couldn't let go. Not yet.

"Am I hurting you?" she asked, leaning forward and hovering over his face.

"You're killing me," he answered before he kissed her, shifted her forward, and began fucking her hard and fast.

"Yes," she hissed. "Right there. Yes, Blaze." She bit his shoulder as her body shook with another orgasm.

When she coasted down, she kissed the red mark she left on him. "Sorry."

"Don't apologize," he chided. "Also, call me Brian," he whispered his name and kissed her ear.

"Brian?"

"My first agent talked me into changing my name years ago."

"Brian. I like it." A smile turned up the corners of her mouth.

He swiveled his hips and turned her smile into something much more beautiful.

With her hands on his chest, she propped herself up and closed her eyes. "I like that, too."

Without interrupting his gyrations, he cupped her breasts and ran his thumbs across her nipples, making them impossibly hard. She seemed to like everything he did.

Holding on for dear life, she dug her nails into his chest and then threw her head back, letting pleasure wash over her. A low keening sound spilled out of her mouth as every muscle in her body clenched and spasmed. Never before had he been with anyone so free. Like a force of nature, all he had to do was hold on.

When she fell forward and kissed him, she rubbed her nipples against his chest. "I could get used to those."

"Me, too."

"But you haven't had another orgasm." She frowned and sucked on his bottom lip.

"I meant yours. Listening to you come, and feeling your pussy clench around me." The thought made his hips jerk.

"It's your fault, Brian," she said.

"Say it again," he murmured. Nothing had ever sounded as good as her voice saying his name.

"Brian," she repeated, tilting her hips down to meet his thrusts. "Yes. Please. Come with me," she begged.

How could he resist? With one final thrust, he growled and came hard. They held each other until their breathing evened out. "I need to clean up." When he shifted her body to pull out, she whimpered and rolled onto her stomach

In the bathroom, he glanced at the mirror and smiled. Between the bite and nail marks, Alex had definitely claimed him. He liked it.

From the doorway, he watched her back rise and fall with each breath. If experience had taught him anything it was wham bam thank you, ma'am, and don't let the door hit you on the way out. She got what she wanted. Didn't that mean it was time to leave? But nothing about Alex was like his previous experiences, so he would have to rely on her lead to know what to do next.

Kneeling on the side of the bed and stroking the curve of her hip, he said, "I should go." He didn't want to, but he couldn't tell her that.

"No, don't go yet," she said, her voice sleepy and warm around the edges. "Lie down, just for a little longer." A pathetic whining noise came from the hall. "But first, will you let Koko in?"

With his hand on the doorknob, he lingered. Did she really want him to stay? Not that he could stay long, anyway. All hell would break loose if Nate found out he had taken the car. The whole thing had been a huge risk, but it was worth it, even if for one night.

Koko bounded into the bed and snuggled to the side of Alex.

"Come back to bed. Please?" she begged, patting the open spot next to her.

"Just for a bit." With an alarm set for five in the morning, he stretched out next to her. That would give him enough time to get back to Dembi before Nate would wake up and notice he was missing, assuming Nate had been busy that night, too. If not, he would already be in trouble and there was no sense in leaving until he absolutely had to.

"Mm," she hummed and wrapped her body around his.

Whether it was the rhythmic thump of her heart or her delicious warmth, sleep claimed him quickly. The next time consciousness invaded his mind, his phone chimed from the nightstand. Every inch of his body protested as he pulled away from Alex and tugged his pants on. Leaving her room was the hardest part. In the dim moonlight that spilled in through the window at the head of the bed, Koko's bright eyes glowed.

"Shh. Don't wake her," he whispered as he closed the door behind him and made his way to the front door. Before he stepped outside, he paused. What would it look like if he just disappeared? It wouldn't look good. That's for sure. So, he rummaged through a drawer in the front room and scrawled a note for Alex to find.

As he made his way up the narrow street toward the parking lot, he had to force himself to keep moving. Torn between Alex's warm bed and keeping their night together a secret, he finally listened to his brain and got in the car.

By the time he got back to Dembi, he was wide awake. His thoughts cycled through the same questions. What would happen next? Would she want to see him again? The answers to his questions would have to wait, but he knew the perfect way to distract his mind. He parked the car in the exact spot he'd taken it from, tightened the laces on his shoes, and started up his trail.

****

"Knock knock," Maggie called out from the front room. "Alex? Your door was unlocked. Are you up?"

"Oh shit," Alex said to Brian, clutching the blanket to her chest, but her heart sank as she realized she was alone. "Hang on, Maggie. I'll be right out," she hollered. She smoothed her hair and pulled a robe over her shoulders as she propelled herself out of bed. Koko whined at the closed door.

"What's up?"

Maggie's eyes swiveled from the tiny piece of paper in her hands.

"What? What is it?" Alex frowned.

"I'm sorry, I didn't mean to…"

Was it bad news? Still half-asleep, worry gnawed at her. *Alex,* she read. *I'm sorry to leave you. I need to keep up appearances. I hope you understand. B.* Emotions welled inside her. Without hearing his inflection, it was hard for her to comprehend what he meant. What did keeping up appearances mean? Was he ashamed of her or was he honoring her wishes to keep their whatever it was a secret?

"He stayed last night, didn't he?" Maggie asked. "Also, I woke you up, didn't I? I'm sorry. I should've called or something."

Alex smoothed her hair again. "It's okay. I don't

usually sleep this late."

"Busy night," Maggie said with a grin.

Alex pressed her lips together but it was no use. Heat spread across her cheeks. Alex wanted to die. "You can't say anything. Promise?"

"Duh. Of *course* I promise. Now spill."

****

When Alex arrived on the set at eight o'clock, everyone was bustling around. The daily meeting with Steve was just ending when Brian sauntered over to them already in costume. Steve mentioned wrapping up filming on Sunday, but she couldn't think about Sunday. Brian was the perfect diversion.

"Nice of you to show up," he said, cocking one eyebrow. Blaze took over in all his glory.

She brushed away his insult and snapped back, "I'm right on time." For the past week, she had been exchanging barbs with Blaze. It was more important than ever to be consistent so no one would be suspicious.

"Some of us have been here for a while," he said.

"Overachiever," she mumbled, making Steve laugh.

Later, during a lull in filming, Blaze jumped around the cluster of boulders she had been leaning against and dragged her to the side hidden from the rest of the world. "Sorry I had to leave this morning. I didn't want to wake you."

"What did you mean by keeping up appearances?" The only way to find out was to ask.

"You said you didn't want to draw attention to us, right?"

Alex nodded.

"If I wasn't there in the morning, Nate would've noticed. Then there would have been questions."

"I understand." She let out a breath she hadn't realized she was holding.

"Sorry about being a jerk in front of Steve," he added.

"I forgive you," she replied, giving him the kiss she'd been waiting hours to give him. "Everyone expects you to be a dick, so you might as well give them what they want, right?"

He shook his head. "Sorry. I wasn't listening. Did you just say something about wanting my dick?"

She laughed a little too loud and covered her mouth. "No, I was saying you *are* a dick. Me *wanting* your dick is beside the point."

With another shake of his head, he said, "That's where you're wrong."

"Do you have to be right all the time?" she asked, kissing him again. That time, she ran her hand down the front of his pants and rubbed against his growing erection. Noises on the set pulled her back to reality, so she withdrew her hand. "Someone is going to see us. You need to get back out there. I'll wait a minute and then get back into position."

"You are a cruel woman," he said and then opened the front of his vest, showing her the faint bruise from where she'd bitten him. "Here's proof." Next, he pointed out the tiny crescents still visible on his pecs.

She chewed on her lip. "Sorry. I didn't mean to leave marks."

"I don't mind them one bit. I'm teasing. It definitely makes it harder to be secretive, though," he added. "I told Javier in wardrobe I bumped into a tree during my morning run."

Heat spread across her cheeks. "What are you doing tonight?"

"You," he replied with a sparkling smile.

"Simmer down, cowboy. No one likes people who presume things."

"I'm not presumptuous, I'm hopeful." He winked and strolled away.

When the sounds of raucous laughter from the stunt team reached her, she knew Blaze had made his way back and it was safe to return to her post. Always the center of attention, Blaze was easy to find. Brian, on the other hand, could blend in with everyone.

To avoid another moment of temptation, Alex went home for lunch, and while she ate, she called Maggie.

"What did he say?" Maggie asked.

"Hello to you, too," Alex laughed.

"Well?" she demanded.

"He didn't want to draw attention to us. We're good. You haven't said anything, have you?"

"Um… Can Jim know?" Her voice went up an octave.

"You already told him, didn't you?"

"Of course I told him," Maggie said. "Are you kidding me? After the note this morning. I had to ask his opinion."

"No one else can know, and he can't tell anyone. How would it look? Like I'm using Blaze to get a good recommendation. It's already bad enough you know since you're my boss."

"I'm not your boss right now. I'm on maternity leave. Besides, what you do in your personal life is just that: personal."

Alex sighed with relief. Maggie was the only person she trusted, but she definitely needed to change the subject. "How's Henry? Are you sleeping well?"

"Meh. I wouldn't say well. But it's all good. Jim's going back to work tomorrow. Just for half the day. They need him to adjust the hops mixture or something."

"With great brewmastery skills, comes great responsibility," Alex joked.

"Definitely." Maggie talked for the next few minutes about nursing at night and diaper changes gone wrong before Alex had to cut her off.

"Sorry, but I need to head back to the set."

"Come over later? I'd love to finish catching up."

"I might be busy," Alex said, trying to keep the excitement out of her voice and failing miserably.

"I get it. I can wait. Don't worry about me."

Alex laughed. "Thanks for being so understanding."

They said their goodbyes and then Alex made her way back to the throng of people still lingering around the food service truck, including Blaze who stood flirting with a handful of beautiful women.

She struggled to hold onto her happiness as she watched him compliment and charm other women, but she cheered up when he slipped her a napkin before he made his way back to the set. When she was alone, she peeked at it to see what was written on it.

Meet me in the parking lot at 7:15. B

The next four hours passed slower than she'd ever thought possible, and checking the time on her phone every few minutes only seemed to make it worse. When filming for the day finally ended, she made sure everything was taken care of in the park, went home and changed, and then got into the bland rental car in the parking lot as discreetly as possible.

"You're right on time," Brian said, pointing to the clock on the dashboard.

"Where are we going?"

"I was hoping you might know somewhere quiet we could go."

"I know just the place," she said with a smile before pointing toward the entrance booth and directing him to a small dirt road five miles away. The ruts in the road deepened, forcing him to slow down. When they arrive at an empty parking lot he turned the car off.

"Is this the place?" he asked.

She shook her head. "No. Now we hike."

"But you're wearing a skirt. Maybe we should just stay in the car." It didn't take a genius to figure out what he wanted.

"This skirt is longer than my shorts, plus I'm wearing hiking shoes. One can never be too prepared in the desert. Come on. I want to show you something before the sun goes down." The only way he would get out is if she did first, so that's what she did.

They followed the riverbed for a little over a mile before it cut toward a sheer cliff where the wind and water had already begun to etch away the stone at the bottom, forming a proto arch. During storms, water flowed over the edge of the cliff, bringing the river to life. It had been days since the last rain, which meant the sand was still hard and cool, but no water remained on the surface.

"How do we go up?"

"We don't," she said. "Look." Behind the branches

of a big sage, she uncovered a blackened layer of rock adorned with ancient designs. "Petroglyphs."

"Is that a goat?" He tilted his head from side to side.

"I think so, but I'm not an expert or anything. This one looks like the sun to me," she said, pointing to a perfect spiral carved into the stone. "Not a lot of people know about this place. There are more over here."

Another cluster of rock art was hidden near a crevice in the cliff, which they spent a few minutes admiring before she pulled him into her arms as she backed against an undecorated portion of the rock face.

"It's beautiful."

"And isolated," she added, guiding his hand up her skirt.

He gasped when his fingers brushed against her sex. "No panties? Now who's being presumptuous?"

"Me," she said before kissing him.

The lines around her eyes became visible when she laughed.

He picked up her hand and pressed their palms together as he laced his fingers through hers. "I like you because you don't have any preconceived ideas about who I'm supposed to be, so I can be myself." That was only one of his favorite things about her. "Plus, you're really smart and dynamite in the sack." Getting to be himself was a bonus.

"Or against a rock," she added, laughing again.

"Either way."

The shadows from the cliff stretched farther and farther with each passing minute.

"I didn't bring a flashlight. We should go before we get stuck here in the dark."

"It wouldn't be so bad, would it?" he asked, sucking one of her fingers into his mouth.

"I don't know. How comfortable are you with scorpions?"

That did it. He moved so fast she had to run to catch up.

"Damn, you're twitchy," she teased.

"Shut it," he retorted.

When she caught up to him, she was still snickering. "Do you want to come over for dinner? I have no idea what you like, but I have eggs."

The invitation made him smile because it meant she wanted him around, with or without sex. "I guess I could stay a little longer, but I really do need to go back tonight." It was tempting to tell her about Nate and the car but didn't want her to have to worry about that, too.

"I know."

Knowing he would have to leave made every

second together matter. "What do you want for dinner?" he asked after a few minutes into their drive toward the park.

"Scrambled eggs are pretty much the only thing I can cook. Sorry."

He laughed. "No one's perfect."

When they got back to her house, he looked around her kitchen, opened every cupboard, snooped in her fridge, and went through her drawers. College students had better stocked kitchens than hers, which made him want to laugh. "Why don't you let me cook?" he asked.

"You cook?"

"Yes, ma'am."

With an eyebrow raised in disbelief, she pulled the apron off the side of the fridge and put it over his head, tying it behind his back. "Be my guest, world's greatest cook."

"I'm not so sure I can live up to that. Let me know after dinner, okay?"

****

Koko rested her head in Alex's lap while Brian danced around the kitchen. While he cooked, she set the table and opened two beers. Within a half hour, he pulled a pan out of the oven and announced dinner was ready. It had been years since anyone had cooked for her.

"I'm impressed," she said. "What is this? An omelet?"

"Frittata. Similar though."

When she took her first bite, she sighed. "I'm *really* impressed. Just one more thing to add to the list."

"List of what?" he inquired, offering a chunk of eggs and cheese to Koko.

"All the stuff you're good at—you're a good cook, you love dogs, you're handsome, funny, easy to talk to, and very generous with orgasms."

He smiled around the bite of food he was chewing.

"Where did you learn to cook?"

"My mom. She didn't want to send me off to college without knowing the basics."

Alex snorted. "The only thing my mom worried about was getting me out of the house. We fought like mad. Still do. We've never been close," she confided. "I miss my dad, though."

"But you're not going home to see them this weekend?"

"No. It's been a few years, but I don't want to. My mom keeps pressuring me to be there for every holiday: Easter, Thanksgiving, Christmas, birthdays, you name it. She has no idea how hard it is for me. My brothers are both moochers and my mom can't see it. She always has an excuse for why they don't have jobs, but she never recognizes the work I do. I'm busting my ass to make something of myself and she thinks I'm camping." The muscles in her shoulders tensed.

"I wish she could see how amazing you are," he said, caressing her arm.

It became difficult to swallow as emotion overcame her. "Why are you so nice to me?"

"Because you deserve it."

****

"Well? Did I live up to your expectations?" Brian asked as he cleaned up the kitchen.

"Yes. And then some. Now stop cleaning," Alex said as she tried to take the sponge out of his hand.

He stopped her. "Please let me. Nate is always

cleaning up after me."

"What's up with him? Are you friends?"

"No. My agent hired him."

"So that's his job? To clean up after you?"

Brian looked away. How could he admit the truth to her? What would she think? "You could say that."

"I don't think I would mind. I've always hated cleaning. My mother thinks a woman's job is in the home. Cooking, cleaning, making crafts. I guess I fail as a woman. My brothers never had to lift a finger because they lack the proper parts. She tried to force me into that role from the time I was little. I rebelled."

"Naturally."

"I studied science." She covered her mouth and gasped in mock horror. "Learned how to tie knots, fix cars, you know, guy stuff. Anything that would drive her nuts."

"And your dad?"

"He filled the man of the house role, whether he wanted to or not. I feel sorry for him. I know what it's like to want one thing and be expected to do another. Secretly, I think he's proud of me."

"For following your dreams?" he asked as he rinsed the last fork and put it in the dish drainer before turning to face her.

With her hands clenched into fists, she said, "No. For defying her."

He touched the side of her face. "You're brave."

"A lot of good it's done me. You heard her the other day. She's awful. If I turn my phone off, she starts calling the office. Last year when my phone died, Maggie got the pleasure of handling her calls. She's a good friend." Alex leaned against his chest and sighed.

"Enough about my mother. Tell me something about you."

"If only I had your strength." If he had her strength, it would be so easy to stand up to Nate and everyone else who treated him like a child. "I know what it's like, except the whole world expects me to be this person I'm not. Wouldn't it be amazing? To be able to tell them to go fuck themselves so I could live happily ever after."

"You probably wouldn't have much of a career after," she said with a laugh.

"True, but it might be worth it." The clock on the wall reminded him how late it was and he knew he would have to go soon before he got too tired.

"Can you stay a little longer?" She looked up at him with those pleading chocolaty eyes and he couldn't resist.

"It's not like anyone's expecting me, I just don't want to raise suspicions. Plus, I'm tired."

"Sit with me?" Guiding him into the front room, she led him to the couch. "You look tense. Let me rub your shoulders."

"I didn't get enough sleep."

"I can't imagine why, what with waking up in the middle of the night, driving an hour, then turning around and working all day." She patted the spot next to her. "Come on."

"Okay, but only for a minute."

"Take your shirt off," she demanded.

"Why?" Not the he cared, it just seemed like an odd request.

"I want to see you half naked again. Just kidding, it helps if I can see your muscle groups."

Who was he to argue with that kind of logic?

After wiggling her body behind him, she rubbed her hands together and got to work. "Damn, you're really tight." She worked her fingertips into his aching muscles and swept one knot after another down and away from his neck. "You need a proper massage." A shiver went through his body.

Words wouldn't form in his mushy brain. Everything she did hurt and felt good all at the same time. "How are you so good at this?" he finally managed to say.

"I studied human anatomy. The key is to know the direction of the muscles. Like this one." With her hands on either side of his spine below his shoulder blades, she pushed out. "It runs along your ribs. But there are muscles deeper that run the length of your spine." To demonstrate, she walked her fingers down his back. "You're the perfect model. I can see everything. This one is still really bad though." Perched on the back of the couch, she put all of her weight on a knot in his shoulder.

He groaned.

"Am I hurting you?" The massage stopped and then she craned her head over his shoulder to look at his face.

"No. Yes. It hurts so good. Please don't stop." No one had ever given him a deep tissue massage before and it was worth every bit of pain. Eventually, his eyes got heavier and heavier until he couldn't keep them open anymore.

"Hey, Brian?" Alex said, kissing down his neck. "Wake up."

He inhaled and straightened his back. "Sorry, I

didn't mean to fall asleep."

"It's okay. It means you enjoyed it, right?"

"You're amazing. I feel great." The tight muscle at the base of his neck didn't hurt, even when he stretched from side to side.

"Glad I could help. Are you too tired to drive back?"

Was she inviting him to stay? What would Nate say? It wouldn't be pretty if he found out. "I'll be fine. I should go before it gets any later. Thank you for another amazing night."

"Thank you," she echoed and held onto him tightly in the doorway, which only made leaving harder.

"See you in the morning," he said before kissing her one last time and ducking out into the cool night. Inside the rental car, he thought about how happy it made him feel that she didn't want him to leave. He smiled and put the key in the ignition.

When he got back to the hotel he couldn't park the car in the same spot. Someone else had taken it. "Great," he grumbled. Nate would definitely notice.

****

Brian's heart raced as he struggled to pull himself out of a dream. No. Not a dream. A nightmare. Nate was telling him he was a fake. That if people knew what he really was, he'd be nothing. No one. The sheets clung to his clammy skin, suffocating him.

A shower helped rinse off the residue of fear, but as he got dressed for a run he realized it wasn't fear. It was anger at feeling like he had to sneak around and lie to Nate about the car. Nate would notice no matter what he did, so he decided to plan for his night with Alex and go to the grocery store in town.

Instead of shopping for one, like he would do at home, he bought enough for two. As he walked past the toy aisle, something caught his eye. A little stuffed raven sat in a basket with other birds, waiting to go home with a bird enthusiast. He knew one of those. It made a little mechanical croak when he squeezed its chest. Next, he picked out a toy for Koko since she would need something to go with her pumpkin treats.

With his hat covering part of his face, he paid for his groceries and drove back up to the hotel just in time to watch the cast and crew get on the vans for the day. Nate had his back to them and was scanning the hills above the hotel.

"Looking for me?" Brian asked from the driver's seat through the cracked window.

Nate frowned and turned to face him. "What the fuck are you doing in there?"

"I'm taking it from now on. I can't stand the bumpy, crowded rides every day."

"Who do you think you are?" Nate lunged for the door handle, but Brian had thought ahead and locked all of them.

"I'm Blaze Fucking Johnson, and you work for me in case you forgot. I've been using it for days. It would be a shame if Alan found out you suck at your job."

"How did you get the keys?" Nate asked.

"It's not my fault if you leave your room open because you're in such a rush to get laid," Brian lied. "I wanted to see if you changed your mind about dinner the other night. How much is Alan paying you?"

"I didn't... That's not..."

"You better get to your ride, unless you'd rather stay here all day?" He nodded toward the last van. "I won't mind."

"Fuck you," Nate spat.

"No thanks. They're leaving," he said.

Nate growled and sprinted for the van. Brian followed behind them, lagging so he wouldn't have to see Nate's face through the back window. When Alan hired Nate to watch over him, Brian didn't have any say in the process. Nate had power, but so did Brian. He knew how much Nate liked his job; he just had to play it right. If he didn't, Nate could ruin everything.

When he drove through the entrance gate he nodded at the ranger on duty and parked next to the vans in the overflow parking lot. The second he stepped out, Nate got in his face again, ruining any chance Brian had of looking for Alex.

"Give me the keys," Nate demanded.

"No. I'm keeping them. In exchange, I won't tell Alan about how lazy you are." With the keys wedged deep in his front pocket, he kept his hand there to block Nate just in case he tried to get them. "I get a little freedom, you get to keep your job." He straightened his back and walked away from Nate; satisfied for once he had said exactly what he wanted.

Chapter Fourteen

Tuesday morning brought a new day and a new reason for Alex to get up: to see Brian. She was beginning to believe all the kind things he said about her and her job, so she no longer put much energy into worrying about screwing up. As long as no one found out about them, she could handle everything else. Living in the moment gave her a little freedom from the familiar confines of her anxiety. Arriving at the set a full thirty minutes early, she nodded to the cast and crew as she anxiously waited for him.

The last van pulled into the overflow parking lot, followed by Brian's little rental car. Alex got as close as she could, partially hidden behind the food service truck and tried to signal him, but he wasn't looking for her.

Nate was yelling at him and following close on his heels, but Brian was too fast.

"I wasn't done talking to you," Nate shouted.

"I was," Brian grumbled.

"Just tell me why you need the car. Where are you going?"

"None of your business." Brian stepped away from him.

"But it *is* my business. That's why I'm here. To make sure you don't screw up again." Nate and Brian walked side by side, their feet visible on the other side of the truck.

Alex frowned. Were they talking about her? Her heart raced.

Brian turned to face him. "I'm not doing anything wrong."

"That car is in my name. If you get caught with—"

Brian slammed his hand into the truck. "I'm not doing anything, okay?"

The next time Nate spoke, his words came out carefully measured, the way a parent would speak to their child, "I'm just trying to keep your reputation safe."

"I need it so I can have a private place to fuck, okay?" Brian replied.

"Why didn't you say so?" Nate ground out. "Who is it?"

"Who do you think?"

"Jennifer?"

"Bingo."

At some point during their conversation, Brian became Blaze. Maybe it had been Blaze all along. The lie came out of his mouth so easily. Perhaps it wasn't a lie. What if he had something going on with the actress, too? Could she blame him? It was okay to get caught with Jennifer, but not her. That much was clear. Alex turned and disappeared into the crowd before they came around the corner.

Why did she ever think she could compete with women like Jennifer? Even for a week. It was a stupid idea. She spent the rest of the day hiding from Brian, trying to save them both from the trouble that would come if anyone found out about them.

Filming ended early that day as another storm

moved in. The crew didn't want to take any chances like last time. One by one, the vans hauled everyone away, leaving Alex enough time to do her regular job. The air hung heavily as the barometric pressure dropped. Distant lightning marbled the sky as storm clouds gathered, blotting out the sun.

Instead of heading to her office, Alex stayed outside. Alone for the first time that day, she could finally process what she had heard. Wind whipped around her, buffeting her with sand, leaving tiny pinpricks across her exposed skin. Once the toppled cairns were taken care of, she moved to a spot a few feet away and hunkered down, setting to work removing a plastic bag tangled in a big sage.

"There you are," Brian called out as his shoes slapped against the rock. "I've been looking for you all…day." He faltered at the end when she looked up at him. "What's wrong?"

"Nothing," she spat. "Everything is just fine."

"You're upset," he stated as he reached out to touch her cheek, but she pulled away.

"It's not going to work out, okay? Please leave me alone so I can get my job done."

The rain started to fall, pattering lightly around them.

"I don't understand." He frowned.

"You better go before the wash floods," she warned.

"I don't want to go," he protested.

Why did he have to make it so hard? Was he trying to humiliate her? "I'm sorry, Brian. I have to go. Your reputation is at stake." With that, she ran off, following the twists and turns of the trail, cutting through the neighborhood to go back to the Visitor Center.

With her back pressed against the building, she watched Brian duck into his car and drive away. It took several minutes before she was composed enough to go inside.

The rain still fell hard when she hurried across the parking lot and down the little road toward her house. When she pulled her keys out of her pocket she noticed an insulated bag tucked against her front door. Groceries poked out the top. She picked it up, unlocked her door, and stepped inside. Koko wiggled between her legs, sniffed the bag, and then smiled at her.

"It's from him, isn't it?" Alex asked. Two poppy seed muffins were propped right on top. Waiting for them. "He was probably going to make me dinner again."

****

Brian gripped the steering wheel and pulled off the side of the road toward the trail they had visited the previous night. He didn't want to leave the park. Nothing waited for him in town except an empty, cold bed. What happened? Nate yelled at him and then watched him like a hawk. His lie about being with Jennifer had been easy since she was always a little too friendly. Staying away from Alex had been harder, but he didn't want to draw Nate's attention to her. When he finally had a chance to talk to her alone, it had ended in disaster.

The rain fell hard, pelting the top of the car. Replaying their conversation didn't help. It was one of those days. The kind where everything goes wrong. Maybe she just needed time to cool down. Waiting wouldn't be easy, but he would do whatever he had to.

He reclined the seat and stretched out. The constant drum of rain lulled him to sleep, but he didn't rest easy as another nightmare began. That time Alex told him she was done with him and that his reputation was too important.

When he bolted upright, he hit his head on the roof. "She must've overheard my conversation with Nate." Oh no. That meant he would have to explain everything to her, which would forever change her opinion of him.

****

Sleep didn't come easily that night. Alex tossed and turned as her head filled with nightmares. She jerked awake at midnight, her heart racing. The storm raged against the windows, more wind than rain. Resigned to her sleepless fate, she got out of bed.

Wrapped in a robe, she padded through the kitchen and made a cup of tea and then scrambled eggs for her and Koko. Just as she sat down to eat, she saw someone walk past her front window. Probably Maggie, trying to soothe Henry.

Nope.

When she pulled the door open, she gasped. Brian paced back and forth, his hoodie soaked with rain and his teeth chattering. Why was he there?

"Can I come in?"

"No."

"Please?" he begged. "I have to talk to you." Water dripped off of him.

Why did he have to look so pathetic? "Um," she said, trying to think of a good reason not to let him in, but nothing came to mind. "I guess, but only for a minute."

When he stepped inside, he shivered as he pulled

his hoodie off. Out of habit, he hung it from the doorknob. Just like she always did with her hat.

"What are you doing here? I told you. It's not going to work," she said, turning her back on him.

"I've been out there for a while, trying to figure out what to say to you." A sigh escaped his lips. "You heard my argument with Nate, didn't you?"

What was worse? Overhearing their conversation or admitting she'd overheard their conversation?

"Let me explain." He came up behind her and put his hands on her shoulders. "I racked my brain trying to figure out what happened. And that's when it hit me. You must've heard what Nate said. Please don't judge me."

"Judge you?" she turned to face him, her eyebrows furrowed. "I don't care what Nate said. I care what you said."

"What?"

"The reason you needed the car. A private place to…" It hurt too much to repeat him.

"No. I had to lie to him so he wouldn't think I was using the car for something else."

"For what?"

"I swear I haven't used in almost a year." He paused and his eyes dipped into his skull looking for the answer. "Actually… Nine months."

Without a clue as to what he was talking about, she frowned. "Used what?"

"Cocaine."

"Oh." Her mind reeled, and he wouldn't look at her.

"My agent hired Nate to keep tabs on me. He doesn't even let me use my phone when I'm working.

To make sure I don't get into trouble. And by that, I mean relapse." He glanced at her briefly. "I'll understand if you don't want me, but I had to explain. You have to believe me. I'm done with that part of my life."

"What about Jennifer?" she asked.

"There's no one else. Besides, you know how I feel about her."

"I thought he was trying to protect you from me," she whispered.

"What?"

"He said he was trying to protect your reputation. He said he didn't want to catch you…" she stammered.

"With drugs. I can't blame him for being suspicious."

"That's why he wanted to know where you were going in the car."

"It's in his name. I just didn't want him to know about us because you're so uncomfortable about…" He motioned between their bodies. "Not that I'm trying to blame you for the argument."

"I had no idea," she said.

He scoffed. "You're the only one."

"I'm sorry I assumed the worst. Are you hungry? You brought groceries," she said, pointing to the bag on the counter she still hadn't unloaded. "I also made some scrambled eggs." When she poked them with her finger she grimaced and emptied her plate into Koko's dish. "Really cold, gross scrambled eggs."

"No," he said. "Are you angry with me? I know I should've told you. It was just so nice to be with someone who didn't know…who didn't judge me."

"I'm not judging you." She shrugged. "People

make mistakes." After locking the front door, she took his hand. "You're freezing."

"I told you, I was out there for a while. I didn't want to wake you, but I couldn't leave without explaining myself first."

"Come on," she said, leading him into her bathroom. "You need to warm up." A nice warm shower was just what he needed, but first she had to undress him. And he let her, lifting his arms and stepping out of his clothes before she turned the water on and pushed him in.

After undressing herself, she stepped in behind him and put her arms around him, which startled him. "I didn't mean to scare you."

"Just surprised," he said as he turned to face her and pulled her into his arms. The warm water flowed between their bodies. "I feel better already."

So did she. With the misunderstanding behind them, she rested her head against his chest and listened to the soothingly rhythmic beating of his heart. Exhaustion was beginning to set in and she couldn't keep her eyes open. "I'm tired."

"Me, too," he said. "Thanks for talking to me and warming me up." He dried them both off and then carried her to bed before going back to the bathroom to collect his clothes. "I'll lock the door behind me."

"Don't go," she pleaded.

By the smile on his face, she figured that was just what he wanted to hear. Without pausing, he dropped his clothes on the floor and slid into bed next to her. They snuggled and fell asleep.

Hours later, her bladder woke her. The first rays of muted sun crept over the horizon as she used the bathroom. Before tiptoeing back to bed, she brushed her teeth. Brian murmured and reached for her, pulling her firmly against his body. Within a few minutes, the sheet tented over his dick. Alex couldn't subdue a giggle, rousing him from his lingering sleep.

"Morning," he said, pointing his face away from hers to yawn.

"Hi."

"What's so funny?" he asked, stretching.

"This," she said, pointing on top of the sheet and clicking her tongue. "Too bad we can't put it to good use."

"Did you throw away the ones I bought?"

"We used them all," she said.

"No, the ones I brought last night."

"Are you telling me there are condoms in the grocery bag in the kitchen?"

He nodded and smiled.

"I'll be right back." She jumped out of bed and then paused at the threshold into the hall. Koko looked up at her, expectantly. Even with the door locked, someone could see through her window, and in order to get to the kitchen, she would have to take a chance. So, she listened hard, took a deep breath, went for it, and skidded to a stop at the counter. As she sorted through the contents of the bag, water ran in the bathroom. The pile of groceries grew as she uncovering bags of veggies, a loaf of French bread, a plush raven, and a thirty-six-pack of condoms. Better than a three-pack. So much better.

She filled Koko's bowl with breakfast, topped it off with a pumpkin treat courtesy of Brian, and then repeated her sneaky moves back to her bedroom, slamming into the wall at the end of the hall and dropping the box.

Brian laughed from her bed, where he had just gotten settled again.

Leaning against her closed bedroom door, she smiled. "Someone is *really* hopeful." The giant box of condoms spilled its contents when she ripped it open.

"One can never be too prepared in the desert," he said, returning the smile. "I borrowed some toothpaste. I hope that's okay."

"I have a spare brush," she offered.

"I guess it would do a slightly better job than my finger. Maybe I'll take you up on that later."

Holding a condom between her teeth, she crawled onto the bed next to him and pulled the sheet down. She placed the thin package on his stomach and turned her attention to his hard-on.

He tucked his hands under his head, making his biceps flex. When she sucked him into her mouth, his eyes closed and he inhaled sharply.

"Are you okay?" she teased.

"Mm," he groaned.

"I'll take that as a yes," she replied before circling the head of his cock with her tongue. She licked his length and then pursed her lips and pulled him into her mouth, gently scraping him with her teeth.

"Fuck," he said with a clenched jaw.

Back and forth, up and down, she swirled her tongue until pleasure coiled and built inside his body. Cupping his balls and sucking him hard and fast, she milked an orgasm out of him which made his muscles twitch for a full minute.

She slithered up his body and snuggled against his

warm neck.

"That was…" Instead of finishing his sentence, he kissed her.

"Okay?" she offered with a small smile.

"Fuck *okay*. Fucking amazing."

Her cell phone rang from the side table, so she stretched across Brian and reached for it. A familiar number displayed on the screen.

"Good morning, Steve," she answered with a smile on her lips.

"Hi, Alex. We're going to delay filming for a bit. I know that will put us behind a little, but…"

Brian sucked one of her nipples into his mouth, making her focus crumble. She moaned and then covered the sound with a cough. "Sorry about that," she said, pressing her lips together to keep future sounds from escaping.

"…they don't want to risk…" Steve's words faded again.

"Mm-hmm."

"The storm is supposed to move out by late morning, so we'll be there around ten," he finished.

"That sounds goo-od." The words fragmented when he rolled his tongue across her sensitive skin. "See you later." She didn't wait for Steve to respond before hanging up.

"Damn it. That was Steve," she scolded but didn't bother moving.

"I know who it was, I could hear everything he said," he answered, moving his mouth to her other breast.

"I'm so ma-ad at you," she said, but even she could hear how half-hearted her words were.

"Mm," he hummed against her skin, scraping her nipple with his teeth.

She twisted and reached for his dick, which, to her delight, came to life again. Now she had to choose between having sex and whatever wonderful thing he was doing with his tongue. Before she had a chance to decide, he gripped her body and positioned her on top of his sheathed cock. She pouted.

Rubbing his thumb across her bottom lip, he asked, "Why so sad?"

"I was enjoying myself," she said, looking down at her ruddy breasts.

"I think I know a way to cheer you up," he said, lifting his hips, simultaneously pushing inside her and shifting Alex toward the head of the bed. Surprised by the sudden movement, she gasped and braced herself against the pillow. Without missing a beat, he opened his mouth just as her breast swung in front of his face and he proceeded to suck and fuck her until she careened into oblivion. Only after her slow descent back to earth did she realize she'd been holding her breath the whole time. The room began to spin.

He stopped moving and cradled the sides of her face. "Are you okay?"

Resting her forehead against his, she said, "Forgot to breathe."

"You scared me. I've never heard you have a silent orgasm. I thought I broke you," he said and then kissed her.

"Only a little."

Chapter Fifteen

An hour later, they still hadn't moved out of bed. Alex glanced at the clock and knew she should be getting ready for work but had a better idea. If the crew wouldn't be there for another two hours, there was no need for her to hurry. Telling everyone else about the delay hadn't crossed her mind yet, so she called the gift shop. "Hey, Lynn. The crew won't get here until ten today and I have a bunch of stuff to take care of at home, so I won't be in until then, okay?"

Lynn responded with, "You're the boss. See you later."

In the past, she had cringed at being called boss, but now it seemed to fit. Everything was working out just right and she was calling the shots.

"What are you thinking?" he asked, dragging his fingers across her back, half tickling, half caressing.

"How great it is we still have two hours together."

"Thanks for inviting me to stay, your bed is so much better than the one at the hotel."

"Are you using me for my bed?" she asked, propping herself up on one elbow so she could scowl at him.

"I guess you would've found out sooner or later," he said, trying to keep a straight face. "Come on, I'll make you breakfast," he wiggled away from her, pulled his pants on, and had his hand on the doorknob before she managed to sit up. Koko came bounding in as Brian strolled down the hall.

Koko licked Alex's face. "He's going to make breakfast. I'll share," she said rubbing Koko's silky ears before pulling her robe on and following the clanging sounds in the kitchen.

"You have the shittiest pans," he said pointing to the stove where her beat up frying pan sat unevenly on the burner.

"I don't cook. Why would I invest in good pans?"

"Maybe if you had good pans you'd be more inclined to cook."

"Whatever. I've had that since I lived in the dorms at college. You're lucky I still have it."

"You should see my kitchen. It's pretty awesome. The last time I went to Spain, I bought a paella pan that is truly a work of art. It produces the most delicious *socarrat.*" He paused and looked at her. "That sounded really pretentious, didn't it?"

Subduing a giggle, she mimicked his deep voice, "The last time I was in Spain, I did things common people wouldn't dream of doing."

"Is that what I sound like?"

"I'm Blaze Johnson and I have fancy stuff." She put her arms around his waist and laughed. "Please go on, tell me more about your *amazing* pots and pans."

"You can't make me," he said, putting his hands on his hips and smothering another smile.

"I bet your paella is the best ever. Am I right?"

"It's pretty good," he said, kissing her and interrupting her teasing. "You'd have to taste it and let me know."

"I don't have a paella pan," she stated.

"No, but I do."

"So, I should just pop over to your house for dinner one night?"

"Yeah, if you ever find yourself in Beverly Hills my kitchen is always open to you," he said.

Just like that. As if it were that easy. As if he meant it. Did he really just invite her over? Instead of asking what she really wanted to know, she said, "What are you making?"

"French toast."

"I may not share with you. Sorry, I'm a liar," she said to Koko, who stood near their feet, wagging her tail.

He laughed and went back to work slicing bread and whisking eggs. While he stood cooking, he plated her food and forced her to sit and eat it while it was hot.

"Holy shit," she said after the first bite. "You should open a restaurant."

"I could serve French toast and sign autographs."

"Shirtless," she added. "That definitely adds to the ambiance. You could call it Hot and Tasty. You're hot, the food's tasty."

With another plate of food and a grin plastered on his face, he joined her at the table. "It's nice having someone who appreciates my cooking."

"I'm grateful you're cooking for me. It's a win-win." Regardless of her desire to keep it all for herself, she saved a tiny piece and shared with Koko. "What's with the stuffed animal?" The plush raven was still perched on the table.

"I thought of you when I saw him, and I promise not to throw rocks at this one."

She narrowed her eyes. "You better not."

"Did you know they can solve complex puzzles?"

"Yes, I did know that. Looks like someone did some research."

"Only a little. Nate made fun of me." A frown ruined his perfect forehead.

"Don't think of him. Think about what you want to do tonight." Getting to plan their evening activities in advance was a novelty, and she would do anything to distract him from thoughts of Nate.

"Are there any more good hikes around here?"

She laughed. "You're in a state park, surrounded by pristine beauty. Of *course* there are good hikes."

"Can we meet in the parking lot after everyone else leaves?"

"Sounds like a plan. I'll bring sandwiches."

****

Brian strolled along the eastern rim trail as he waited for everyone to show up for the day. No one needed to know he'd stayed the night. From his vantage point, he could see a string of vans arriving, which was his cue to head to the costume trailer so he could start his day of work. The sooner it started, the sooner it would be over and he could be with Alex alone again.

Alex stood, watching guard over the desert, totally focused on her job. When he did tricks on his horse, trying to show off, she rolled her eyes.

"Remember what happened last time," she called out.

Travis laughed and Brian hit his shoulder playfully. "How could I forget?"

She put on a good show for everyone, and he would've believed it if it weren't for the way she looked at him when she thought no one else would notice. To everyone else, she was a hard-ass ranger who took her job very seriously. To him, she was everything he'd ever wanted in a woman.

****

They managed to avoid each other for most of the day, and when Alex was forced to interact with him, she remembered that he was Blaze. Thankfully, though, she was used to it by now.

Blaze by day, Brian by night.

Blaze played a good game, making everyone believe his cocky swagger. Everyone except Alex. Brian lurked just under the surface, and it thrilled her to get to keep him all to herself.

If only for a few more days.

As they strolled hand-in-hand down an isolated trail back to his car later that night, he asked a question out of the blue. "Your parents really named you Alex? School must've sucked."

"No. My name is Alexis. My mom still calls me Ally, like I'm six. I hate it."

"Alexis," he repeated, rolling her name around in his mouth, as if he were tasting the rise and fall of letters. "It's beautiful."

Alexis never seemed to fit her, too soft for someone like her. Too feminine. But the way he said it was like magic. She wanted to be Alexis, just so he would say it again. "Thanks," she whispered.

As they approached his car, Alex said, "Do you want to come and watch a movie at my house tomorrow night? It's usually just Maggie and me, but I figured if you could come, maybe Jim could too. We could all hang out. If it's okay with Maggie. I need to ask first before we plan on anything."

"I'd love to if it works out. If not, I'll just keep you all to myself." To demonstrate what he had in mind, he pressed her against the passenger door and kissed along her jaw and then down her neck.

"I can't believe filming wraps up on Sunday," she said. That fact had been eating her up since Steve told her. What would happen after? Between her and Brian?

His mouth froze. "Oh."

"I wasn't sure if you knew," she added.

With his face nuzzled into the crook of her neck, he wrapped his arms around her. "I don't want to leave. This is the best vacation ever."

Was that all the last few days had been? A vacation from his real life? It was so much more to her but she couldn't admit it now. She had allowed herself a little too much time in her fantasy world, the one where she and Brian would live happily ever after. But it seemed like all he wanted was to be happy for the week. Nothing more.

****

The drive back to Dembi was long and lonely. Brian hated leaving her. Now more than ever. Filming would wrap in four days. Four more days of work and four more nights with Alex. "Why didn't I ask her if I could stay? I'm an idiot."

The night went downhill when he pulled up to the hotel and found Nate waiting in the parking lot for him.

"Look who decides to grace us with his presence," Nate slurred.

"You're drunk." Brian pushed past him.

"So what?" Nate shoved him. "Give me the keys. They belong to me."

"I'm paying for the car. It's mine as much as

yours."

"Why do you have to be such a dick?" Nate swiped at his arm but missed.

"Don't touch me."

"I've been thinking about what you said." Nate narrowed his eyes. "About me leaving my door open. They close automatically. I tried it out earlier."

"So?"

"You lied to me. You broke into my room and stole my keys. I should have you arrested."

"It's my word against yours. How do you think Alan would feel about me being hauled to the local jail? Imagine the look on his face. You haven't told him, have you? You don't have the balls." All the rage and anger swelled to the surface as he laughed bitterly. "Where would that leave you? Unemployed. A wannabe-thug hungry for power with nowhere to go."

Nate pulled his hand back and let loose before Brian could step out of the way, his knuckles connecting squarely with Brian's forehead. Luckily Nate was too drunk to do much harm, but it stung nonetheless. "You're nothing but a washed-up drug addict."

"You don't know the first thing about me," Brian spat as he pushed away. On his way to his room, he considered calling Alan and telling on Nate, but he wasn't sure Alan would believe him.

In his room, he checked his eyebrow in the mirror. It wasn't bleeding, but it would be bruised by morning. After a trip to the ice machine down the hall, he settled into his bed with a cold washcloth. When the throbbing stopped he packed his belongings into his duffle bag. Now he had to think about how to ask Alex if he could stay with her for the rest of the trip.

That would create a new problem: he might be seen with her and she didn't want that. He would have to convince her that being caught would be worth it.

****

Brian slept with his packed bag, waking at the slightest noise. If he could get into Nate's room, that meant Nate could return the favor. Too groggy for a run, he did a final check in his room, loaded the car, and headed into town. If he was going to make his case to Alex, he couldn't show up empty-handed.

With the trunk full of groceries and all his belongings, he drove to Twisted Juniper, hoping to get there before everyone else. Sure enough, the overflow parking lot sat empty. As he walked down the road toward her house, he sighed and practiced what he was going to say. When he approached he could see her standing in the kitchen eating cereal, wrapped in her robe, her hair wet.

He rapped on the window and then pulled his hand back when he remembered the venomous spider living there. Alex's face lit up and Koko rushed to the door and whined to greet him.

"What are you doing here so early?" Alex asked as she opened the door and then her smile fell. "What happened to your eye?"

"Nate."

She frowned. "He hit you?"

Brian nodded. "He was drunk and angry. It was ugly."

"I'm sorry." Resting her head against his chest, she hugged him, holding like that for a while, soothing his hurt and erasing his unpleasant night. "I missed you."

It was the perfect time to ask to stay, but the words got stuck in his throat. The proximity of her body had the usual effect on him, one he didn't want to ignore, so he slid his hands down her back and cupped her spectacular ass.

"It's almost seven," she murmured as she rubbed against his straining dick.

"And?" He tugged the hem of her robe upward, uncovering her soft, warm flesh.

"They'll be here soon." As she spoke, she unbuttoned his jeans.

"Do you want me to stop?" he asked, waiting for her response.

"No, I want you. Now," she said before kissing him.

He lifted her easily and sighed when she wrapped her legs around him. As he carried her down the hallway, she untied the belt holding her robe closed, letting it fall. The bedroom was apparently too far away, so she wiggled out of his grasp and finished undressing him in the hall, her hands frantic and impatient.

No one had ever made him feel as desirable as she did. "That's better," she said before shoving him onto her bed and retrieving a condom from her bedside table. Before he had time to catch his breath, she tore the package with her teeth and straddled him. He squeezed his eyes shut while she sheathed his cock, her fingers caressing everything all at once, driving him wild. And then his dick pressed against her slippery sex.

When she sank down on him it took his breath away and ignited his passion. They both stilled, basking in the initial moment of their union. "So good," she mumbled and then she started moving. Every time their bodies met, she cried out, and then her face morphed as pleasure consumed her. He knew that face and what came next. And he wanted to give it to her.

Dipping his fingers between their bodies, he rubbed her clit and slammed up into her.

"Yes," she screamed and her pussy fluttered around him.

Wanting to make her come again, he fought to remain in control, but his body had a different idea. His cock swelled as he joined her in orgasmic bliss. When he tried to roll her off of him, she refused to move.

"Give me a minute." Pinning him to the bed, she melted against his chest, her heart hammering. Eventually, her pulse and breathing slowed.

"I need to clean up," he said and she relented, letting him go to the bathroom. When he finished, he joined her in bed. "I'm sorry that didn't last—"

She put her finger against his lips. "Don't ever apologize for anything that spectacular. Besides, we didn't have time for marathon sex."

"I'll make it up to you later," he promised.

"I'm sure you will. You always deliver."

The clock read *7:20*. "Have you talked to Maggie about tonight?"

"No, all the lights were off last night after I got home, so I thought I'd play it safe and wait until today."

"When you talk to her, ask her and Jim if they want to join us for dinner."

Alex pushed up to look at him. "Are you planning on cooking again?"

"I'd like to."

"When did you have time to shop?"

He shrugged. "This morning."

"You really want to cook dinner for all of us?"

"Yes," he said emphatically. "I like your friends. They're nice."

"*You're* nice."

"Shh, don't tell anyone," he said. "I need to get the stuff out of the car so the produce doesn't wilt." Dressing proved trickier than he thought since his clothes were strewn all over the place. Alex laughed from the bed, which didn't help. As he made his way through the parking lot with the bags of groceries, the first van arrived for the day, so he picked up his pace and ran back to Alex's house.

Alex stood in the front room buttoning the shirt of her brown uniform, which made him sad since he had hoped for a few more minutes in bed with her.

"The first van just got here." Koko wove through his legs as he made his way to the kitchen to unload the groceries. When he gave her a pumpkin treat, she wiggled to say thanks.

Alex came up behind him and wrapped her arms around him. "Are you feeding the whole cast?"

Brian laughed. It wasn't all for dinner, but he couldn't tell her that. And he had to admit that three days of groceries looked like a lot set out on her tiny counter. Now he had to work up the nerve to ask if he could stay. "If they can't make it tonight, I'll cook for just us. It's not a big deal. Don't pressure them, okay?"

"I won't."

The clock on the wall ticked, reminding him he needed to leave sooner rather than later.

As if she could read his mind, she sighed and said, "We should both go."

He nodded and they walked to the front door together.

"If you follow the wash between my house and Neal's, you can get to the eastern trail. He lives on the other side of me," she added, pointing away from Maggie's house. "Just don't let him see you."

Brian nodded and pulled his hood over his head. "See you later."

"Thanks for this morning." She grinned and kissed him before he darted away.

The morning air cooled his cheeks as he ran along the trail. As he approached the costume trailer, he found Nate waiting outside.

"Did you enjoy your drive alone, princess?" Nate asked.

"As a matter of fact, I did." Brian straightened his back and touched his bruised eyebrow. "If you'll excuse me, I need to see makeup about covering this up."

Nate looked away.

Brian turned toward the makeup trailer but stopped mid-step. "By the way," he said, getting Nate's attention. "If you ever touch me again, I'll break your fucking arm."

Nate didn't respond.

Chapter Sixteen

When Alex went home for lunch, she stopped at Maggie's and tapped lightly on the door.

Maggie stepped outside and whispered, "He's asleep."

"Great. How are you holding up? Is Jim at work again?"

"Yeah, he's been going in for a few hours here and there. It's fine, mostly. Every day is a little easier. One of these weeks I might even feel up to going to town with him."

"Speaking of being social," Alex started, "How do you feel about hanging out tonight...with Brian?"

"Who's Brian?"

Alex shook her head. "Sorry, Blaze. His real name is Brian. Anyway, I miss you, but I also want to be with him, so I thought maybe we could have a movie night for all of us."

"Sure. I'll tell Jim. Seven?"

"Six. Brian offered to cook us dinner."

Maggie smiled. "I'll have Jim pick up a movie."

"Great. Thanks for being so understanding." Alex checked her phone. "I need to get back to the set. See you tonight."

When Alex got back into position, resting against a large boulder, Brian came up alongside her. "We're on for tonight," she said.

"Good. Can I come over early? There's something I want to talk to you about," he added in a quiet voice.

"Sure. Is everything okay?" Worry twisted her stomach into a knot.

"I think so." He offered a small smile and checked his phone. "I need to go. We'll talk later, okay?"

"Okay," she replied. Whatever it was he needed to talk to her about didn't seem to be bad news. She couldn't help but replay the conversation over and over again as she tried to figure out what it could be.

When filming ended for the day, she was dying to talk to him, but after changing back into his regular clothes he took off on one of the trails. Slowly but surely the overflow parking lot emptied.

Alex tidied her front room while she waited for Brian. Only when the last van disappeared over the hill did he arrive at her door, his cheeks rosy and his breath ragged. "What did you want to talk about?" she blurted, unable to wait another second to ask him the question that had been on the tip of her tongue for half the day.

"I wanted to ask you a favor," he said, but he wouldn't look at her.

"What?" She chewed on her lip.

"I wanted to… I hoped I could stay…with you. After what happened with Nate." Their eyes met for a second before he went back to staring at his feet.

Saying goodbye every night had become more and more difficult. Having him stay with her would make her beyond happy, but she knew the only reason he asked was to escape Nate. "Tonight?"

"As long as you'll have me," he said.

She threw her arms around him and looked up at his handsome face. "I would love for you to stay."

"I may or may not have brought a duffle bag full of clothes," he mumbled, looking away again.

"Maybe you should go get it," she said.

Within two minutes, he returned with a bag slung over his shoulder. "I was so nervous," he said with an uneasy laugh. "I didn't want to assume it would be okay."

Once they were in her room, she pushed her clothes to the side. "My closet has plenty of room. Put your stuff in here."

As he unpacked his things, he said, "It's like I'm moving in."

"Temporarily. To keep you safe from Nate. You don't need to spend the next three days with a bully like him."

He nodded and finished unpacking without another word.

****

Alex got out of the way while Brian bustled around the kitchen. Wonderful fragrances filled the air and then Maggie and Jim arrived promptly at six, with a baby and dog in tow. Alex set the table and helped Jim with the portable swing for Henry.

Brian served everyone and opened a bottle of sparkling cider, pouring a little into four wine glasses. "Cheers," he toasted.

Everyone dug in, complimenting him on the meal. Jim said, "Wow. You can cook."

"That apron's not a joke anymore," Maggie added, pointing to the lettering on Brian's chest. "You really are the world's greatest cook," she said.

Alex laughed. "I think you should keep it," she said. But keeping it meant him taking it when he left. In three days. And she didn't want to think about him leaving.

"To good food," Jim announced, raising his glass, clinking his way around the table.

"And good company," Brian added.

"To movie night," Jim said. "I've never been invited before," he confided in Brian. "Thanks for making that happen."

"I didn't do anything, I just cooked." Brian smiled. "Alex planned everything."

Everyone looked at her. Could they tell she had been thinking about Brian leaving? "So, Jim how's work?"

"Can't complain. I think you'll like what we have brewing right now. It's a rye-based pale ale."

"Sounds good," Alex said.

"You're a brewmaster, right?" Brian asked.

Jim nodded. "It's my dream job. I mean, it's not as cool as acting, but…"

"You get to taste everything you make, right?" Before going on, he waited for Jim to nod. "That sounds pretty cool to me."

Jim smiled wide. The conversation veered from Jim's job to Henry, who decided he couldn't wait any longer for his dinner. Maggie picked him up and excused herself to nurse him in the front room. While they were gone, Alex, Jim, and Brian discussed filming, but only after Jim swore up and down not to tell anyone the details of the movie. So far, the media hadn't gotten wise to the fact Twisted Juniper hosted some of the biggest names in Hollywood.

"It's a shit storm when they find out," Brian said, leaning back in his chair. "That's why I try to keep a low profile when I'm on location."

"By hanging out with a ranger," Jim added with a sly smile.

"That's a bonus," Brian added.

Alex avoided the attention by clearing the table. "Maggie, are you ready for us yet?" she called to her friend.

"Almost."

Alex started in on the dishes and Jim came to help her. When Brian stood, they both shooed him back to the table. "You're not going to cook *and* clean up."

"Fine."

"Thank you for dinner," Jim said, drying the clean dishes Alex handed him.

"You're welcome," Brian said.

"Did Alex tell you what we're watching?" Jim asked him.

"Don't make fun of me, Jim, or you won't be invited over for movie night again," she warned.

Jim laughed. "I wouldn't dream of it."

"I happen to like old westerns," she said a little too defensively.

"I do, too," Brian added. "They remind me of stage acting. The story always focused on the triumph of good over evil, fought by real people instead of all the CGI bullshit in movies today."

Alex smiled and kissed him, right there in front of Jim. She couldn't help it.

When they put on the movie, Jim joined Maggie and their sleeping baby while Alex and Brian snuggled together. He wrapped his arms around her and pulled her against his chest, so she reclined against him. Being surrounded by his warmth and the scent of his skin made her brain a little fuzzy. Despite her love for the movie, all she noticed was the way Brian's body tensed when the good guy got captured and then cheered when he won.

At the end, Brian said, "That was awesome."

"I'm glad you liked it," Alex said.

"Thanks for hanging out with us," he said to Jim and Maggie. "And for being so understanding about the need for discretion."

"No worries," Jim said. "You're welcome to stop by for a beer at Dembi Brewing any time."

"I will gladly take you up on that." Brian grinned. "Hey, we'll probably be having a wrap party before we leave. Could we have it there?"

"I don't see why not. We could definitely use the publicity." Jim's back straightened. "That would be cool. Really?"

"Yeah. Sunday," Brian said.

Alex laughed.

"What's so funny?" Brian frowned.

"Sundays in Utah are interesting," Alex said. "Most places are closed, including Dembi Brewing. It took me a while to get used to that."

"I'm sure I could pull a few strings for a private party," Jim said, winking at Brian.

"Okay, I'll talk to Mr. Reid about it. What's the best way to get in touch with you?"

While they exchanged information, Alex and Maggie said good night.

"He's really great," Maggie said.

"I'm glad you think so." It was nice to have feedback from her best friend because she certainly thought he was great.

"Too bad he's leaving," she added.

"I know." Alex's shoulders fell.

"I'm sorry, I shouldn't have brought it up. Just live in the moment, right?"

Alex nodded because she planned to enjoy every second she had left with him. "Thanks for coming over."

"Thanks for inviting us," Maggie said.

"It was fun," Jim added, giving Alex a quick hug and shaking Brian's hand. "Thank you for everything. We'll be in touch."

Pelli led the family procession back to their house, leaving Alex and Brian alone.

"They're so great," Brian said.

"They really are."

"So are you," he said as he pulled her into a hug.

"I can't believe I get you all to myself." It didn't matter that it was only for three more days. Living in the moment meant not focusing on the future. "What should we do first?"

With a smile on his lips, he locked the front door and scooped her into his arms. "I believe I owe you a few more orgasms."

He delivered on his promise and so much more.

****

Brian stretched carefully when he woke the next morning. The sun was almost up, which meant it was the perfect time for a run. Trying not to disturb Alex, he slid out of bed and got dressed. Even though he was quiet, she stretched to fill the gap where he'd been and mumbled in her sleep.

Koko's tail thumped against the mattress and she followed him out into the hallway. "Want to go for a run?" he asked and her ears perked up. "Come on," he whispered. In the front room, she nudged her leash with her nose. "Good girl." He ruffled her ears and clipped her. "Sit and stay. I need to leave your mom a note so she doesn't worry." In the kitchen, he scrawled a note and crept into her bedroom to leave it on his pillow.

At first, the dog wanted to smell and pee on everything and had no interest in running, so he ran in place. "Come on, Koko. Let's run." She tilted her head to the side. "Yeah, let's go." Tugging at her leash, he started moving toward the eastern trail. When he picked up the pace, so did she. Before long, they were running together, Koko matching his stride with ease.

They reached the farthest rocky edge of the trail just in time to watch the sun show itself, tingeing the desert gold. The return trip along the sandy trail was filled with the sounds of their synchronized breathing. Instead of completing the path around the park, they finished a loop to and from Alex's house. The full path would have to wait for when they had more time. Just like in town, he didn't run into another person on the trail that early in the morning, but that changed when he approached the row of houses.

Neal was in the process of walking to work when he bumped into them. "Good morning."

"Morning," Brian returned.

"Out for a run?" Neal asked. A frown settled on his forehead as he looked at Koko.

"Beautiful out there," Brian replied as his stomach filled with dread. How could he explain why Koko was with him? He couldn't. "See you later."

Neal nodded. "Later."

Brian ran past Alex's house and kept going until he

was sure Neal would be gone, and then circled back and let himself in. He unhooked Koko's leash, returned it to the hook on the wall, and groaned. No matter how much he wanted to crawl under a rock, he knew he had to tell Alex what happened.

The water ran in the shower so he went into the bathroom.

"Brian, is that you?" Alex called out.

"Yes." Time to come clean. "I fucked up."

She turned the water off, pulled the curtain back, and frowned. "What happened? Is Koko okay?"

"She's fine. We had a great run. Until we saw Neal."

"Oh shit."

"Exactly. I'm so sorry. I should've left her at home, but she followed me and begged to come with me. I didn't think it through."

Alex reached out of the curtain and tugged on his clothes. "Join me. There's no sense in feeling bad about it now. It's in the past."

When he looked up at her, she smiled.

He undressed quickly and stepped into the shower just as she turned the water on again. "I'm so sorry."

"It's okay. I'm sure she had a great time and don't worry about Neal. I'll talk to him."

"Why are you so understanding?"

She smiled and caressed his face. "Because you deserve it."

****

Despite her calm reaction to Brian's news, Alex had some major damage control to do. They left her house at different times and in different directions. While he meandered along the trails, she went directly to the Visitor Center.

"Hey, Lynn," she greeted at the gift shop. "Have you seen Neal?"

"Nope. Must be out somewhere. You want me to call him?"

"That's okay. I'll find him." The last thing she wanted was a confrontation over a walkie-talkie frequency the entire staff could hear. After visiting his usual haunts she finally found him tinkering with a bat house wedged under the back eave of the Visitor Center.

"Hey," he said as she approached.

"Hey," she echoed. "Do you need a hand?"

"No, I'm good. I noticed this box had fallen off one of the hooks. Probably in that crazy wind we had. Bats won't use it if it's crooked."

"They're so persnickety," she said.

"True." He teetered on the ladder while he struggled with the box, so she reached out and steadied it. "Thanks."

"You're welcome." Their conversation baffled her. It wasn't the confrontation she had been expecting, and she couldn't figure out what to do next.

Neal descended the ladder and faced her. "Thanks for helping me."

"I didn't do much. Um. I actually wanted to talk to you about something."

He nodded. "I figured as much."

Heat crept up her neck. "It's about when you saw Koko this morning." When he didn't respond at all, she went on. "With Br—Blaze."

"It's none of my business," he replied.

Her mouth hung open. Things definitely hadn't

gone as she expected. "I don't want you to get the wrong idea. You have to know I would never let a relationship interfere with my work."

"You don't need to justify anything to me."

"If Mr. Howard found out, I would be in serious trouble," she added.

"He's not going to find out from me."

Alex let out a long, shaky breath. "Is it obvious? Me and him?"

Neal shook his head. "No. I wouldn't have believed it except I saw it with my own eyes. Blaze is such a dick to everyone on set, especially you."

"That's just for show." Not too long ago, she had felt the same way. "Thanks. I mean it. I'm so grateful."

"Don't mention it." Neal inclined his head slightly. "Before we get going, I'll say one thing. Tell him to be more careful. I'm not sure Beth would be as quiet."

Alex laughed. "I will."

They walked to the set together and split up. Neal stood near the costume trailer. Alex went to Steve to check in for the day. After they discussed the day's shoot, he turned the conversation to his property.

"My sister couldn't wait for me. She met with a man from the wildlife trust and set everything up. I'll have to sign some paperwork when I get home."

"That's very exciting."

"All thanks to you," he said with a smile. "Would you ever considered moving to California to work for me?"

"Um." The loose thread on her brown shirt suddenly became very interesting, so she rolled it between her fingers. Anything to get her mind off Steve's question.

"My sister said we need to hire someone to do a wildlife survey, and then they could stay on as the manager," he said.

"Neal is an excellent naturalist. I bet he would be happy to help. You could ask him," she said, nodding toward her friend.

"I'd like you to do it. It's your idea, after all, and you know so much about everything. Blaze was telling me the things he's learned from you while we've been on location."

"I wouldn't know the first thing about doing a wildlife survey," she lied. She had, in fact, helped Maggie with one in the spring. It became increasingly difficult to hold still. "Thanks for meeting with me. I should probably get ready. Mr. Reid is here. I bet he's going to call everyone to the set soon," she said as she inched away from him.

Steve nodded, but before she left he said, "Think about it, okay?"

Chapter Seventeen

The cast and crew bustled around Alex, including Blaze. Larger than life, full of swagger, and goofing around with the stunt guys. "Hey," she called out. "Stay on the designated trails."

He threw his hands up in the air and strutted toward her. "Now you're just busting my balls."

"You'd have to have balls first," she said.

Nate sniggered.

Blaze glared at his assistant before breaking away from the group to confront her. "I was *on* the trail."

"I'm just doing my job, buddy," she said loud enough for everyone to hear before whispering, "Neal's good. He's not going to say anything."

"Good." A smile softened his face, and his shoulders relaxed. "Are you going home for lunch?"

"Probably best if I do." Anything to avoid another awkward conversation with Steve.

"Will there be anything else?" he said loudly as he straightened his back.

"I suggest you get back to work," she replied.

In an exaggerated movement, he rolled his eyes and turned on his heel. Nate scurried over to him and mumbled something while looking at Alex but Blaze shook his head. "I think she still wants my autograph. Poor thing doesn't know how to ask for it."

She almost laughed, but that would undermine his

act, so she scowled at him instead.

The morning passed quickly, and when lunch arrived, she stood in line for a plate and carried it home. Koko sat at her feet and waited patiently for her share, but after a few minutes, she lost interest and whined at the front door. A knock followed.

Brian waited just outside, still dressed in his costume.

"Did anyone see you?" she asked as she opened the door and ushered him inside. To avoid anyone invading their privacy, she pulled the curtains over her front window.

"No. I checked."

"You shouldn't be here during the day."

"I know." He kissed her. "But I missed you."

Couldn't argue with that. "Neal was surprisingly cool about everything."

"I feel so much better. Thanks for talking to him. Do you mind if I keep you company?" In the chair next to her, he hooked his boots on the bottom rung.

"I need to finish eating." The plate was still more than half full.

"I need to check on Ozzie. The webcam at his daycare is only live during the day, and I can't check it around Nate. Plus, reception is spotty out there." He opened the browser on his phone and waited for the video feed to load. "There he is," he cooed.

Alex craned her head. "You didn't mention he's a border collie."

"Border collie and something else. His legs are too long for his body. Look," he said, tapping the screen. "See this little scruffy-looking dog? They're friends. I called to check in on him a couple of days ago."

"He looks so sweet."

"You would love him," he answered softly.

There it was again, another comment that implied she should go to Brian's house. In California. What was she supposed to do when he said something like that? At a loss for words, she focused on the screen.

They watched together until Ozzie disappeared through the dog door out into the fenced yard. Brian turned his phone off just as she took her last bite. "It's surreal."

"What?"

"You being here in costume. It's like I'm in the movie."

"Are you going to say your shitty lines now?" he joked.

Mimicking Jennifer's voice, she reached over and touched his bare chest and said, "Oh, Buck. What are we going to do?"

Just like on set, he removed his hat and leaned toward her. "I reckon I could call the sheriff."

"Wait. Something's not right," she said in her normal voice before unbuttoning her shirt until the top of her breasts showed. "There. That's better."

"Yes. Yes, it is." He grinned and then pulled her onto his lap.

"Buck, you cad," she protested and then he buried his face in her cleavage. That was not in the script, but she didn't mind. Especially when he pulled her bra out of the way and sucked a nipple into his mouth. "Oh shit," she murmured. He gripped her ass and moved her body against his, crushing her clit against the bulge in his pants, and forcing a moan out of her mouth. She reached between their bodies and pulled his dick out and started pumping him with her hands.

"Fuck," he said and then sucked on her other nipple while he rubbed her slit through her thin pants. No one had ever touched her with such skill.

As her orgasm neared, her breathing became erratic, but her hands never stopped moving. "Come with me," she begged before kissing him. When she cried out, his dick swelled in her hands and he painted his bare stomach and chest with cum. They clutched each other, trying to breathe while their bodies trembled.

"I need a towel," he said.

"Let me." She wiped at him with a napkin, but he tried to take over. "I insist. It's my mess."

He smiled and leaned back in the chair.

"Good thing you're not wearing a shirt." When he was clean, she tucked his dick into his pants and patting him lightly, eliciting a groan from him.

"Good thing your shirt opens in the front." To get even, he caressed her ruddy breasts, making her jerk on his lap.

"That's the best lunch break I've ever had."

"I second that."

The alarm on her phone chimed, reminding her lunch was almost over. "We should get back. Just in time too. You're good as new."

"Better than new. Thanks for letting me stay."

She lifted off of him with wobbly legs. "You should get a head start."

****

Brian kissed Alex long and hard before he poked his face out the front door and scanned the neighborhood. Nothing stirred for as far as he could see, so he ducked outside and headed for the trail so he could loop back to the set without drawing attention to himself. Unable to run in his boots, with only a few minutes to spare, he shuffled along and pushed his phone deep into his back pocket so it was out of sight. Nate hadn't mentioned his phone and wallet. Maybe he hadn't figured out Brian had taken them, too.

A minute later, he found Nate leaning against the saloon, flipping through his phone.

"Where did you go?" Nate asked. Ever since their fight, he had been walking on eggshells around Brian. It was the only thing that made his presence tolerable.

"For a walk."

Nate flashed his screen. "You missed out. I got Stacy's number." He frowned. "Or is it Steph? Whatever. I'm finding the closer we are to wrapping, the more desperate they are to hook up. Especially because I know you."

Leave it to Nate to name drop to get laid. "What happened to Charlotte?" Brian asked.

"I'm done with her. She's way too needy."

"That's too bad. She really seemed to like you."

Nate snorted. "This place is crawling with pussy. You, of all people, can't expect me to settle. What time did you get in anyway?"

"Late," Brian lied. Nothing could convince him to return to the hotel.

"Pounding it hard, right?" Nate grabbed an imaginary partner by the hips and thrust into the air.

"You know it," Brian said. Letting Nate believe he was out with women until all hours was better than having him question where he really was. "How are things going with planning the wrap party?" he asked, wishing more than anything to change the subject. During his morning meeting with Mr. Reid, he had proposed the idea that Nate take care of organizing the party. It was the perfect distraction. Nate felt important, and Brian got a little more space.

"Good. I talked to a guy who works there and we hashed it out. How'd you find such a cool place?"

Brian shrugged. "I have my sources."

"One of your fuck buddies?"

"That's for me to know…" He looked for Alex, and relief flowed through him when he saw her coming down the trail toward the set. There was no way she had heard their depraved conversation. "I better get back to work."

Later that night, when the bustling set transformed back into a peaceful park and he didn't have to hide on the trails anymore, Brian walked to Alex's house. The curtain was still drawn across the front window, but the lights were on and the door was unlocked. She was waiting for him. Nothing had ever felt so good.

"Honey, I'm home," he called out as if he were in an old sitcom.

"In here," she replied from the kitchen. The hem of her robe rode up in the back as she bent to look in the fridge, giving him a spectacular view. "How was work?" she asked playing along as she wiggled her ass against him.

"Same old, same old," he said as he ran his fingers down her back. "There was this ranger on set today who gave me a hard time."

"Oh yeah?" she asked as she turned to face him. "What were you doing wrong?" When she opened the front of her robe, it was obvious she wasn't wearing a bra.

"Me? Why would you assume I'm at fault?" Unable to resist, he dipped his hand inside and squeezed her nipple.

She moaned. "You know how you get with the boys," she said with a smile as she untied the belt. She wasn't wearing underwear, either.

Coherent thoughts left his brain and his mouth went dry. "Um, I wasn't doing anything wrong. She just yelled at me."

"Poor guy." Alex clicked her tongue and unbuttoned his jeans. "For her to take her frustration out on you like that. So unfair."

Trying to follow along with their banter became more difficult, especially when she wrapped her hand around his dick and twisted. When she ran her thumb along the head, his knees wobbled.

She kissed him and sucked his bottom lip into her mouth, nibbling on it lightly as she twisted her hand the other way. They both shuddered when she pressed her body against his.

Too impatient to find out what she was going to do next, he lifted her onto the counter by the sink. A smile tugged up the corners of her mouth and then she opened her legs and pulled him toward her. Encircling the head of his dick, she spiraled her wrist and brushed her sex with her knuckles. Another moan spilled out of her open mouth.

"I need to…" he mumbled. Less than an inch separated their bodies. If he pushed forward, he would be inside her, but he couldn't do that. They needed to be safe. "Get a condom," he finished.

It was clear by her pout that she didn't like it

either, but they didn't have any other choice.

With his cock jutting out of his open jeans, he raced to her bedroom, grabbed a condom, tore the package open, put it on, and ran back to her. Still sitting on the edge of the counter, she shook out of her robe and crooked her finger, beckoning him to get closer. How could he resist? His mouth descended, kissing his way down her arm and moved laterally toward her heaving breasts. Another moan escaped her lips as she wiggled closer to the edge of the counter and arched into his mouth. She reached between their bodies and gripped the base of his dick. Positioned against her opening, she wrapped her legs around his ass and urged him forward.

They moaned in unison when he leaned forward and pushed inside her. It didn't take long before her pussy quivered as an orgasm worked its way through her body. Moving his tongue in time with his hips, he thrust into her mouth while she dug her fingernails into his shoulders. The soft mewling sounds spilling out of her mouth drove him crazy. At the cusp of release, he slammed into her hard repeatedly, taking her breath away and sending a pile of mail to the ground as she scrambled to hold on while he fucked her.

When she screamed, her body tensed and he came with her that time, unable to hold off any longer.

A warm, pink blush covered most of her body as she leaned her head against the wall and panted. "I'm glad you finally came home, I was still hungry after lunch."

"Me, too," he said while he ran his hands along the curves of her body, which made her twitch. "You are so beautiful."

When she sat up to kiss him, he started sliding out of her. "Hang on, I'll be right back." That was the biggest downside to using condoms. If he stayed inside her too long it would slip off and then what would be the point of using one? After disposing of it and cleaning up in the bathroom, he tucked himself back into his jeans.

Alex was pouting when he returned to the kitchen. "Why are you dressed?"

"Because I thought I'd cook us dinner." The ingredients waited for him on one shelf in the fridge, where he'd put everything the night before. "I learned the hard way not to cook naked."

She pulled her robe back up over her shoulders and started tying the belt, but he stopped her.

"*You* don't have to get dressed. I'm enjoying the view far too much."

"You want me to sit here naked while you cook?" she asked, lifting one eyebrow.

"I may have to postpone cooking." He wedged his body between her legs and kissed along her shoulders. "Maybe I should have dessert first."

****

Only a sliver of doubt remained in the back of Alex's mind when she went to bed that night. Wrapped in Brian's arms everything seemed wonderful, but the rest of the time she wondered how he really felt about her. If she believed what he said to her, everything was great between them. If she believed what he said to everyone else, she needed to worry. Was he attracted to the countless beautiful women on set he flirted with on a daily basis? Or was he just doing that to keep up appearances? Even so, how was she supposed to look the other way? If she meant something to him, wouldn't he stop all that?

In that moment, listening to his slow and even breathing, she tried to silence her racing mind.

"What is this?" she whispered.

He answered with a deep exhale.

****

"What's your favorite restaurant?"

Alex frowned and stopped chewing her cereal. "Where? In town?"

"Yeah," Brian responded casually.

"There's a great Japanese restaurant with private tea rooms. I've only been once, but it was really good. Why do you ask?"

Brian shrugged. "Nate asked for a recommendation."

"I don't know why you're even talking to him." If she were in his shoes, she wasn't sure what she would do to a dick like Nate, but it sure as hell wouldn't be pretending everything was okay.

"I have to."

"You're going to talk to your agent about him, right?"

"Definitely." The bruise over his eye was nearly gone, but Brian touched the spot carefully.

Talking to his agent meant he'd be home. Without her. Day after tomorrow. Reality hit hard. Their time together was coming to an end and it made her sad.

"Are you okay?" he asked.

"Yeah." Lying about her feelings had become easy. "Just thinking about work. I'll be meeting with Steve in a half hour so I should probably finish up." On her way to the sink she paused. "That reminds me. He said you've been talking about me."

Brian nodded. "I told him about the fairy shrimp. He has a very high opinion of you. Rightly so."

Had they been talking about Steve's nature reserve, too? "Whatever." Ever since it came up, she couldn't stop thinking about Steve's offer.

"Why do you always do that?"

"Do what?" she asked defensively.

"Dismiss my compliments. You think I'm not being sincere?" He turned her away from the sink so she would look at him.

"I think you're biased."

"Steve isn't biased and he thinks you're amazing, too."

"I have a hard time believing either of you." Since she was a little girl, her mother had always told her she would never amount to anything. Feeling insufficient came naturally.

"I wish you could see yourself through my eyes," he said.

She hugged him because that was easier than changing the way she viewed herself. "Okay, so I'll see you later?"

"For lunch?" A grin split his face in half while he wiggled his eyebrows.

"You shouldn't. Your presence is needed on set. Reputation to uphold and all that."

"It's boring without you there."

"I can't—" Admitting her insecurities, seeing him interact with other women, wasn't a good idea. "I can't leave Koko inside that long," she finally said. "And you can't get caught coming here."

"I have to wait all day to kiss you again?" he

whined.

"Yep, so you better get it out of your system." With her eyes closed and her lips ready, he still managed to surprise her with a hundred kisses.

The alarm on her phone rang. "We need to go."

"One more," he begged and then cradled her face in his hands and kissed her one last time so tenderly it took her breath away. "Have a good day." He opened the front door and paused to check for other people.

"You too," she replied, still dazed. Even after her five-minute walk, she was still practically floating.

Chapter Eighteen

Alex spent the morning near the saloon making sure no one strayed too far from the set. Thankfully, Brian wasn't working near her that day. Focusing on work was twice as hard when he was around.

Someone nearby exhaled, getting her attention. Alex swiveled toward Jennifer and looked at her very carefully. Something was wrong. Alex stepped toward her just in time to catch her as she fell. Jennifer's body went limp and someone screamed.

"Call the medic," Alex shouted as she guided Jennifer onto the wooden platform outside the saloon, cradling her head in her lap. Jennifer was breathing, but it was very shallow. People bustled around them and a minute later the medic ran up the stairs.

The man checked Jennifer's pulse and shined a tiny flashlight into her mouth and under her fluttering eyelids.

When Jennifer tried to sit up, they both stopped her. "I'm so embarrassed. I fainted. I guess I locked my knees."

"Your costume isn't helping," the medic pointed out. "Your diaphragm is supposed to fill with air, not be compressed."

Jennifer gave him a sheepish smile. "Maybe my corset is a little too tight today."

"Can you get up?" he asked.

She nodded, but Alex helped her anyway.

"Go to costume and change," he said. "Drink some water, too. You're dehydrated."

Jennifer nodded, her face pale.

"I'll walk with you," Alex offered.

"Thank you."

"It's a warm day, that probably didn't help," Alex said as they moved together up the trail toward the overflow parking lot.

"Thanks for catching me."

Alex smiled. "No problem. That's what I'm here for, to keep you safe."

"I'm glad you were standing right there."

"Me, too," Alex agreed as they made their way to the costume trailer. "Can you manage on your own?" When Jennifer nodded, she said, "I'll get you a bottle of water."

Jennifer smiled and thanked her again before heading into the trailer.

When Jennifer reappeared, Alex offered her the bottle. Most of the color had returned to her face and her waist wasn't nearly as tiny as it had been.

"Feeling better?" Alex asked.

Jennifer sighed. "Loads. Thanks for this." She opened the cap and took a long swallow.

"Are you feeling well enough to go back?"

Jennifer nodded. "Will you help me, though? These shoes are ridiculous."

Alex smiled and offered her arm as they started the trek back to the set.

Jennifer held on tight. "I should've been more careful. I wasn't paying attention. My mind was somewhere else. I was thinking of my boyfriend," she added in a whisper. "I get to see him in just two more days."

"Boyfriend?" Alex repeated.

"Yeah, don't tell anyone. My agent says I need to be seen as being available. That's how it is in Hollywood. The second you're off the market your fans lose interest and then you stop getting cast. Blaze has that part down pat."

"How do you mean?"

"He claims to never date anyone. The way I hear it, you think you're with him, but he'll deny it up and down to anyone who will listen. I got warned to stay away from him, but who knows? He seems sweet to me." They had arrived on set, so Jennifer got back into position outside the saloon with a smile on her face. "Thanks again for helping me."

"No problem," Alex said. All the headlines she'd read about Blaze claimed one relationship after another, but when she asked him about them, he had denied them all. Just like Jennifer said he would. Was that going to happen to her? Mr. Reid called her and pulled her out of her head.

"Miss Mitchell?" he repeated.

"Yes, sir?" she said as she approached his chair where he sat behind the camera.

"I heard you were helping Jennifer. Thank you for taking care of her," he said. "Warm day." Without another word, he turned his attention back to the screen.

"Yes, sir." It was the first time he'd thanked her. As luck would have it, she was in the right place at the right time, and Mr. Reid noticed. Maybe she wasn't such a failure after all, at least not when it came to her job.

When Alex went home for lunch, she watched the door; wondering if Brian would join her despite their agreement. What would she say to him? Was it fair to judge him based on a bit of gossip?

She smiled when Maggie knocked on the window.

"Hey, mind if I join you?" Maggie asked in a whisper, trying not to wake Henry who was asleep in her arm. "I saw you come home a few minutes ago, but I wanted to wait to make sure I wasn't interrupting anything."

"Oh." Heat crept up Alex's cheeks. "He's staying on set for lunch. Do you think anyone else noticed yesterday?"

Maggie shrugged and then carefully lowered Henry onto the couch, patting his chest when he stirred and sat down next to him.

"How have you been?"

"Henry slept for five hours straight." Maggie grinned. "The longest yet." She laughed. "I never thought I would be celebrating five hours of sleep."

Alex shared her lunch with her friend while they talked quietly about Henry.

"How are things with you?"

Alex beamed. "Mr. Reid thanked me for doing a good job today."

Maggie grinned. "See? I told you you're good at this."

"Jennifer fainted on set." Alex conveyed the entire story about the medic and how she caught her before she fell. "Jennifer also told me something about Brian, and I don't know what to think of it." She took a deep breath before telling Maggie the rest.

Maggie frowned. "That doesn't sound like him.

He's nice."

Alex nodded. "In private. On set, he's totally different."

"Didn't he say he was just keeping up appearances?"

"I guess that's all it is." She wanted to believe it.

****

At every opportunity, Brian checked the clock on his phone. Impatient for the day to be over, he counted down the hours until he could be with Alex again. Right on cue, he smiled, recited his lines, and threw fake punches better than ever. He didn't want to be the reason to have to film a scene more than once.

During slow moments, he thought about Alex's reason why they couldn't be seen together. It wouldn't look good if she were using him for a good recommendation, but that's not what she was doing. Maggie and Neal both understood and he was sure the other rangers would, too. And then there were directors, producers, and other bigwigs from the crew. The letters would carry a lot of weight, but she worried too much about them. It was time to show her that their relationship didn't bother anyone.

At the end of the day, Mr. Reid gave him an approving nod. "Good work today."

"Thank you, Mr. Reid." Getting on his good side had taken a lot of work, and the validation put him in a good mood. But it didn't last long.

Nate sidled up to him and said, "In trouble again?"

"No." Brian didn't say anything else. Nate didn't deserve more.

"You should join me tonight. Shit is about to get real." Nate glanced at a handful of extras waiting outside the costume trailer.

"I have plans," Brian said. Holding his finger and thumb like a gun, he clicked his tongue and pointed at Jennifer. She giggled and waved.

"Showoff," Nate grumbled before he stormed away.

A satisfied smile tugged at Brian's mouth. Jennifer was out of Nate's league, and she played along beautifully to foster the envy Brian had been hoping for.

Brian disappeared along one of the trails and found the spot where he got the best cell coverage. After a quick search online, he made a reservation for dinner.

When he opened Alex's front door later, she smiled from her spot on the couch.

"Come on. Get dressed."

She looked down at her brown uniform. "I am dressed."

"I mean dressed up." In her bedroom, he sorted through her closet. "I thought I saw a dress in here."

"Where are we going?" she asked as she put her hand on top of his.

"I lied. The restaurant recommendation wasn't for Nate. I want to take you somewhere special while I have the chance. We have a reservation at seven."

Alex narrowed her eyes. "Like a date? In public?"

"Yeah."

She frowned. "But—"

"No buts. I've been thinking about it. The press hasn't gotten wind of us being here, so there's no chance of me being recognized."

"That's not true. You have fans all over the world."

"I've been to Dembi a few times, walked around,

eaten at restaurants. No one has recognized me. I know how to blend in."

"But what if Mr. Reid saw us? Or Steve? I'm trying to impress them, not—"

"They're impressed. Besides, what are the chances that they'll be at the same restaurant at the same time?"

Before he could go on, she shook her head. "I can't."

"Please? Let me take you out. I want to be a normal couple. Just for the night," he pleaded. It worked. As he watched her face, her resolve crumbled. A sly smile tugged at her lips as if she secretly wanted to be wined and dined.

"Okay," she finally said. "But we have to be discreet."

"We will," he promised and then kissed her. He changed into the only button-down shirt he had packed. It would have to do.

She pulled two dresses out of her closet and held them up to her body, one after another. "Which one? Green or purple?"

"Purple." They would both look good on her, but the purple one had a deeper cut in the front, which would greatly improve his view. Sitting on the edge of the bed, he watched her slip out of her uniform, remove her bra, and tug the purple dress over her head.

"Hang on," she said before ducking into the bathroom. When she emerged, she had brushed her hair and put on lipstick.

"I didn't see any makeup in there." Brian grimaced. "Not that I was snooping."

"I don't have much, but we're going out so I thought I would get fancy." A warm laugh filled the room. "Lipstick is my version of fancy, so you know."

"I do now." He grinned. "Are you ready?"

After grabbing a pair of flats out of her closet, she nodded. "I am. Do I look okay?"

"You're beautiful." It was the truth, if only she would believe him.

She shook her head but smiled anyway.

"I think we should take a picture to commemorate our first real date." With his phone at arm's length, he pulled her into a hug. "Say monkey butts."

Alex burst out laughing and Brian got the whole thing in a series of pictures.

"Monkey butts?" she asked when she finally caught her breath.

"No one expects monkey butts. It's always cheese or smile. Boring."

Without releasing his hold on her, they walked to the parking lot together and he opened the passenger door of the rental car. "After you."

Alex kissed him before taking her seat. "Thank you."

Behind the wheel, he started the car, and pulled onto the quiet road. After a while, she opened her hand. "Can I see the pictures?"

He unlocked his phone and handed it to her. The sound of her giggling distracted him from the road. Nothing could beat that sound.

"These are actually pretty good. You need to share these with me." After a second of her typing something on his screen her phone chimed. "Done."

"Does that mean I finally have your number?"

"Yep. I'll update your contacts." The keyboard on his phone clicked as she typed. "There, I'm in your phone."

He glanced at her just in time to see her smile fall. "What is it? What's wrong?"

"There are so many." The light from his screen lit up her sad face as she scrolled. "Amber, Amy, Angie, Anna." The screen went dark and she stared at the windshield. "That's just part of the As. Are they ex-girlfriends?"

"They're people I know through work. Networking is very important for my job."

No answer.

"I have nothing to hide from you."

"It's none of my business anyway," she finally said.

"Yes, it is." The car coasted to a stop on the desolate road to Dembi, and he turned in his seat to look at her. "They don't mean anything."

Pressing her lips into a thin line, she sighed.

He brushed his thumb against her cheek, turning her face toward his. "You're the only one who matters."

****

Alex exhaled. "It's hard." This conversation had been on the tip of her tongue for days, but she hadn't known how to bring it up. Thinking about him with other women made her want to cry.

"What is?" Brian responded.

"The jealousy. I try not to let it get to me, but it's not easy. There are so many women."

"I'm sorry. It's part of my job." He hung his head.

"I'm not trying to make you feel bad, just trying to explain myself. I get it. You have to act a certain way or people will start asking questions. But it's hard not to believe the lie."

"That's all it is," he reassured her. "I should've explained what I was doing. I assumed you knew I was flirting to throw Nate off, especially since you didn't say anything."

"I didn't feel like I could say anything." Keeping their relationship light and fun meant ignoring the green monster inside her. No matter how much time she spent with Brian she had to admit Blaze was a huge part of his life, and Blaze could do whatever he wanted.

He picked up her hand and kissed it. "I'm sorry. You're the only one."

"It's okay," she said with a smile. "Sorry to derail our date. We should get going."

"Are you sure? We can talk about this more. As much as you like."

"I'm sure," she said. "Let's go before it's too late." Everything he'd said had been reassuring. No one else mattered and she believed him. Why shouldn't she?

A few awkward seconds passed.

"We're good. I promise. Go," she demanded.

"Yes, ma'am." He chuckled and started down the road again.

When they pulled into the parking lot, Brian opened her door and offered his hand. Before getting out, she looked all around them. No one stopped and stared or said anything. At that moment, they were a regular couple going on a date.

"Thank you," she said as she swung her leg out onto the pavement. A cool breeze blew across her thighs, reminding her just how much skin showed. Brian noticed, too. His eyes glazed over and she laughed. "You wouldn't think you'd be so easily distracted."

It was as if he hadn't heard a word she'd said. "What?"

"I'm amazed at how easily distracted you are by a little leg." She pulled the hem of her dress up and he swallowed hard. "Considering you work with the most beautiful women in the world."

"They're nothing compared to you," he said. "You're stunning."

Unable to ignore him and the warm feeling that crept into her heart, she said, "Thank you."

He blinked and smiled. "Did you just take a compliment?"

"Maybe."

"I'm finally getting through to you."

"More like wearing me down," she said with a laugh. "Maybe I needed to be worn down."

"However you want to look at it," he said and then pulled her the rest of the way out of the car and into his arms.

When he kissed her, she truly believed everything he said.

The reservation was under her name, and after apologizing for being a few minutes late, they followed the hostess to a tea room near the back of the restaurant. They slipped their shoes off and ducked around the silk curtain hanging in the opening of the private dining area.

Alex tucked her feet under her body and wiggled under the edge of the short table until her feet were down on the sunken floor. She giggled when Brian struggled to follow suit.

"My legs are bigger than yours," he said. After a few seconds, he managed to fold himself into the small space and get comfortable.

The menu was just the right size to hide her smile.

A minute later, Alex and Brian listened while their server listed the specials and his personal recommendations and then disappeared to give them time to decide while he got their drinks.

"See?" Brian said. "No one is going to pay any attention to me when I'm with you."

One of the reasons she had hesitated to agree to a date was because she feared Blaze might make an appearance. He did every time they were in public. Why should this be any different? But there wasn't a trace of Blaze. Just Brian and his seemingly never-ending string of compliments. It was unsettling for a completely different reason.

When they were alone again after ordering Alex said, "Why are you so quiet?"

"I'm nervous."

"Why?"

"This is our first date. What if I say the wrong thing and you don't return my calls?" A hint of a smile played at the edge of his mouth. "A lot is riding on this."

"First dates aren't that bad. All we have to do is talk about work, hobbies, and family." She shook her head. "Scratch that. Let's not talk about my family."

"That leaves work and hobbies."

"So, Brian, what do you do for work?" she asked.

"I dress up and lie to people."

A laugh erupted out of her. It took a minute to compose herself. "Do you like it?"

"Most of the time. How about you? Have you always been a ranger?"

"For about ten years. Do you have any hobbies?"

"I like to cook. You?"

"Can't cook."

Brian sighed. "Well, we're out of first date material. Should we move on to more advanced conversation?" He waited for Alex to nod before going on. "When did you first realize you liked me?"

Chapter Nineteen

Alex narrowed her eyes. So far, she had been playing with him, pretending to get to know someone she'd been living with, but now she had a real answer for him. "When I saw you in town."

At that, he smiled. "It wasn't that first day? When I walked up to you and you were practically drooling?"

"I wasn't drooling, I was still mad at you for throwing a rock at that raven." Reaching across the table, she smacked his hand with her napkin. "And no, it was definitely in town. And then I wanted to kill you."

The smile disappeared from his face. "What? Why?"

"Because you were flirting with Jennifer. You gave her a flower and told her how pretty she was." Despite knowing the truth about Jennifer, and knowing how silly it was to hold onto a feeling not founded in reality, the jealousy still hurt.

"That flower was for you," he said.

"It was?"

He nodded. "I lost my nerve. I wanted to kiss you. In town that day."

"Too bad you didn't. We could've skipped to the good part." That time, she reached across the table and put her hands in his. "That first night at my house, did you drop your towel on purpose?"

223

The server brought their appetizer before Brian could answer, but the second he was gone Alex said, "Well?"

Brian pressed his lips together but didn't answer.

"You did, didn't you?"

"It was all part of my plan to woo you. When you're accustomed to getting your way using your one asset, you use it."

"And you thought it would work?" That night was when everything changed. The kiss in the car had done it though, not his trick with the towel. That was just fodder for her dreams.

"It did, didn't it?" he said with a laugh.

"How about you? When did you decide you liked me?"

"When you gripped my wrist and told me not to hurt that raven. You were so tough and intimidating. You scared the shit out of me."

Alex nibbled on edamame. "You like that about me?"

Brian nodded. "You're so strong and passionate and opinionated."

"In your face, Mom."

"I thought family was off the table."

"I couldn't resist. She always told me no one would ever want me if I didn't learn how to keep my mouth shut."

"Should we call and tell her she's wrong?" A sly smile turned up the corners of his mouth.

"Absolutely not," Alex warned.

"Fine." He lifted an eyebrow. "You didn't make it easy though. You kept rejecting me."

"You kept being an ass," she reminded him. "But

then you made it all better. And here we are."

"Here we are," he echoed. "How am I doing so far?"

"Good, but the night is young. Still plenty of time to ruin your chances of getting lucky. What next?"

"Tell me something no one else knows," Brian said.

Alex opened her mouth and to her surprise, her biggest secret spilled out. "When I lived in Texas about five years ago, my boyfriend asked me to marry him."

Brian frowned. "No one else knows that?"

Alex looked at her plate of edamame husks. "No. I broke up with him right after and moved to Oregon."

"You didn't tell your parents?" All the humor left his face.

"No. My mother would've loved him. That's why I ran away. He wanted me to quit my job and settle down. Start a family. There he was, the kind of man my mother told me to find, asking me to marry him. I couldn't do it. Relationships scare me. That's why this is perfect," she said motioning between them because she couldn't admit she wanted more with Brian. He had clearly defined what they had—a fun vacation. Not a relationship. There was no sense in wanting more because she wouldn't get it from him.

Silence surrounded them, and for a minute Alex regretted sharing that information with him. And then he spoke.

"I was high for most of the movie I filmed two years ago," he admitted.

Her mouth hung open. "Seriously?"

"At first it was for fun, but after a while, I couldn't function without it."

"No one noticed?"

"I got sloppy near the end of filming. The director said he would never work with me again. I may or may not have punched him at a Christmas party. That got the attention of my agent."

"Did you go to rehab?"

"Not at first. I thought it didn't matter where I woke up, or the fact that I couldn't remember driving somewhere. Ozzie brought me back."

"Your dog?"

"Ozzie wouldn't understand if I never came home."

"I'm glad you did it for him."

He squeezed her hand. "Me, too."

Everything she felt for him came to the surface. It was more than happiness. It was love. Not that it mattered because his vacation was coming to an end and that meant he would be going home. There was no room in his Hollywood life for her, so she took all her feelings and swallowed them down, keeping them locked up where they belonged.

When he cleared his throat, he interrupted her thoughts. "Tell me something else. Something that's maybe not so—"

"Depressing?" she finished. When he nodded, she went on. "I tried to steal a candy bar when I was in junior high, but couldn't follow through with it. I overcompensated by paying for it with a five dollar bill and telling the guy to keep my change."

Brian laughed. "When I was little, I loved peeing outside. In Kindergarten that didn't go over too well. My mom didn't think to warn me."

A laugh bubbled up out of Alex. "That must've

been an interesting call from the principal."

"It's one of my mom's favorite stories to share…at dinner parties."

"Oh, here's an obscure one. I love the sound of really sharp scissors opening and closing. When I was little, I used to steal my dad's best scissors so I could sit in my room and listen to the sound while snipping tiny pieces of paper." She laughed at the memory. "He always knew where to find them when they were missing."

Brian laughed, too. "Here's something most people don't know: I hate going to the gym."

"That must suck, considering your occupation. As Maggie said, you're paid to look good."

"You two talk about me, huh?" he asked as he lifted an eyebrow.

"Of course we do."

If she wasn't already smitten, his dazzling smile would've done her in. "Anything you want to share?"

She shrugged. "The usual. How good of a cook you are, how much Koko loves you. That sort of thing." The truth was Maggie knew almost every detail of their relationship, but Brian didn't need to know that.

Their conversation lulled when their meals came out. Their server filled their drinks and then disappeared.

They shared food and continued talking about everything and anything for the next hour. Most of the time passed with Brian talking about the places he had visited. Alex hadn't been out of the country, so his stories captivated her.

"This is, by far, the best first date I've ever been on," Alex said.

"I'm glad you gave me a chance."

When the server came with the check, Brian put his finger up, indicating he should wait while Brian opened his wallet. He slid two large bills into the black folder with their check and said, "Keep the change, Mark."

"Thank you, sir. I hope you have a wonderful night," he replied before disappearing one final time.

"How did you know his name?" Alex said.

"He said it earlier when he told us the specials. I waited tables when I was in college. It always made my night when someone called me by name." He smiled. "A big tip didn't hurt either, so I always make a point to do both."

Just what she needed, another reason to love him. "Thank you for taking me out. It was perfect."

"Thank you for letting me."

She took his arm and he led her to the car, unlocking the passenger door for her and guiding her into her seat. "Thank you, kind sir."

"My lady," he replied, kissing her hand before letting it go.

****

Brian sat in the driver's seat and started the car. Once he pulled onto the highway headed to Twisted Juniper, Alex grabbed his hand and laced her fingers through his.

"What a great night," she said, her voice sleepy. She leaned against the headrest and closed her eyes.

"You make every night great."

A smile spread across her face, but she didn't respond.

During dinner, her revelation about her marriage proposal had shaken him. What did that mean for him?

The only way to find out was to ask. "Do you think your mom would like me?"

"You're kidding, right? Do you remember how excited she got when she recognized you during our video chat?" Wiggling her shoulders deeper into the seat, she yawned and then said, "She would love you."

That sealed the deal. Didn't it?

While he drove, her breathing slowed and evened out and then her grip on his hand loosened.

"Does that mean you're going to run away from me?" That was the question he really wanted to ask, but the only reason he asked it now was because he knew she wouldn't respond. "I have a better idea. I'm leaving the day after tomorrow. You should come with me." As the fantasy played through his mind, he smiled. Alex would run after the plane and demand to get on. And then he would tell her he loved her and she would move to California because he would ask her to marry him. Only that time, she would say yes.

Except she wouldn't. He knew that now. If her long term boyfriend in Texas couldn't convince her, what made him think he could? What did he have to offer? A tiny knife twisted in his heart.

When they finally got back, he parked in front of her house, took her keys out of her purse, and unlocked the front door and greeted Koko. "Your mom is asleep. Stay here."

Koko got onto the back of the couch and watched through the window as Brian lifted Alex out of the passenger seat. Alex wrapped her arms around him, nestled against his chest, and mumbled in her sleep.

"Shh, it's okay, we're home."

"Home," she echoed in her sleepy voice when he

closed the front door behind them. "That sounds nice when you say it."

He put her down gently on her bed. "I need to move the car."

Koko returned to her perch by the window while Brian moved the car, and then followed him to bed. Alex had tried to undress but hadn't gotten very far. One shoe still clung to her foot and she had only managed to get the zipper halfway down on her dress, making the material sag against her shoulders.

"Help, please," she mumbled against the pillow with her hand still wedged behind her back where she fumbled with the zipper.

Brian chuckled and pushed her hand out of the way. When he got the zipper down, he tugged while she lifted. They were the perfect team. Lying face down, she didn't stir while he undressed, but when he joined her in bed, she wiggled toward him.

"Sorry, I'm so sleepy. No getting lucky tonight," she murmured as she wrapped her arm and leg around him.

"Good night," he said. It wasn't that he didn't want her. He did, but holding her was just as good. Maybe better. In the moments before sleep and again before waking, she was unguarded and vulnerable. It made his heart ache to think he wouldn't get to experience it again, so he stayed awake as long as possible.

****

In the morning, Alex rolled onto her back, covered her face with a pillow, and groaned. "How is it Sunday already?" Two whole days of domestic bliss were coming to an end.

"I don't know," Brian answered. "The wrap party

is tonight."

She peeked at him to see how he felt about that, but his face was unreadable.

"Is everyone going to be there?" he asked.

"Lynn offered to stay behind. We can't all be gone at once."

"You're coming, right?"

"Well, not at the moment, but..." she trailed off and smiled at him.

"I can fix that," he said.

And he spent the next half hour making that happen.

Alex marked the occasion in her brain—the last time they would have morning sex. The list grew throughout the day. The last time she checked in with Steve. The last time she anxiously watched a cameraman hug a cliff to get the best shot. And the last time the crew gathered on the set.

A list of firsts grew as well.

It was the first time in a while she dreaded the end of the day. When work was done, Brian would have to leave. Watching him pack was also a first. She didn't like either.

"Are you sure you have to go?" she asked. "No one would notice if we didn't show up, would they?"

Brian laughed. "Pretty sure everyone would notice if I wasn't there. Especially Nate."

Instead of crying, she went into the kitchen and grabbed the apron hanging on the side of her fridge. With any luck, it would remind him of the week they spent together. After folding it neatly, she tucked it into his packed bag. He was leaving. Really leaving.

As if he could read her mind, he said, "We still

have tonight." And then he caressed her cheek and kissed her sweetly before stuffing his toothbrush into his duffle bag. "I need to go. Travis wants to grab a few drinks before the party."

"I'll see you there," she promised, kissing him again. It wasn't goodbye. Not yet.

Koko's tail swished against the floor when he bent down to hug her. Over the past few days, he and Koko had spent a lot of time together and it showed.

It took twenty minutes for her to stop crying and another hour before she could consider facing a crowd.

Maggie and Henry had gone into town with Jim in the afternoon to prepare for the party. Everyone would be there. Even though she wanted to, she couldn't stay home and wallow. A promise was a promise.

By the time she arrived at Dembi Brewing, the party was well underway. Jim had arranged a few servers to come and help, but he buzzed around the room delivering beers and appetizers. Maggie stood near the bar with Henry tucked in the sling wrapped around her torso, rocking back and forth and chatting with Neal. She waved across the room, beckoning Alex to join them.

"How's it going?" Alex asked as she joined their conversation.

"Good," Maggie answered. "I think everyone is here." The *everyone* she was referring to was Blaze, who was sitting with the stunt team, laughing loudly and taking pictures in the Dembi Brewing T-shirt Jim had given him, which would be featured in dozens of selfies and most likely boost the popularity of the local pub.

Alex nodded. "How are you, Neal?"

"Not as busy as you, but I've been good."

The heat of a blush crept up her neck.

"I meant work," he said, but he followed her gaze to the loudest table in the room. Looking from Maggie to Alex he whispered, "Does she know, too?"

"Wait, Neal knows?" Maggie said.

Alex hushed them both. "You're the only ones. Please keep your voices down."

Neal pressed his lips together. "I thought everything went well," he said, changing the subject. "You're a good boss."

The blush spread. "I survived," she said. "I'm anxious to hear what Mr. Reid thinks." Worry creased her forehead as she glanced at the director, who was deep in discussion with Steve. Mr. Reid only seemed to have one emotion—serious.

"I'm sure it'll be fine," Maggie said.

As the night wore on and the beer started to work, Alex relaxed. Just like on the set, she avoided Blaze. Making her way around the room, she shared stories and laughed with the crewmembers she'd come to know.

Steve waved at her, signaling her to join him. "Alex."

"Are you having fun?"

"I am. Have you given any more thought to my offer?" he asked, his words slurring together a little.

With everything else going on, his offer was more than she could process. Accepting would mean moving *and* being in charge full time. "I'm not really comfortable being in a managerial position," she admitted.

He blew air out loudly. "You're a natural. You're

the only person I would trust with the job. Will you think about it? Please?"

"I, um…" The hem of her brown shirt had a loose thread she couldn't resist, a nervous habit she couldn't break.

"As a favor, to your friend?" he added, pointing to himself with both of his thumbs.

"I'll think about it."

A little later, Mr. Reid sat alone, so she took the opportunity to ask him the question she needed and dreaded hearing the answer to.

"Hi, Mr. Reid," she said, approaching him.

"I've been hoping to speak with you tonight." The somber lines around his mouth became more visible.

Oh shit. She held her breath and braced herself.

"I wanted to express my gratitude for everything you've done to make filming this movie a success."

Alex blinked.

"Thank you for taking our safety concerns so seriously and educating the crew. I look forward to working with you again."

"Thank you, sir," she said once her brain started working again. "Thank you so much. That means a lot."

"I'll have my people handle things with the governor's office."

Two weeks of worry erased with one sentence. "Thank you, sir. Thank you," she repeated, and then, to her horror, she bowed. Mortified, she gave him a tight smile and then darted for the hallway leading to the bathrooms. Leaning against the wall, she closed her eyes.

"What did he say?" Brian asked.

A squeak of surprise escaped her lips and then she

glared at him. "You need to wear a bell."

He smiled. "Mr. Reid. What happened?"

"I bowed for some reason. I'm so stupid. But he said he appreciated me and he would make sure his people would handle things with the governor's office." For a moment, she forgot where they were, and she grinned and then threw her arms around his neck.

"I told you there was nothing to worry about. You're amazing. Everyone can see that," he said, his mouth inches from hers.

When she kissed him, she let her worries slip away and focused on the tingling feeling spreading through her body as his hands spread across her ass.

Their moment of bliss didn't last long.

Something flashed and then Nate said, "Holy shit." The bathroom door closed behind him. "This explains everything."

Brian stalked toward him. "Hand it over, Nate."

"Or what?" Nate asked, trying to stand his ground as Brian pushed him into the door. "Why didn't you just tell me you were slumming it?"

"Fuck you." Brian jabbed Nate in his chest.

"No, fuck *you*." Nate smiled and looked down at his phone.

Brian grabbed it and threw it against the far wall. Pieces of plastic and glass rained down, clattering onto the floor.

"Asshole," Nate shouted before grabbing the mangled remains and storming off.

"What just happened?" Alex asked, stunned.

"He's looking to get his ass kicked, that's what. He doesn't know me," he said with disdain.

Nate had looked at her like she was pathetic, and

Brian had stood up for her. It made her heart race. "We should probably get back to the party before someone else notices us."

"Can I see you later? I'm in room 212; it's right by the stairs."

Someone's voice traveled down the hall.

"Please? It's our last night together."

"Yes, I'll be there." Before they got caught again, she kissed him quickly and then pushed him toward the men's room before joining the party.

Eventually, the party wrapped up and Alex stayed behind to help Jim clean up long after everyone else left.

"Will you keep Koko tonight? Maybe tomorrow, too?" Alex asked Maggie as she stacked chairs on tables. Without a clue about Brian's travel plans, she had arranged to take Monday off.

"Of course," she said, smiling. "You should go. We'll take care of the rest."

"Thanks," Alex said, jogging toward the exit.

Chapter Twenty

The wrap party moved from the brewery to the hotel. No one wanted the night to end, least of all, Brian. With one last glance at Alex, Travis dragged him outside to the waiting vans, but she didn't look at him. When she showed up, he would get to see her again. What if she didn't show up? It wasn't a good idea to think about that. After all, she had promised.

Back at the hotel, several rooms on the second floor were open. People flowed in and out, moving from one conversation to another. Brian led Travis into the room across from Nate's, which was just a few doors down from his own. He had to keep an eye on his door.

Someone thrust a beer into his hand and clinked against his bottle. "Cheers."

"Cheers," he echoed but didn't drink because he'd had enough. Enough noise, enough partying, enough of everything. All he wanted was Alex.

From the doorway, he watched the hall and nodded and laughed along with the rowdy banter. It seemed to never end and his cheeks hurt from holding a fake smile in place.

Nate mouthed the word *asshole* as he walked by with two women.

Brian leaned against the doorjamb, determined not to beat the shit out of him. Bullies like Nate would lose interest if he didn't react, so that's what he did. Standing there and smiling at him worked like a charm. Nate skulked into the room after flipping him off.

After waiting for almost an hour, the door to the stairs opened. A flash of silky brown hair made his heart pound.

"Hey, hold this, will you?" he said to Travis.

Travis nodded but didn't pay much attention to him.

Brian walked out of the room and down the hall. He had one night to show Alex exactly how he felt about her.

****

Alex kept her head down when she entered the lobby, passed the elevators, and followed the signs that read, *IN CASE OF FIRE USE STAIRS*.

That's what she wanted. The stairs.

The heavy door clicked behind her and the concrete walls echoed every breath and footfall. Each noise layering on top of the other until it sounded like an army surrounded her. When she stopped and held her breath, the noise stopped with her. Only a few more steps and she would be on the second floor. Brian's floor.

Once she opened the door, all she could see was people roaming the corridor, talking loudly as they crossed from one room to another. The textured walls and plush carpet partially muffled the noisy conversations spilling into the hall. Wait. Was that why he invited her, so she could go to a party with him?

No. That couldn't be it. Blaze probably loved a good party, but not Brian. And that's who had invited her. After taking a deep breath and hiding behind her hair, she made her way toward room 212. Keeping her back to the gathering down the hall, she knocked softly. No one answered. "Brian?" she whispered as she knocked again.

"Yes?" he answered right behind her.

When her initial shock subsided, she relaxed into his arms, which he wound around her as he inserted his keycard into the slot. The light flashed green and beeped twice and then they were inside the room. "You scared me," she said.

Instead of answering, he kissed the side of her neck and cupped her breasts.

"Are you going back to the party?" she asked, hoping he wasn't.

"No," he said against her skin. "I was waiting for you."

"Oh. It's just us?" she clarified.

"Just us," he repeated.

For one last night. With the tension gone from her body, she could focus on his mouth. Unlike every moment before, he took his time, moving slowly over every inch of her exposed skin. When she turned in his hands to face him, his mouth latched onto hers, sucking on her lips and grazing them with his teeth.

In an attempt to speed things up, she tugged at the hem of his shirt, but he wasn't having it. Winding his fingers through hers, he stilled her movements.

"We have all night. There's no rush," he said, kissing her again.

Resigned to let him take the lead, she sighed when he pushed her against the wall and kissed his way from her mouth to the opening in her brown button-up shirt. He slid the top button out of position and kissed her, and then the second, third, fourth, and fifth, his tongue and lips moving languidly across the top of her breasts. Anticipation built and her pulse quickened. She knew the pleasure waiting for her and postponing it drove her insane.

Just as slowly, he pushed her shirt off her shoulders and then kissed the length of her arms. Following her ribs to her spine, he slid his fingers across her skin where they teamed up to unhook her bra. When the material relaxed against her body, he pulled it off and caressed her breasts until her nipples hardened. His mouth joined a moment later, rolling the rigid buds with his talented tongue.

Arching her body toward him, she moaned and leaned her head against the wall. The things he was doing with his mouth were almost enough to do her in, and then he stroked her through her pants. When she came, her legs wobbled and her breathing became erratic.

Next, he fell to his knees and set to work on the button holding her pants closed, kissing along her waistband, and peeling her pants off. Only stopping to untie her hiking shoes, he lifted her leg over his shoulder. She dug her fingers into his hair and held onto him.

The remnants of her first orgasm still lingered as he kissed her slit. When his warm, wet tongue slid across her slick folds, another vibration shot through her body. Acutely aware of the presence of people in the room next to them, she held her breath and tried to remain silent. But when he started alternately thrusting his tongue inside her and flicking her clit, she moaned.

Cupping her ass and holding her in place, he

moved his tongue and lips, bringing her to the brink again. A strangled cry forced its way out of her closed mouth as she fell down the chasm of orgasmic ecstasy. Once her breathing evened out, he carried her to the bed.

He stood between her legs and lifted the hem of his T-shirt, exposing his rippling muscles. In slow, even movements, he kicked his shoes off and then unbuttoned and unzipped his jeans. It was impossible to look away. The hollow just below his defined hipbone came into view as he tugged his pants off his ass. The material of his boxer briefs was stretched to the limit and soon joined the pile of clothes on the floor as he finished undressing, freeing his hard-on and revealing his powerful legs. Her breath caught in her throat.

And then he started touching himself, his large hand encircling his cock, moving from the base to the tip, collecting the pre-cum and coating his length with it. Alex's hips lifted each time the head of his dick appeared. She could almost feel him pushing inside her. Almost.

"Please," she begged, unable to wait any longer as the wanting drove her crazy.

"What?" he asked, giving her a cocky smile and caressing the inside of her thigh with his free hand. The next time he thrust into his hand, he pushed a finger between her folds in the same unhurried rhythm he used to pleasure himself.

"Yes," she said between gasps for air. Before she could come again, he pulled away from her, retrieved a condom, and took his sweet time putting it on.

"Please, more," she begged.

"Tell me what you want," he said, dick in hand.

"You. I want you." More than anything. More than ever before. Wanting him consumed her.

He kneeled on the bed between her legs, nudging them farther apart, positioning the head of his dick against her opening. "I want you, too," he said before pushing inside.

Alex pulled a pillow over her face, muffling the moan he forced out of her. Brian pulled it out of her hands and hovered over her.

"They'll hear us," she whispered, trying to concentrate on speaking while he thrust into her again.

"Let them. I want to hear you come," he said as he put his hand between their bodies and rubbed her clit.

Fighting the desire to vocalize her pleasure was a battle she would lose. "I can't. We already got caught once tonight."

As a solution, he put his mouth over hers, swallowing her words and her next moan. They separated to breathe, but then their lips locked again. Each cry spurred him on, making him slam into her harder and faster. The veins in her neck bulged when she came, her body arching while his hips vibrated and his cock swelled inside her.

Panting and slick with sweat, they held each other until breathing became easier. When he pulled out of her, her body trembled and so did his. After a quick trip to the bathroom, he returned to the bed and spooned her. The heat of his breath caressed the nape of her neck. "I'm going to miss you," he murmured against her skin.

She didn't respond because she couldn't. Not without crying, so she snuggled against his arm and closed her eyes.

****

Alex jerked awake at the sound of banging. The sun hadn't come up yet. What time was it? Six.

"Wake up," someone shouted from the other side of the door.

Brian groaned and tightened his grip around Alex's waist.

Bang, bang, bang.

"Go away," Brian shouted.

"Wake up, asshole."

"Fuck off, Nate," Brian replied, finally sitting up.

Nate mumbled something and then his footsteps retreated.

"What time are you flying out?" she asked.

"We need to be at the plane by seven." Falling back into bed, he groaned. "Why is it morning already?"

Alex rubbed the sleep from her eyes and made a quick trip to the bathroom to splash water on her face. "I should go," she said, picking up her clothes from the floor and trying to get dressed. It wasn't easy because her limbs hadn't woken fully.

"You should come back to bed," he said, tugging on her waistband and dragging her toward him.

It didn't take much to pull away from him. Enough was enough. It was time to say goodbye. "I shouldn't have stayed. You need to go." She focused on her shirt, one button after another.

"But—" he whined.

"You're going to be late if you don't get your lazy ass out of bed." After slipping her feet into her shoes, she bent over him in bed. With her face buried in the crook of his neck, she inhaled deeply, savoring the scent of his skin still tinged with sleep. Allowing herself one final kiss on his cheek, she whispered, "I have to go."

When she pulled away, he tried to hold her again. She couldn't make him late.

The words goodbye didn't come. It wasn't really goodbye, was it? All the times he had invited her to come see him had to mean something. That was the only thing that kept her moving. Knowing she would see him again. When she got home, she would find out how much it would cost to fly to California.

"Alexis," he called after her.

But it was too late; she was already at the door, opening it to the bustle of crewmembers filling the hallway with luggage. Hiding behind a curtain of hair, she ran for the stairway and pushed the heavy door open. Alone, she slumped onto the stairs and numbly tied her shoes. Once she reached the main floor, she filed outside with a crowd of people and then headed toward her car, fumbling with her keys before getting inside.

But she couldn't leave. Not yet. She had to see him one last time. From where she was parked, she got a glimpse of everyone who exited the lobby heading toward the Red Rock Rental vans that lined the front curb. One by one, the vans pulled away filled with passengers, just not the one she wanted to see.

Brian's voice carried out into the still morning air even through her closed windows. And then she saw him, arguing with Nate.

"Why do you care who I fuck?" Blaze came to the surface.

"It's my job," Nate shouted. "Why? Why her?"

Alex slumped down in her seat while Nate and Blaze approached the rental car parked close to her. The trunk slammed shut.

"Because it was convenient. Is that what you want to hear? That I have needs, and she was willing? That I wanted—" The rest got cut off as he got into the rental, followed immediately by Nate.

His words tore into her heart. Tears spilled down her cheeks as she watched the white car pull away, taking with it her hopes and dreams.

On the way back to Twisted Juniper, she had to pull over, unable to see through the tears. She had believed it all: every smile, every line, and every lie. But his final words erased everything. Convenient. That's all it was. He was slumming with her, just like Nate had said.

The sun finally arrived and illuminated her pathetic life. It should be raining. The sky should reflect how she felt, but it didn't. Bright puffy clouds dotted the horizon mocking her pain.

And it only got worse from there.

Chapter Twenty-One

"Just let it go," Brian shouted, his voice deafening inside the cramped car. They were almost to the airport. All he had to do was stay calm for a few more minutes. The barrage of questions from Nate over the last half hour had pushed him to his breaking point.

"It's not that easy," Nate replied.

"Yes, it is. What Alex and I have isn't anyone's business but ours."

Nate chuckled. "It's clear you didn't think this through, so let me explain it to you: a ranger offered sexual favors so she could get a raise."

Heat licked at Brian's neck. "That's not how it was."

"Wasn't it? Everyone knew she needed you on her side. What better way? She took advantage of you. Can't you see that?"

"That's not how it was," he repeated and tightened his hands into fists.

"Beyond that, your reputation is at stake. Everyone will question your motivation since they know hers." Nate pulled into the parking lot at the tiny airport and turned the car off.

"No one knows. I haven't seen a single camera this entire time."

A smug smile slid onto Nate's face. "Except mine," he said and then got out of the car.

Brian followed. "What does that mean?" Most of the cast and crew stood nearby waiting to board the plane that waited at the end of the runway. The private jet that would take him home hadn't arrived yet. This was the part where Alex showed up in his fantasy, running toward him and flying away with him so they wouldn't have to say goodbye, but she didn't come.

Nate's hand stilled as he pulled his bag out of the trunk. "Consider it payback for being such an asshole."

"What did you do?"

Nate turned and faced Brian. "I showed the world who you really are. A pathetic man being led around by his dick by a manipulative, basic bitch. Your fans are going to be so disappointed when they see the picture."

Brian could take insults all day long, but he couldn't listen to Nate question and insult Alex for a second more. He pulled his fist back and aimed at Nate's mouth. Pain shot through his hand and up his arm as he made contact. Nate cried out and blood gushed out of his nose. "You're a piece of shit," Brian spat.

Someone in the gathering crowd gasped. Brian looked away for only a second, but it was a second too long. Nate hit him hard on his temple. Stars shot across his vision for a few seconds and then he focused enough to retaliate. Just as Nate pulled back for another punch, Brian dodged and grazed the side of Nate's ribs followed by an uppercut that made Nate's teeth clatter.

Before Brian could land another blow, someone pulled him away. He yanked out of the hold and turned to face whoever was restraining him.

"What's going on?" Travis asked.

"I need to warn her," he replied as he pulled his

phone out of his pocket, but before he could unlock it to text Alex, Nate knocked it out of his hand and sent it falling toward the asphalt.

"There." Nate spat blood onto the ruined phone and then stomped on the screen with the heel of his shoe. "We're even."

Brian lunged at him, but Travis held him back again.

"It's not worth it. *He's* not worth it," Travis said behind him. "Let it go."

Rage coursed through his veins, making his heart hammer while he dug his fingers into the palms of his clenched fists.

"Walk with me," Travis said.

Brian exhaled and nodded.

"Don't let him get to you. That's what he wants." Travis looked over his shoulder.

"I can't sit with him for two hours. I can't do it."

Travis patted his back. "Take my flight and I'll take yours. I'll make sure he doesn't get out of line."

"Thanks, man. I owe you one." Brian stretched his neck from side to side, trying to get the ringing in his ear to stop. His pulse pounded against the corner of his eye and his vision had already started to blur.

"Don't worry about it. I knew you didn't get along, but I had no idea it was this bad. Hang on a sec." Travis jogged over to the rental car, retrieved Brian's bag, and returned.

A group of women surrounded Nate and were making a big fuss over his bloody nose. "Oh, you poor thing," one of them said as she looked at Brian with contempt.

Brian scoffed. "Poor thing? He's lucky to be

standing." Inside the airport, he and Travis sorted out their tickets before boarding began. The same man stood behind the counter, moving just as slowly as he had the night Brian arrived.

Travis shook Brian's hand as they stood in line together. "I'll keep an eye on Nate."

"Have a few drinks. That helps," Brian called over his shoulder as he passed through the security screening area. Two police officers were working, tripling the staff at the airport.

"Will do," Travis replied.

Brian followed the stream of people and waited to board the crowded aircraft. The aisle was narrow and the plane vibrated under his feet, but it was better than sitting next to Nate. Once he got into his seat, he buckled up, leaned his head back, and closed his eyes. He couldn't get home fast enough.

****

The first thing Brian did after getting off the plane was take a cab to the daycare where Ozzie waited for him. The woman behind the desk told him what his dog had been doing for the past two weeks, much of which was a recap from what he already knew from calling and watching the webcam.

"He made so many new friends," she said. "We went to the park every day. He's such a good boy."

Brian nodded and smiled and then Ozzie rushed out to see him and nothing else mattered. After a few slobbery kisses, Ozzie circled Brian's body and snuffled every inch of his clothes. They were, in fact, the same clothes he'd worn when he left Alex's house. "I cheated on you," Brian admitted. "You'd love her though. Maybe you'll get to meet her one day, and her mom."

When they got home, Brian couldn't imagine doing anything else but unpacking and relaxing with his dog. Even though he had a thousand things to do, nothing was more important than decompressing. Checking in with his parents would have to wait until he got a new phone, he just hoped they would understand. Just thinking about his fight with Nate made him furious. He needed a break from anger.

The next morning, he tried to get a new phone, but to his surprise, someone else had already gotten one under his account.

"I'm sorry, sir, but that number has already been activated."

Brian frowned and then he realized his mistake. How could he have been stupid enough to leave his phone on the ground at the airport? Anyone could've picked it up.

"May I borrow your phone for a minute?" he asked, trying to remain calm.

The salesman nodded and handed over a cordless office phone. Brian dialed his number and waited, but it went to voicemail. Unrelenting, he dialed again and again and finally, someone answered.

"What?" the voice snapped.

Brian recognized it immediately. "Nate?"

"Who's this?"

"Blaze," he ground out. "You damn well know who this is. What the fuck are you doing with my phone?"

"You left it behind and I'm cleaning up after you, as per usual. That's what Alan hired me to do. I'm also supposed to remind you we have a meeting with him on

Friday."

"I need my phone. You had no right to replace it."

"I have every right. You shouldn't have had it. You stole it from me, remember?"

Brian clenched his jaw. "Give it to me."

Nate whistled. "There are some great pics on here. Your girlfriend looks pretty good when she makes an effort."

"Fuck you," he spat. Remaining civil wasn't an option. Not when Nate insulted Alex.

"Have it your way," Nate replied before disconnecting.

The phone creaked in Brian's hand as he squeezed the plastic a little too tight.

"Everything okay, sir?" the salesman asked from a safe distance.

"No. I need a new phone. Now."

The salesman nodded and got to work. By the time Brian got home, his stomach churned and his back ached. Because he didn't have her number memorized, he had no way to get in touch with Alex directly and it was killing him. The number at the park was busy, no matter how many times he tried calling.

With his new, empty phone in hand, he grabbed Ozzie's leash and started on a run. Ozzie's tongue lolled out of his mouth as he ran by Brian's side, which made Brian laugh and he needed to be in a good mood if he was going to write a letter of recommendation for Twisted Juniper. Mr. Reid had asked him to write one at the wrap party and he had jumped at the opportunity. He and Travis were meeting that afternoon to work on it together before faxing it to Mr. Reid's office. Anything to help Alex. But in that moment, he needed to run. He could deal with the world later.

****

Alex knew she would eventually have to explain to her best friend she had been an idiot. But not yet. How could she admit she had given everything to someone who didn't care? Keeping his words bound up inside her where they couldn't hurt her again, she threw herself into her work and pretended there wasn't a hole in her heart.

Brian didn't call. Not that she would've answered.

On Tuesday, Mr. Howard called, and she had to talk to him about the filming and agree it had been a huge success.

"Good work," he boomed.

"Thank you, sir," she said, trying to muster some enthusiasm.

"Besides the little hiccup near the beginning, I would consider this a slam dunk," he added. "We received a donation and *two* letters of praise."

"Great." And it was. Everyone would get a raise which meant she should be happy, but she wasn't. Celebrating was the last thing on her mind.

The next day, a picture circulated the Internet of Blaze kissing an unidentified ranger, her Twisted Juniper patch visible on her shoulder. Wild speculation filled social media, and as much as Alex wanted to stop reading about it, she couldn't.

And then it happened. Another picture surfaced. The one Brian had taken of them before their date. That night had been real, hadn't it? But the hashtag under the picture said it all: *#anothernotchinmybelt*.

Within the day, someone identified her.

Like a kick to the gut, her brother texted her,

asking if it really was her with Blaze and how she had managed to trick him into kissing her. Almost immediately, her mom tried to video chat, so she turned her phone off and stashed it in her desk drawer. No good would come from answering any of the calls or reading any further texts.

By Friday, the pictures made the front page of the gossip magazines displayed in every store in Dembi:

OO LA LA BLAZE JOHNSON GETS A TASTE OF
LOCAL CUISINE
WHAT DOES PARK RANGER ALEXIS MITCHELL
HAVE TO OFFER?

Each headline was worse than the last, implying she wasn't worthy of someone like him. Of course, she wasn't and everyone knew it.

****

On Friday, Brian pushed into Alan's office, prepared to do battle with Nate. Not with his fists, but with his words. If he lost his temper, he didn't stand a chance, so his strategy was to get Nate to flip out first. Unfortunately, Nate had arrived early, giving him the advantage.

"Nate has been telling me about your trip," Alan said as he leaned back into his plush leather chair and laced his hands behind his head.

"Oh?" Brian replied as he took a seat next to Nate across from Alan.

Nate smirked. A hint of double black eyes still remained, the same ugly yellow as Brian's eyebrow. "I was just telling him about the incident at the airport."

"The part where you confessed to leaking a picture that would expose me and the staff at the park?"

"No, the part where you punched me in the face."

Nate bristled and sat forward in his chair. "There are witnesses."

"I'm aware."

"It's true?" Alan interjected.

"Yes," Brian admitted. "I'm actually glad we're all here. Sir, I'm afraid Nate isn't a good fit. His behavior on this trip was dangerous."

"Dangerous?" Nate shouted.

"Drinking, sleeping around, and interfering with my work schedule." Brian shook his head. "You were supposed to be my assistant, not use me for your personal gain. Not to mention when you got drunk and hit me the first time." He looked at Alan and ignored Nate. "I had to spend an extra twenty minutes in makeup the next morning to cover it up."

"You lied to me. You took the keys," Nate protested.

"To the car I rented." Brian went on, "He also broke my phone and then replaced it without my permission or knowledge. He's been using it all week."

"But... But I..." Nate stammered.

"I've heard enough." Alan silenced them both. "I've already spoken with Mr. Reid and Mr. Frederick. Blaze, they were both pleased with your work and said you never showed up late or missed a day."

"That's not true, Mr. Reid—" Nate said.

Alan glared at him. "Are you calling Mr. Reid a liar?"

Nate shrank in his chair.

But it was true. The director had lied for him, but why? Had he known how much was riding on his evaluation or had Brian made up for his tardiness with hard work?

"It might be time for me to trust you again," Alan said to Brian. "Do I have your word you will continue to meet with your addiction support group?"

"Yes, sir," Brian answered without hesitation. He was damn lucky to have Alan as an agent, and he wasn't about to jeopardize their work relationship again.

Alan stood and offered his hand to Brian. Brian got up and shook it.

"Do you have his phone?" Alan asked Nate.

"Yes," Nate grumbled as he pulled it out of his pocket. It was identical to the one he had broken at the airport.

"Your services are no longer required," Alan stated as he took the phone from him. "Please leave before I have you escorted from the building."

Nate nodded and stormed out of the office without another word.

After being fired by Alan's agency, Nate wouldn't be able to get a decent job anywhere in Hollywood. Knowing that made it easier for Brian to be silent. "Thank you, sir. I won't let you down."

"You better not. Have a look at this." Alan handed Brian a stack of papers. "It's a script for a new movie I think you'll like. Casting thinks you'll be a perfect fit."

Brian nodded and took the papers from him but kept his eyes on his phone.

"Go on, I have work to do." Alan shooed him toward the door.

"My phone, sir," Brian said. Waiting was torturous.

"I'll be in touch." Alan dropped the phone into Brian's hand and opened the door.

Brian stepped out into the hall, pushed past a group

of people, and turned his phone on. Thankfully, Nate hadn't bothered to set up a lock screen.

He texted Alex.

Hey. Nate had my phone so I couldn't text. I tried to warn you about the picture he took. I'm sure you've seen it by now. I've been hiding out and hope you have, too.

He got fired if that's any consolation. I promise I'll make it up to you.

Plans to fly her to California formed in his head, making him smile. The screen on his phone remained unchanged, so he texted her again because he couldn't wait for her response.

I miss you.

Because she was probably busy with work, he would have to wait until the end of the day. As he walked to the stairs, he scrolled through his notifications and found hundreds of replies to a picture he had posted on Wednesday. Scratch that, it was a picture *Nate* had posted. Anger built inside him as he opened the app and found the picture everyone had been commenting on—he and Alex on their way to their date. When he read the hashtag Nate had typed below it, he stifled a shout. In a blind rage, he stumbled down the stairs and stormed out of the building.

Deleting the picture from his account would only get him so far. Another picture meant another explanation and another apology. Alex would understand, wouldn't she? All he had to do was tell her Nate had his phone and posted the picture. It would all blow over soon enough and then they could be together again.

Chapter Twenty-Two

Alex stayed out of town and avoided everyone in the park. It was easier that way; to retreat into her own world where no one could hurt her.

A tornado of media coverage hit and lasted for a week with reporters flocking to Twisted Juniper like ravenous migratory birds. Mr. Howard was thrilled at the increased traffic and didn't seem to care why they were there. All he cared about were the letters and the donation. Alex's personal life didn't appear to matter to him one bit.

The phone in her office rang off the hook, so she unplugged it and let her voicemail deal with them. At the end of each day, she listened to the messages if the caller bothered to leave one.

All the rangers at the park pitched in to keep her out of sight during the chaos, for which she was eternally grateful. There was plenty of work outside to keep her busy, so it was easy to hide. Working long days made the nights shorter, anything to delay going home. Everything there reminded her of Brian, which meant she spent most nights crying. It didn't matter that she knew the truth, she still missed him. Missed his sweetness, even if it had been a lie. Koko missed him, too. For two weeks, Koko looked past Alex whenever she came home, obviously expecting him to be right behind her.

Eventually, the story lost its hold on the public so the reporters left. The calls slowed to a trickle, giving Alex room to breathe again. At the end of another long day, she listened to a voicemail from Steve on her work phone. "Hey, Alex, it's Steve Frederick. I hope you've considered what we talked about because we're gearing up for our wildlife survey and getting you out here to discuss your vision for the future is the first step to making our dream into a reality. You said you'd consider it, so call me, okay?"

Alex sighed and deleted the message. Worrying about his job offer was just another thing weighing her down. That night, when she finally dragged her sorry ass home, Maggie paced the length of the driveway between their houses with Henry strapped securely to her body in his wrap. Up until that point, Alex had managed to avoid any conversation with her best friend.

A shadow darkened Maggie's normally cheery face. "I'm worried about you, Alex. Have you been sleeping?"

Alex shook her head. "I fucked everything up."

"No, you didn't. You did a wonderful job, and we're all going to get raises."

"I mean in my personal life. I knew I shouldn't have gotten attached to him. I knew it wouldn't work out, but it happened anyway."

Maggie's mouth fell open. "Are you in love with him?"

Alex squeezed her eyes shut and nodded. "What am I supposed to do? Everything here reminds me of him. It's killing me."

Maggie frowned. "Time heals all wounds."

"It's been almost three weeks. It's not getting

better. I want to move on, but I can't."

"You need to find happiness. That's all," Maggie said. "You're not happy here anymore."

"I was…until *Blaze* ruined everything." Alex slumped against her house.

"There's a whole world out there. I'm sure you'll find something that will make you happy." Maggie smiled. "You have a ton of experience. You're hard working. You're—"

"Stupid. Unprofessional. A failure," Alex said.

"You're not a failure. All you ever focus on is work." Maggie paused. "Except when he was here."

Alex looked up. "Yeah, and we all know how that turned out. Literally. The whole world knows who I am now."

"You need a new adventure."

"A new adventure?" Alex's heart thumped against her chest harder. Did Maggie know about Steve's offer?

Maggie clicked her tongue. "You need a fresh start so you can really move on."

"I don't want to let go. My memories of him are all I have."

"Those memories aren't doing you any good."

Maggie was right. She was *always* right.

****

Brian's hopes slipped away with each passing day he didn't hear from Alex. The apron she gave him hung from a hook in his kitchen, reminding him of what he was missing. Despite the sheer number of times he'd tried to contact her over the past few weeks, she didn't reply to his texts or return any of his calls. The park number wasn't any better.

"Relationships scare me," she had told him. What

they had was perfect for her—a secret affair revolving around sex.

Or maybe it was just a way to get a letter of recommendation. It killed him to think Nate had been right about her. Every time he went out he got asked questions about her. Where she was, what their relationship meant, but he didn't know, so how could he answer?

He threw himself into his work and prepared for his upcoming role. They would start filming in January. Until then, he focused on anything that would keep his mind off Alex. Flying home for Thanksgiving turned out to be harder to plan than he anticipated.

"How long can you stay?" his mom asked over the phone.

"A week. I'm between jobs, so it's pretty quiet around here."

"Are you bringing anyone with you?" Her voice lifted with hope.

"Nope, sorry, Mom," he whispered.

"Do you want to talk about it?"

"Not really." The need to talk about it was driving him crazy, but he couldn't admit what had really happened. The wound was still too fresh.

"Hon, did you hear me? Is Ozzie coming with you?"

"Yeah, of course."

"Good," she said. "It wouldn't be Thanksgiving without my grandson."

"Thanks, Mom." He cleared his throat. "I need to go. I love you. See you in November."

"I love you, too," she replied just before he hung up.

All he had to do was get through the rest of October, and then November, and then every day for the rest of his life. Alone.

****

Alex spent a lot of time thinking about what Maggie said. Alex had to change in order to move on. And for the first time in her life, she realized moving on wasn't the same as running away. It was time for something bigger. Something better. Something that would help her let go of the lingering memories of Brian, which caused her more pain than she cared to admit. Although he hurt her, he also taught her to trust herself. Fear had always held her back—worried she would disappoint someone, afraid she wasn't good enough. But she *was* good enough.

Which meant it was time for her to run a nature reserve.

Alex waited until Maggie returned to work full time before she called Steve. She had to be certain everything would be okay at work without her, and sure enough, Maggie stepped back into the park manager role without missing a beat.

After a long day of culling infected pines, Alex returned to her office and picked up her phone. Her fingers shook as she dialed.

"Hi, Steve, it's Alex Mitchell," she began. "I was hoping we could talk."

And they did; for half an hour, they discussed the job and everything it would entail: a full-time position, first doing a wildlife survey, and then running the show. Knowing she couldn't afford housing anywhere near Beverly Hills she voiced her concerns, but Steve immediately offered his grandparent's house, which would double as the Visitor Center, and of course, she could bring Koko with her. Everything fell into place.

After they worked out all the details, Alex skulked into Maggie's office.

Maggie frowned from behind her desk. "What's up?"

"I'm officially putting in my two weeks." Those words were harder to speak than she anticipated. "I'm taking a job in California. During filming, Steve talked to me about turning a piece of property he and his sister inherited into a nature reserve. He wants me to help with the wildlife survey and then manage it. I think it's time I start my new adventure." Alex gave a little smile.

"That's great news. Why do you look so sad?" Maggie rushed over to hug her.

"Because it means leaving you and your family and… And…" Her eyes filled with tears.

"You think a few hundred miles can keep us apart? I love California and now I have a reason to visit."

Alex laughed through her tears. Maggie, always the optimist, saw the silver lining in everything.

****

Alex's remaining time at Twisted Juniper was filled with a mixture of excitement and sadness. The rangers threw her a going away party and all promised to keep in touch. Most of her time was spent with Maggie, including staying with her the night before she was supposed to leave.

With a small trailer packed with her belongings, Alex and Koko took one last look at the park that had been their home for over a year. The sun had just come up, bringing warmth to the cool November morning. The desert was oddly quiet as if it were saying goodbye, too.

Maggie and Pelli stood next to her. "We're going to miss you," she said.

"Am I making a mistake?" Alex had been asking herself that question for weeks.

"No. You're moving on to bigger and better things."

Alex shook her head. "It can't get much better than this."

Maggie hugged her. "Sure it will. Just wait."

Alex's shoulders sagged as she wrapped her arms around her friend.

"This isn't goodbye," Maggie said. "I'll see you later, okay?"

Alex nodded and smiled as she pulled away. "I'll see you later," she echoed. "Give this to Henry, okay?" she drew the stuffed raven from her jacket pocket. It was her only physical connection to Brian and as much as it pained her to give it away, keeping it hurt worse.

"I will," Maggie replied, cradling the shiny black bird.

"Come on, Koko, time to go." She opened the passenger door and waited for the girls to say goodbye to each other. "Take care of your family, okay, Pelli?"

"Let us know when you get there," Maggie said.

"I will," Alex replied as she got behind the wheel. Koko whined from her seat, her head hanging out her window. "I know, baby. We'll see them soon, okay?" Alex waved to Maggie and drove away. Halfway to Dembi Koko finally relaxed in her seat and fell asleep.

Alex stopped for gas in Barstow and turned her phone on for the first time in months. The voicemail was full and she had over fifty text notifications. The thought of going through them was daunting, so she called Steve to let him know where she was so they could plan a time to meet at his grandparent's house. Next, she called Maggie. Apparently, there were already five applicants for Alex's position at the park, a fact Maggie had kept secret just in case Alex changed her mind. Interviews would begin the following week. The guilt she had been holding onto slipped away.

That evening, after many stops along the way, Alex and Koko spent a full hour sitting in traffic in Los Angeles. By the time they made their way up Live Oak Canyon, their snacks and patience had been depleted, but as they drove, most of the noise of the city fell away. Enormous mansions dotted the landscape, and she was sure if she looked hard enough, she could find movie stars. Stars like Blaze Johnson. Even after everything, she couldn't help but think of him. Part of moving on was letting go of him and her remaining memories. That would take time.

Following the directions Steve had given her, she finally found the long, winding road that would take her to his grandparent's estate. She parked in a massive gravel drive in front of a beautiful Spanish hacienda-style house, hooked Koko to her leash, and stepped outside.

Steve greeted her from the heavy wooden front door. "Welcome."

"It's spectacular."

"Wait until you see it during the day. Come on, I'll take you on a tour of the house." He bent down and patted Koko's head, making her tail wag.

"This is Koko."

"Nice to meet you," he said, shaking the dog's

paw.

Alex laughed and then followed him inside. The house and property had obviously been a ranch or farm at some point and was different from many of the mansions she'd passed on her way up the canyon. It had been well cared for over the years and original details remained intact. "When was this house built?" she asked.

"In 1920. My grandparents were friends with the Dohenys. They owned most of the land around here, so when my grandparents were trying to find a place to settle down, the Dohenys offered to sell them a parcel. It was before the real estate boom, so they sold it for next to nothing. It's been in my family ever since. My dad died in January, so now it belongs to my sister and me." A smile formed as he touched the rough stucco walls. "I have so many fond memories of this place."

"I can see why." Between the smooth tile floors and great arching doorways, the house had more character than anything she'd seen. A door at the back of the house opened into a spacious courtyard connecting the main structure to another smaller building that ran parallel. "What's that?" she asked as they walked outside.

"Servant's quarters and stables," he replied. "My sister and I used to play in there. Once upon a time, my grandparents had horses. The man who managed the stables lived there, but it's storage now." He unlocked the door and flipped a switch and smiled when the lights came on. The walls had patches of caramel bricks showing through where chunks of plaster had fallen over the years, giving her a glimpse into the past. Massive beams of wood supported the ceiling, which matched the rustic cabinets in the tiny kitchen. It was perfect.

"This is where I want to stay."

Steve frowned. "But the house is so much more spacious. And clean."

"That'll make a perfect Visitor Center," she said. "Believe me, this is more than enough room for the two of us."

They walked through the house, which was easily twice the size of what she was used to. The floors had smooth tiles, exactly like the main house; they were just dirty. Nothing a little tender loving care couldn't fix. The bedroom she chose had a massive window overlooking the property. It would be beautiful in the daytime. All the utilities worked and better yet, she wouldn't feel bad about her eclectic furniture ruining the authentic look of the main house. One of the other rooms was packed with old tables, chairs, and dressers that had probably been stored for a half a century.

"Are you sure? It's not much. We didn't clean out here. We thought you'd prefer to stay in the main house."

"I'm sure. I'm not afraid of a little cleaning." She picked up an ancient broom and started sweeping to prove her point. A few of the bristles fell onto the floor so she made a note to buy a new one.

"Okay. What can I help you carry inside for tonight? You can also take anything you like from this room. There might be a bed frame in here somewhere," he said studying the piles of furniture.

"My mattress and two pieces of luggage are all I need for now. You really don't mind?" They cut through the courtyard, and she unlocked the trailer.

"I wouldn't offer if I did. I'll bring help tomorrow to carry the rest."

"That would be great since you're the only one I know around here." The mattress was wedged firmly on top of everything else, and she grunted as she pulled it out and held it so it was sandwiched between them.

"That's not entirely true, is it?" he asked from the other side of the mattress. "What happened...with Blaze?"

She winced. "I thought I knew him. Turns out, I was wrong. You saw the pictures, huh?"

"I saw you on set, too. He spent an awful lot of time near you. And then I read those horrible headlines about you. It didn't seem to fit with what I saw during our time at Twisted Juniper."

The memories made her skin flush—his hot breath on her neck, his hands on her hips, and that stupid sexy smile that melted her heart. She sighed. "I thought he liked me, but he didn't. He said some really hurtful things. It's been hard."

"I'm sorry. I don't mean to pry. I just wondered what really happened."

"You and me both," she replied, grateful for the mattress between them hiding her face. They walked side by side into the old servant's quarters. When they dropped the mattress on the floor, dust flew out in every direction.

"Are you *sure* you want to stay here tonight?"

"Yes."

"Well then, welcome home," he said and then he left.

Alex flopped onto her mattress and dialed Maggie. It rang five times before the generic answering voice asked her to leave a message. "I'm here. This place is amazing. I'm dying to tell you all about it. Call me," she said and then hung up.

A few minutes later, her phone rang. Alex smiled as she pulled it out of her pocket, ready to tell Maggie everything, but her smile fell when her mom's number glowed on the screen. It would be days before she could deal with her mom, so she spent the rest of the night tidying up and ignoring her phone. She didn't want to start her new adventure by reliving the nightmare of her past.

Chapter Twenty-Three

When Alex opened her window the next morning she was greeted with golden rays of sunlight bathing the rolling hills that extended as far as the eye could see. Birds sang softly, insects hummed, and a soft breeze carried the sweet perfume of something she couldn't quite put her finger on. In that moment reality set in. It had finally happened; her new adventure had begun.

Just as Steve promised, a crew of volunteers were ready to help her move her belongings and rearrange anything she needed. After a week, she had transformed the servant's quarters into her home with a mixture of her belongings and the relics Steve had given her permission to use.

Alex talked to Maggie on a regular basis while she got situated with her new job. Thursday nights were still movie nights and they watched a classic together albeit on the phone. It wasn't quite the same, but it helped both of them. They talked about work, dogs, and Henry and then made plans for Maggie's family to visit after the reserve opened. They would come for Christmas.

Steve and his sister, Linda, organized a thorough cleaning and repairs of the main house while Alex got to work with the wildlife survey. It meant she spent many of her days climbing hills and exploring caves in the arid wilderness with Koko. Eventually, between hard work and lots of time with her dog in nature, she found her happiness. For the first time in her life, she was fulfilled. Her peace had been waiting for her all along. Steve had been telling her she was the perfect person for the job, and she could finally admit he was right.

****

"Are you ready to see your grandma?" Brian asked as Ozzie wiggled inside his kennel at the airport. "She's going to have treats in her pocket. I'll bet you anything."

As soon as he made his way through the security gate, he saw his mom, smiling from ear to ear. "Happy Thanksgiving, honey," she said and then she kissed his cheek. Before he could respond, she squatted down to say hello to Ozzie through the bars of his cage. "And how's my baby? Was the flight okay? I hope they treated you well." She pushed two tiny bone-shaped treats through the front of the cage.

"You know he can't answer you, right, Mom?"

With a wave of her hand she dismissed him. "Let's go to the car so we can get him out of there."

Brian nodded and started toward the door, but before they got outside, a camera flashed in his face.

"Traveling for the holiday?" the man asked as he flashed another dozen times.

Brian smiled. If he smiled, they would leave him alone faster. That was the way it happened. Backing away from his mother and Ozzie's kennel, he continued to smile.

"Blaze. Over here," someone shouted as they positioned their phone so they could take a selfie with him in the background.

A group of young women squealed and mobbed him. "Can we take a picture with you?" one of the women asked.

"Of course." Once he opened his arms, the women squeezed in while a friend took their picture with one phone after another. His face hurt from holding a smile long enough to get through all seven of them.

"I can't believe it," one of the women said. "Thank you." Just as she leaned up and kissed his cheek, a camera flashed. "I kissed him," she shouted triumphantly as she rejoined her group of friends.

The man with the camera who had started the whole thing said, "Are you here with Alexis Mitchell? Has she been with you for the past two months? No one has been able to find her." He craned his head to look around for her.

"I traveled with my dog," Brian said. "Now if you'll excuse me, my family is waiting for me."

The photographer took another handful of pictures but didn't follow Brian as he rejoined his mom and Ozzie.

Outside, his mom shook her head, pulled a tissue out of her pocket, and wiped at his cheek. "You have lipstick on your face." She sighed. "I don't know how you deal with that all the time."

"It wasn't so bad today. No one recognized me on the flight. That was nice."

A few car lengths away, his dad waved from the curb. They hugged briefly and then Brian set to work collapsing the kennel while his mom took Ozzie into the back seat with her.

"I had to move a few times. What took so long?"

September Roberts

his dad asked as he got behind the wheel.

"Paparazzi," his mom explained.

Brian sat in the passenger seat and relaxed. "It's nice to be home. What's on the menu this year? I'm starving."

"Just wait until you see what I've already made. Now that you're here, we can finally get the turkey ready."

His dad laughed. "Don't you two ever think about anything besides food? Thanksgiving isn't for another two days."

Brian smiled. "You never seem to complain about our brined turkey."

"You're right about that," his dad said and twisted a pretend key to lock his mouth shut.

****

Brian and his mom moved around each other in the kitchen, stirring, cooking, and chopping in perfect harmony. "Oh, I brought almonds and dates from California," he said.

"Perfect," his mom said. "We'll add them to the stuffing."

"Is Ozzie your date?" his dad called out from the front room where he relaxed on the couch with the dog.

"Very funny, Dad." Brian rolled his eyes and his mom laughed.

"Speaking of dates," his mom started. "What's going on with you and Alexis? You two looked pretty cozy in those pictures. I was hoping to meet her."

All the times he'd called home he had managed to avoid all conversations about Alex, but he couldn't in person. "I don't know. She won't return my calls."

"The man at the airport says no one has been able

to find her. What if she's in a coma?"

"I don't think she's in a coma, Mom."

"Did you call the local hospital? The desert is a dangerous place. What if she got stung by a scorpion?"

"It would only hurt, not hospitalize her. Besides, she's careful and carries a special light to search for them at night."

"Sounds like you know her pretty well."

"I do. Well, I thought I did."

"Well? What happened?"

"It didn't work out."

"But you both looked so happy."

"We were. It was just…fun. She got what she wanted and then it ended. That's it."

A frown creased her forehead. "You're making it sound like she used you."

"That's how it feels." Unable to face her, he turned away and took a deep breath.

"I'm sorry, honey. I didn't mean to upset you." She touched his back and patted it lightly. "It's okay."

"No, it's not," he admitted. "I miss her. I…I love her."

His mom gasped. "You love her?"

With a quick nod, he let out a shaky breath. "But it doesn't matter. I need to move on just like she did."

****

Brian's parents didn't mention Alex again while he was visiting, but he felt their pity every time they looked at him. That's why he didn't want to tell them about her in the first place. The reminder of how much he had lost wasn't necessary.

On his last day, he flopped on his old twin bed and stared at the ceiling. It had been two months since filming ended and he missed Alex more than ever. Dialing by heart, he called her, but her mailbox was still full. Next, he called the park.

"Twisted Juniper State Park, how can I help you?" a man answered. Finally. It took Brian a few seconds, but he figured it was Neal.

All the times he had called in September and October, the line was always busy. "Is Alex there?"

Neal sighed into the phone. "Alex no longer works here. Please stop calling." The phone creaked as if Neal were about to hang up.

"Neal?" Brian said.

"Yes," Neal replied slowly.

"It's Blaze. I um," he stalled and cleared his throat. "I'm trying to find Alex."

"Sorry man. She's not here."

"Where is she?"

"You should call her and ask," Neal said.

"I've tried. No answer."

Neal exhaled. "Then I guess she doesn't want to talk to you. I'm sorry. She asked us not to tell anyone. It was pretty crazy for a while."

"Okay, thanks anyway," Brian replied before disconnecting.

****

Near the end of November, Steve and Linda met a final time with the California Wildlife Trust to set up a plan to maintain and monitor the environment and with Alex's survey, the Frederick Nature Reserve took shape.

Now all they needed was money.

Steve had been paying Alex's salary, but if they could attract attention from the community and solicit memberships, she wouldn't be a burden on him. Of course, he didn't see it that way and assured her he made enough money to pay her, but the whole idea of setting up a reserve was to make it self-sustaining. In any case, they needed to hire a few part-time positions to help since the property needed a lot of work. The land had been changed almost a century ago by livestock and orange groves, both of which had left a lasting mark. Alex wanted desperately to return it to its native habitat but knew she couldn't do it alone. Hiring a few assistants was at the top of the list...once they had money. While Alex cleaned up the grounds as much as she could, Steve and Linda arranged for their grand opening event.

To help promote the reserve, Linda put together a pamphlet and invited a local artist to create a piece of work that would capture the beauty of the area. For a week, Alex worked nearby as the artist painted the serene landscape, and when the piece was done, she could see herself and Koko in the background. They fit right in.

****

"Steve Frederick called in a favor," Alan told Brian at one of their meetings.

"A favor?" Brian frowned. They had been discussing casting calls, costuming, and everything else related to the job he would be starting next month, which made him wonder if Steve was going to be part of his new gig.

"He's trying to rustle up support for a new project," Alan said.

"This?" Brian asked as he tapped on the script sitting on the desk between them.

"No, some nature park or something." Alan slid a pamphlet toward him. "They could use the press."

"You want me to make an appearance, smile, and sign autographs?" Brian was still proving to Alan he didn't need a babysitter. If he did what he was told he wouldn't have to deal with another Nate.

"Yes. That's exactly what I want you to do. I could send someone else, but you have the best press. I'll let Steve know you'll be there."

When Brian opened the pamphlet and saw the painting inside, his heart sped up. On the edge of a stunning sunset, sat a woman and a dog. Alex and Koko. At least that's what he thought it looked like. It was probably a shrub or something. A lovesick heart could make a couple of shrubs look like a dog and the love of his life. It happened all the time: in shadows at night, at the store, and on the street. It wasn't her. It never was. Wishful thinking wouldn't bring her back.

****

"I wish we could be there," Maggie said over the phone the morning of the party.

"I'm nervous," Alex replied. "Tonight is the night Steve announces me as the official director to potential members." It was happening. Finally. All her hard work was about to pay off.

"You're amazing. It's going to be great. You're providing city dwellers the chance to get away from the hustle and bustle for a while. Who wouldn't want that?"

"I don't know. Ugh. Let's talk about something else."

"It snowed last night. Our first of the season, I'm sure," Maggie said in a flat voice. "I hate the cold."

"Clearly you need to move to California," Alex

said, trying to persuade her friend to move closer for the hundredth time. "When you get snow, we get rain. It sounds great on the clay tile roof."

"I just might. I always watch the job boards. And Jim can get a job anywhere. Everyone drinks beer."

"I'm going to show you around when you get here and try and convince you all. I know all the best places to eat."

"Two weeks."

"I can't wait." She grinned. "I need to go. Linda just got here." Alex peered out her front window, across the courtyard, where the lights had just come on in the main house.

"See you soon. Good luck tonight," Maggie said.

"Thanks, bye." Alex disconnected and then went to lend a hand.

Linda was also nervous, so they spent the rest of the day commiserating. Before she left to get ready, Linda produced a stack of newly printed tri-fold brochures. "These are for tonight. What do you think? We've been sharing them all over town."

Alex opened one and smiled. She had taken most of the pictures inside and written the description of the wildlife, all except the beautiful painting featured in the middle. It was her favorite. Linda had added historical details about the house and property. Steve and Linda had decided on a membership price list, which was on the right panel of the brochure. It was perforated so it could be detached and submitted with annual dues. "It looks amazing, but you already know that. You didn't change them from last time, did you?

"No, I wanted to make sure you still like them."

Alex laughed. "Do you know who's coming

tonight?"

Linda shrugged. "Hollywood types, I'm sure. I invited a few people, but Steve was mostly in charge of that." For the tenth time, she checked her watch. "I need to get ready. See you tonight."

Alex nodded. "I probably should get ready, too."

"The caterers will be here at five."

"I'll take care of it," Alex said before waving her out the door. In a hurry to get ready, she threw on the viridian dress she bought for the occasion. Since leaving Twisted Juniper, she had actively avoided the color brown and her new wardrobe reflected that. As she brushed her hair, her hands shook. Having Steve's friends there meant mingling with directors and producers, someone who might recognize her and say something.

Despite her disheveled emotional state, the house and the grounds were perfect. The caterer arrived right on time and, with Alex's instructions, the team of servers set up trays of food and drinks. Everything was ready.

"Wish me luck, Koko." Alex filled a bowl with dog food. Koko wagged her tail and gave a little doggie smile. Alex patted her head, took a deep breath, closed the door behind her, and headed to the main house. "I can do this."

Steve and Linda arrived first with their spouses. Alex plastered a smile on her face and greeted the seemingly never-ending stream of visitors. One after another, she discussed the reserve and the benefits of a membership. It wasn't hard for her to convince them since she cherished every inch of the land.

Steve got the attention of everyone in the room by

tapping his ring against a glass of champagne. "Thank you very much for coming tonight," he started, holding up his glass. "Without your support, the Frederick Nature Reserve wouldn't be possible." The audience gave a polite round of applause. "I would like to introduce you to our director, Alex Mitchell, who has worked tirelessly to make our dream a reality." He swept his hand toward her and motioned for her to join him. "Alex, would you like to say something?"

After taking a deep breath, she started the speech she'd been practicing for a week, "Thank you, Steve, for having faith in me. I have loved exploring every inch of our fifty-seven acres, and I know you will too. Your membership will give you access to pristine beauty, breathtaking views, and..." As she looked around the room at the smiling face, she stopped when she found Blaze, his countenance impossible to read. The rest of her speech forgotten, she mumbled, "Thank you." The heat in the room seemed to crush her, so she darted outside and pressed her back against the rough wall.

With each ragged breath, her shoulder blades dug into the stucco. Of all the Hollywood types, she didn't expect to see him. How could she have been so stupid? It was bound to happen sooner or later and she kicked herself for not being prepared.

Before she could collect herself and head back to the party, the lights came on in the room to her left, casting a soft glow into the dim courtyard.

"You didn't mention she'd be here." Blaze's muffled voice floated out to her, making her inch closer to the window.

"Alex is the reason this place exists. Of course

she's here," Steve replied. "The only reason *you're* here is because your agent insisted you come. I asked him to send someone else. You think I wanted to invite you? I care too much about Alex to do that to her."

Keeping her back to the wall, she peeked at them through the window.

"What's that supposed to mean?"

"You broke her heart, you idiot." Steve's shoulders tensed. "If I were twenty years younger, I'd beat you to a bloody pulp."

"*I* broke *her* heart? She's the one who disappeared. She's the one who didn't return any of my phone calls. She got what she wanted and never looked back."

Chapter Twenty-Four

Alex's mouth fell open. That's what he thought? That she used him? What about the pictures and the things he said about her?

"That's not the way I heard it." Steve puffed his chest out.

Blaze clenched his jaw. "I haven't done anything wrong, and I don't need to justify myself to you." An echo of a door slamming snapped Alex out of her stupor.

"Didn't do anything wrong?" she muttered to herself. "He never called me." Pushing off the wall, she stormed across the courtyard to her house. Koko had been whining and waiting for her, but as soon as Alex stomped inside, Koko disappeared.

Alex flopped onto her bed and snatched her phone off the nightstand. "What an idiot," she shouted as she swiped at her screen, scrolling through the massive list of texts. There were more than twenty from her mom, a few from Maggie, but most of the list was unknown numbers demanding information about Blaze Johnson. Back and back she went until she found the first of a string of texts from Brian, his smiling face pressed to hers on his contact picture.

Hey. Nate had my phone so I couldn't text. I tried to warn you about the picture he took. I'm sure you've seen it by now. I've been hiding out and hope you have, too.

He got fired if that's any consolation. I promise I'll make it up to you.

Stunned, she scrolled to the next text.

I miss you.

The date and time stamp showed they had come through the day the papers in town had a heyday with her personal life. No wonder she had missed them. Within an hour, he sent another one.

I just saw the picture of us Nate posted under my account. I'm so sorry. I could kill him, but he's not worth it. Please believe me when I say I didn't share it or write that. You were never just another notch in my belt. Nate was out to get me. I guess he got us both. Sorry.

Tears welled in her eyes, blurring the screen in front of her, but she couldn't stop reading the thread. Koko nudged against her arm and licked her cheek.

Alex? Are you getting these? Are you mad at me? Please call.

Hello?

Alex? Please call.

I miss you.

A sob escaped her lips as she opened her voice mail. The mailbox had filled by the end of September, right around the time her number was leaked to the press. More than twenty messages waited from numbers she didn't recognize, and then there was Brian.

"I hope you're not mad at me. I swear I had nothing to do with those pictures. That was Nate. All Nate. You know I wouldn't do that, don't you? I keep wishing I was still there. Before it all went to shit. I hope you're doing okay. Did they find you? I get mobbed every time I step out of my house. Like sharks following the scent of blood. It's awful." He sighed. "Please call me. I miss your voice."

"I miss you, too," she said to her phone as she played the message from the next day.

"Today sucks. Everyone is living their lives like everything is normal, but it's not because we're not together. I know we never set up anything official, but you should come out. You could meet Ozzie and I would make you dinner. And breakfast. And lunch. We wouldn't have to go anywhere. It would just be us. Think about it?"

It sounded wonderful. Better than that. Amazing. To think she had missed an invitation to escape the worst part of her life because she turned her phone off for a few weeks. "Wait," she said and Koko stopped licking her and sat down.

"What about the stuff he said? I heard that with my own ears," she explained to Koko. "He said I was convenient and willing to meet his needs," she whispered the words that had been stored inside her for so long. "I heard him."

What was she supposed to believe?

****

Brian slammed his hand against the steering wheel of his car, sending out a distorted honk into the quiet street where he had parked outside the reserve. "Fuck," he shouted. He hadn't been prepared to see her.

"What is she doing here?" Pulling away from the curb and following the winding road down the canyon, he struggled to process what had happened. By the look on her face, she was just as surprised as he was. Steve knew but obviously hadn't told her.

After all the time that had passed, he assumed she had fallen off the face of the earth, but in reality, she had been right around the corner. Avoiding him.

Bile rose in the back of his throat and he had to will it to go away by taking a few deep breaths. Nothing good would come of thinking about her anymore. Not after what she had done.

****

"What am I supposed to do?" Alex asked her best friend over the phone.

Maggie sighed. "You should go talk to him. That's probably what you should've done from the very beginning."

"I couldn't. Not after what he said." When she called Maggie the whole truth came out, and just as she would expect from her loyal friend, Maggie was outraged.

"It sounds like you need to get his side. If he really misses you, then you need to know. If he was using you because you were convenient, you need to kick him in the balls."

Alex laughed. "I thought you told me not to hit him."

"Nope. This is different. You're not working together anymore, and if that's how he really feels about you I give you permission to kick him in the balls. Really hard. Either way, you need to go talk to him."

"I'm a mess," Alex protested.

"Wash your face and go talk to him before he leaves the party."

"But—"

"No buts," Maggie chided. "You need closure. Go

now."

"Okay." Alex swallowed hard. She had to do it.

"Call me later?"

"Yep. Talk to you soon," Alex said before disconnecting.

Koko followed Alex into the bathroom and wagged her tail while Alex splashed her face with cold water.

"I have to do this," she told her dog. "I don't want to, but I have to."

Alex walked across the courtyard and pushed into the crowd. If Brian was still there, she couldn't see him.

"There you are," Linda called out to her.

Alex turned to face her, and Linda put a hand over her heart.

"Have you been crying? Is everything okay?" Linda said, pulling her aside.

Alex touched her puffy eyes and shook her head. "No. I need to find Brian. I mean Blaze. Is he still here?"

Linda frowned and motioned for her brother to join them.

"Is he still here?" Alex asked Steve.

"No," Steve grumbled. "He stormed out of here about twenty minutes ago. We had words."

Alex bit her lip and nodded.

"You heard?"

She nodded again. "Thank you for standing up for me. I really appreciate it."

"I knew there was a chance he'd be here tonight. I'm sorry I didn't warn you." Steve looked at his shiny black shoes.

"It's time I stop running away from everything. I have to talk to him."

"Are you sure?"

Even though her stomach flipped, she nodded. "Do you have his address? This isn't a conversation we should have over the phone."

"I can get it for you." Steve pulled his phone out and started dialing.

Linda rubbed Alex's shoulder. "Is there anything I can do for you?"

"Forgive me for missing so much of tonight."

"Of course." Linda pulled her into a hug. "You haven't missed anything. Go. We'll clean up tomorrow."

Steve slipped a piece of paper into Alex's palm and squeezed her hand shut around it. "Call me if you need anything."

"I will." Alex clutched the piece of paper to her chest as she ran back to her house. "Got it," she announced to Koko as she entered Brian's address into her phone. "Come on, I need backup."

****

Brian paced the length of his front room. He had come face-to-face with the truth and he didn't like it. A part of him had been holding onto hope, but now he had nothing left.

Rain fell outside, mirroring how he felt inside.

Ozzie whined from the couch, bringing Brian back to reality. "I'm sorry I'm in such a bad mood," he said as he slumped down next to his dog. Ozzie nuzzled against his chest and whined again. "What is it, baby?"

Ozzie's tail thumped against the cushions as he looked out the window. And then his ears perked up, and he trotted to the front door.

Brian frowned and followed him. "No one is

out…here," he finished as he opened the door.

Alex stood just outside with her hand raised, ready to knock.

"What do you want?" he asked, trying to keep his voice level even though his heart was racing. She couldn't know how much she hurt him.

"I want to talk," she said as she shoved her hands into the pockets of her jacket. A light sheen of water clung to her hair and face.

Ozzie tried to push between his legs, but before he could greet her, Brian stepped outside and closed the door. "What do you want to talk about?" He crossed his arms over his chest and straightened his back. Ozzie whined and snuffled the seam of the door.

Alex held her head high. "What you said to Nate."

"I got Nate fired."

"I know…now," she added and then frowned. "I listened to your messages tonight."

How could he believe her? "The ones I left for you in September?"

"I turned my phone off. It was easier that way. Someone gave them my number. Once they started calling, they wouldn't stop. They were almost as bad as my mother."

"Paparazzi?"

She nodded. "They descended like a plague."

"Here, too." A lack of privacy was something he had gotten used to, but she had been thrown in the deep end. Pity replaced a little of the anger.

"You mentioned," she said.

"Fucking Nate."

"Did you mean it?" Her chin wobbled. "What you said?"

287

"Of course I did. I wouldn't have said all of those things if I didn't mean them."

She pressed her lips together and nodded. "I understand," she whispered and turned away.

Anger boiled to the surface, and when he touched her shoulder, she practically jumped. "That's it? That's all you have to say? After everything?"

When she turned to face him tears streaked down her cheeks. "What do you want me to say? How honored I am to help you meet your needs?"

He frowned. "What?"

"That's all it was. A matter of convenience."

"What was convenient?" What was he missing?

"Us," she shouted; her eyes flashed fire and then she slapped his face.

Stars flickered across his vision as he rubbed his cheek.

She gasped and covered her mouth before turning again, that time running down the sidewalk toward her car.

His bare feet slapped against the wet concrete, as he chased her and then he gripped her wrist tightly. "Wait."

"Let go of me," she demanded, whirling around, her face a mixture of anger and grief. Koko cried in the car a few feet away.

"No. What are you talking about?"

Twisting out of his grasp, she faced him, her hands clenching into fists. "I heard you. The morning you left, I was still in the parking lot. I heard you tell Nate I was convenient, that you had needs, and I was willing," she whispered, her shoulders crumbling.

"That's not what I said."

"Yes, it is. This hurts enough. Don't lie to me, too."

"No. Nate wouldn't leave me alone. Please listen," he begged, holding her arms so she couldn't hit him again. "That's not what I *meant*. I was asking him if that's what he wanted to hear…that I was some kind of depraved loser who went around fucking women because I was bored. He wouldn't shut up, badgering me the whole way to the car. I shouldn't have said anything to him. He wanted to know why I was with you, and it made me so angry he couldn't see it for himself."

That's why she never called, and he'd had no idea. If that's what she believed he didn't blame her for being angry. But it was time to set the record straight.

Chapter Twenty-Five

Alex relaxed a little, but she still couldn't make sense of what he was saying.

"You heard an argument and only part of it at that."

She blinked, took a deep breath, and looked up at him with her bleary eyes. Staring back at her was Brian, his face open and honest just like she remembered him. But no matter how much she wanted to believe him, how could she?

"Even if I told him why I was with you, he wouldn't believe me. Everyone wants something from me: fame, money…" He laughed bitterly and shook his head. "That's pretty much it—fame and money. And then when I didn't hear back from you, what was I supposed to think?"

"I wasn't using you," she said. "I don't want your fame or money."

"I thought you were done with me," he admitted. "I called and called and never heard back."

"I thought I was another notch on your belt," she said, quoting the picture.

"I'm sorry. I didn't see it until it had been up for four days. I tried to warn you about the first picture at the airport that morning but Nate broke my phone. Like an idiot, I left it there. Apparently, he took it to the store, transferred my data to a new one, and started using it. I didn't get it back for almost a week, but by then the damage had been done. I called Twisted Juniper and talked to Neal. He said it was pretty nuts there."

"You could say that again. I couldn't go anywhere near people for two weeks. Everyone had to lie about knowing me."

"Did you get in trouble with your boss?"

"He didn't care. I thought he would, but all he cared about was the increased traffic to our park and those damn letters."

"I wrote one," Brian said.

"You did?"

With a shrug he said, "Well, me and the stunt team. I thought you knew."

She shook her head. The second letter is what had sealed the deal with Mr. Howard. No wonder it carried so much weight.

"Will you come in so we can talk without getting wet?"

"Why does this always happen to us?" she asked with a weak laugh.

"I don't know, but it's starting to pick up."

"Can I bring Koko in?"

"Definitely."

As soon as Alex unlocked her car and opened the door, Koko jumped into Brian's arms, making Alex smile. "I think she missed you."

With that, he hugged her close to his body and then ran toward his house. When they all got on the front porch, he opened the door a crack. "Koko, meet Ozzie. Ozzie, Koko." They both pressed their faces into the gap and wedged it open so they could meet each other the right way, by sniffing each other's butts.

After a minute of waggles and whines, they all moved inside. Ozzie pressed his front legs against the ground and wiggled his lower half, inviting Koko to play with him, and she happily joined him in a game of run around the furniture. Brian grinned from ear to ear as he watched them play.

"They're friends." Alex leaned against the doorjamb. "She's been so lonely without Pelli, I feel just awful about it."

"Please, come in." He motioned to the couch.

Alex slipped out of her shoes and hung her jacket on the doorknob. When she sat down she gasped in surprise as the damp fabric of her dress pressed against her legs. She smoothed her wet hair away from her face and wiped at her eyes.

They sat for a while without saying anything. The dogs were more than enough entertainment.

"How long have you been running the reserve?" he asked.

"Since early November. Steve and I talked about it a lot during filming. He and his sister inherited the land, but they didn't know what to do with it. I suggested they preserve it, and they loved the idea. He kept asking me to come work for him, but I didn't think I could do it."

"You can do anything you set your mind to," he said.

"You taught me that. That's why I said yes. You believed in me, so it was a little easier to believe in myself. Plus, it was hard being at Twisted Juniper without you."

He nodded and picked up her hand. "It was worse than withdrawals."

"You shouldn't joke about that."

"I'm not." When he kissed the back of her hand, she knew everything was going to be okay.

"I should've called you," she admitted.

"Or answered your phone so I could explain. I'm sorry for everything you've been through."

"It wasn't your fault. I'm sorry for you, too."

"I don't blame you for hiding from the world. It's hard to get used to all the attention. I'm just glad you're here. You're my raven. I've been lost without you." Pressing her hand to his cheek, he closed his eyes. "I should've told you how I felt before I left, but I kind of ran out of time. I was also worried you didn't feel the same."

The sound of her thundering heartbeat muted all other sounds. Did he feel the same way she did? She didn't have to wait long to find out.

"I love you."

"I love you, too," she replied and then kissed him. When he pulled her onto his lap and wrapped his arms around her, all the pain and misery she'd been holding onto for the past three months slipped away, replaced by his strong, warm body. "I don't deserve you," she said against his lips.

"That's where you're wrong," he replied. "I don't deserve *you.*" That time, he kissed her, and she melted against him.

"I've missed you so much."

"I thought I'd never get to see you again and here you are."

"Here I am," she replied.

Cradling her face in his hands he said, "Since I screwed this part up last time, I'd like to clarify a few things."

"What?"

"I like you. A lot."

She grinned and kissed him again. "Me, too."

At that moment, Koko and Ozzie jumped onto the couch, each carrying a large chew toy. "Our dogs enjoy being together."

"They do."

"I hate sleeping alone," he said. "It's too…lonely. No offense, Ozzie."

Ozzie's tail thumped against the cushions as he chewed on his toy.

"What are you getting at?" Even though she had a good idea what he was going to say, she wanted to hear him say it.

"I've wasted enough time being alone. I want you with me, all the time."

"Are you asking me to move in?"

He nodded. "Yes. What do you say?"

"Well…" As she looked around the simple, yet elegant room she knew it was a great idea. "Maybe you should show me around first. How do I know your house is any better than mine?"

"Your house?"

"At the nature reserve. I'm living in the old servant's quarters."

"Sounds glamorous."

"It's lovely. You should see the view in the morning. The way the sun makes the hills glow."

"I'd like that."

"I'm not sure Steve would be crazy about you living there, though. He wanted to kill you."

"That settles it, then."

"It does."

"It makes sense to pick up where we left off, right?"

"Right. We've already lost enough time."

"No one has to know. Except my parents. Can I tell my parents? They are going to be so excited things worked out."

"You told your parents about us?"

"We talked about you when I went home for Thanksgiving. You're going to love them."

A knot formed in her stomach and she groaned. "Does that mean I have to tell my family?"

"Nope. I can be your secret for as long as you want."

"You're funny. You think the paparazzi won't notice? You're the most eligible bachelor in the world," she quoted. "You said it yourself, all people want from you is fame or money. And that's what it's going to look like if I show up in your life again."

"Good point. We shouldn't hide. We should come out as a couple," he added. "We could explain it's not about fame or money. We're in love."

"But they said the worst things about me." The horrible headlines echoed through her brain. What does she have to offer? Why was he with her?

"They don't know you like I do, but they will," he said with a smile. "Especially once I propose to you. Then they'll know I'm serious."

Propose? As in marriage? Panic gripped her and her heart felt like it might stop beating.

"Oh shit, did I say that out loud?"

Despite everything, she laughed. "Yes. Yes, you did."

"You're not going to run away, are you?" Worry creased his perfect face.

"No." A million questions filled her mind, but there was only one she needed to know the answer to. "Why would someone like you choose someone like me?"

"Oh, Alex," he said as he pulled her into another hug. "One of these days I'm going to convince you that you're amazing, and I plan on spending the rest of my life trying."

About the Author

September Roberts writes romance erotica in a variety of genres. Whether it's paranormal, new adult, or contemporary, you'll always get the happy ever after you've come to expect from her. She creates true-to-life romance, smart characters, strong heroines, intimate scenes, and plenty of humor. Please review and follow September at http://septemberroberts.wordpress.com.

~*~

To chat with September Roberts and other Wild Rose Press authors of erotic romance, join us at www.groups.yahoo.com/group/thewilderroses.

Also Available
Gray's Promise
A King Security Novel Book 2
By Anni Fife
http://a.co/e84p1KY

Zoey Morgan seems to have it all as a successful surgeon in Boston. However, perfection lies only on the surface. Plagued by nightmares and amnesia from a tragedy that ripped her family from her fourteen years ago, she finds the courage to reach out to the only man who can make her feel safe. She's buried the memory of their love, but her heart—and her body—responds to the ex-Marine in ways that are all too familiar.

Grayson "Gray" Walker's heart shattered when Zoey chose another man over him. Since then, he's built an impenetrable wall around his emotions. But from the moment she implodes back into his life, her vulnerability breaches his defenses. His skills as an elite member of the King Security team cannot shield him from the devastation of learning he might have left Zoey high and dry when she needed him most. Now, Gray must navigate the tripwire of helping her heal while protecting himself from being hurt again.

As the embers of their potent love reignite, an old threat awakens, leading to greater danger than ever before.

Maximilian Westfield has resurrected his family's company under the controlling eye of the major shareholder—his mother. To keep the company, he must marry the woman she chooses, no matter how inane or spineless. He is resigned to go through with the arranged marriage until he meets a feisty costume designer who will never meet his mother's standards. A stolen kiss spurs his lustful cravings. Once he tastes the spirited beauty's charms, he knows he has to find a way to keep her and his company. No other woman will do.

The daughter of a powerful British businessman, Teresa Medici Staffordshire leads her life as Tess Medici to avoid men out to please her father. Then she meets Maximilian, a sexy uptight CEO. From the moment he unleashes his expert fingers on her skin, she's hooked. His erotic games make her body hum with pleasure. Determined to lure Max out to play, every encounter becomes a game of enticement. But his commitment to his family business and his mother's determination to marry him off makes it impossible to take the relationship public, and Tess refuses to be his guilty little secret.

Choices become consequences, their future is on the line, and Max and Tess are running out of time.